INFINITY
SON

ALSO BY ADAM SILVERA

More Happy Than Not

History Is All You Left Me

They Both Die at the End

What If It's Us (with Becky Albertalli)

INFINITY
SON

ADAM SILVERA

Quill Tree Books
An Imprint of HarperCollinsPublishers

Library of Congress Cataloging-in-Publication Data:

Names: Silvera, Adam

Title: Infinity son / Adam Silvera.

Description: First edition. | New York : HarperTeen, an imprint of HarperCollinsPublishers [2020] | Audience: Ages 14 up. | Audience: Grades 10-12. | Summary: "In a world where some people are born with powers and some people take them, brothers Emil and Brighton Rey get swept up in a supernatural turf war generations in the making."— Provided by publisher.

Identifiers: LCCN 2019033533 | ISBN 978-0-06-245783-7

Subjects: CYAC: Magic—Fiction. | Supernatural—Fiction. | Brothers—Fiction. | Gays—Fiction.

Classification: LCC PZ7.1.S54 In 2020 | DDC [Fic]—dc23

LC record available at https://lccn.loc.gov/2019033533

Typography by Erin Fitzsimmons

21 22 23 24   PC/LSCH   10 9 8 7 6 5 4 3 2

❖

First paperback edition, 2020

For those who don't believe they can be heroes. It's time to fly.

*Shout-outs to Amanda and Michael Diaz, for all the nights
spent obsessing over Harry Potter theories and for reading
my fan fiction. My first fantasy novel is for you.*

Fear is a phoenix.

You can watch it burn a thousand times

and still it will return.

—LEIGH BARDUGO,

CROOKED KINGDOM

ONE
BROTHERS

EMIL

I'm dead set on living my one life right, but I can't say the same for my brother.

No one's expecting Brighton to be full-grown when we turn eighteen at midnight, but he needs to step it up. Long gone are those days where we were kids acting like we have powers like all these celestials roaming the streets tonight. Their lives aren't all fun and games, but he stays ignoring the dark headlines we see every day. I can't get him to see the truth, but I can check myself. I'm done dressing up as the heroic Spell Walkers for Halloween, and I'm done watching celestials and creatures wrestle in steel cages with their natural-born powers. I'm done, I'm done, I'm done.

I got to chill because we're close as hell, don't get me wrong. You step in his face and you'll find me in yours, even though I can't swing bones for the life of me. But man, there's been a few times I wondered if we're actually twins, like maybe Brighton got switched at birth or is secretly adopted. That nonsense no doubt comes from all the comics about chosen ones I've read over the years.

He's running wild at this all-night block party, trying to score interviews left and right for his online series, Celestials of New York, but no one's about it. Everyone's busy celebrating the arrival of the Crowned Dreamer, a faint constellation against the dark sky, which is hanging around for most of this month and then goes back to sleep for another sixty-seven years. No one really knows how far back celestials have existed or how they first received their powers, but all signs throughout history point to their connection with the stars. Like maybe their eldest ancestors fell out of the sky. Whatever the truth is, constellations are always a major event for them.

It's good to see celestials partying for a change. The only time I see gatherings like this lately is to protest the acts of violence and injustice against them, which have doubled in the last nine months. Being gay isn't rainbows and sunshine all the time, but ever since the Blackout—the worst attack New York has seen in my lifetime—people have been treating celestials like terrorists.

Tonight reminds me of when I attended my first Pride

parade. I was out to my family and friends, and all was good there, but I couldn't pretend there wasn't still a knot in my stomach from wondering if strangers would be cool with my heart; reading minds would've come in handy. During the parade, I felt relief and security and happiness and hope, all tied up like an indestructible rope that bound us together. I breathed easy around strangers for the first time.

I wonder how many celestials are taking that breath tonight.

Brighton is standing behind his tripod, capturing footage as people course through the tents before angling his camera toward the massive and flickering crowned figure in the sky. "Everything is changing tomorrow, I can feel it," Brighton says. "People are going to want to film us too."

"Yeah, maybe."

Brighton is quiet long enough for it to be awkward. "You never believe me. Just watch."

"Maybe this is the year we let it go," I say. "You got a lot to be excited about already with college in a new city next week and your series and—"

"People can gain powers on their eighteenth birthdays," Brighton interrupts.

"In books and movies."

"Which are all based on celestials, who've historically come into their powers when they turned eighteen."

"But how rare is that?"

"Rare makes it unlikely, not impossible." Brighton's always

got to win an argument, so I shut up. I'm not trying to fight while we ring in our birthday. Problem is, he doesn't recognize silence as a white flag. "The timing is perfect, Emil. The Crowned Dreamer is elevating every celestial's power, and if we have even a flicker of gleamcraft in us from Abuelita, it might ignite into something greater. I just . . . I sense it already."

"You sense it? This another psychic prank?"

Brighton shakes his head and laughs. "Good times, but nah. I'm serious. I can't explain it, but it's this tightening feeling in my blood and bones."

"Let's bet twenty dollars on this blood-and-bones feeling." Easy cash to buy another graphic novel.

"Bet."

We fist-bump and whistle, our signature move.

Brighton's had his eye on this rooftop rave, and we get in line as more people are being let into the brownstone. We're behind two women who are wearing the half capes that are customary to celestials. I fight back an epic cringe as I remember how up until two years ago we owned some for fun, completely clueless as to how sacred the capes are until our best friend, Prudencia, explained the traditions. I quickly donated ours to a local shelter. Once the women are let in, we go up the stoop, but this low-key bouncer blocks the door.

"Celestials only," he says.

"That's us," Brighton says.

The brown of the man's eyes is swallowed by glowing galaxies for a few moments, the telltale sign of every celestial. "Prove it."

Brighton pointlessly stares back, as if his eyes will swirl with stars and comets if he tries hard enough.

"Sorry to bother you." I drag Brighton down the steps, laughing. "You thought you could lie about having powers, like your eyes are some fake ID?"

Brighton ignores me and points to a fire escape. "Let's sneak up, get some exclusive footage."

"What? No. Dude, it's a party. Who's going to care about that?"

"Might be a ritual."

"It's not our business. I'm not going up there."

He detaches the camera from the tripod. "Okay."

I check the time on my phone. "It's our birthday in fifteen minutes, let's just hang."

Brighton stares at the rooftop. "Give me five minutes. This could be good for CONY."

I sit on the curb with his tripod. "I can't control you."

"Five minutes," Brighton says again as he climbs the fire escape. "And stop slouching!"

Not everyone cares about stiff posture or toned muscles. Some of us camouflage our scrawny bodies in baggy shirts and slouch, just waiting for the day when we can fold into ourselves and vanish completely.

I can't beat the Instagram impulse while I'm waiting for Brighton, so I hop online. My favorite wildlife videographer pops up first. She captures phoenixes—birds of fire that resurrect—in all their glory. Her latest is a video of a blaze tempest phoenix flying into a storm in Brazil. I scroll to find the fitness dude whose abs I've become very familiar with the past couple months, and even though I'm playing around with his workout plan, I'm nowhere near looking like him or the dozen other gym bros I follow. His motivating caption isn't doing it for me tonight, so I put my phone away and try to breathe in the real world.

This block party is everything.

There are children running on air and people grilling food with sunlight beaming out of their palms. I hope Nicholas Creekwell, the first dude I ever legit liked, is celebrating in his own little way tonight. He was my lab partner, and he loves chemistry so much he's going to pursue alchemy lessons for potion brewing in college. He was good-looking and better company and surprised the hell out of me when he dematerialized the door of my busted locker so I could get my calculator for my algebra midterm. I kept Nicholas's secret from everyone, especially Brighton, but even though he trusted me, he claimed he wasn't ready for a relationship, so we stayed friends. Can't help but wonder if things would've been different if I had a six-pack going for me.

Someone's selling these beautiful silver binoculars. I'd love to drop bank on a nice pair, but Ma will be the first to remind me that college textbooks don't pay for themselves. Especially since she's still caught up paying Dad's mountainous medical bills from an experimental trial with blood alchemy that made his bone cancer worse before he died in March. Dad was fascinated by the stars and looking forward to the Crowned Dreamer himself. Maybe I'll get to see the full marvel of this constellation when I'm older and can afford binoculars, and Dad will see it in another life, if you believe in that kind of thing.

Heeled boots pounding the gravel catch my attention, and I turn away from the tent to find a twentysomething woman approaching. Sweat glistens like she's been running for blocks. She's wearing an ill-fitting blazer that's missing a sleeve, and her arm looks sunburnt compared to her pale face; not exactly dressed for a late-night jog. Two figures are pursuing her from the air. One is a girl who's about ten feet above the ground, and the other is a boy who's being carried by winds that are sweeping up all sorts of trash as he passes.

I jump to my feet and backpedal from whatever is about to go down. I turn to the fire escape, where Brighton is four stories high. "Brighton, come back!"

The woman trips against the curb and slams into the concrete. I should stop being a punk and help her, but fear has a tighter grip and pins me to the wall. She stands and grabs the pole of the tent, and it glows orange. White fire runs up her arm as if she's been doused in gasoline and set alight. The canopy stands no chance—a mountain of fire bounces to the other nearby tents. This pandemonium definitely isn't going to help how people view celestials as dangerous.

Someone grips my shoulder, and I drop the tripod.

"You okay?" Brighton asks. He was quick getting down here.

I catch my breath. "Let's go."

"Wait a sec." Brighton is spellbound by the mayhem and holds up his camera.

"You're kidding." I grab his arm, but Brighton breaks free.

"I got to document this."

"The hell you do."

For someone who was our school's salutatorian, Brighton can be pretty damn stupid. If he were anyone else, I would straight ditch. This is why I don't have it in me to be a hero like I used to pretend. I want to live too much to risk my own life. But Brighton dreams of getting this kind of action for his series. Most of the celestials in the area are smarter, not sticking around to see how this will play out. Some are teleporting so quickly I would've missed them if I'd blinked.

The figures in the air break out of shadow and into the moonlight, the Spell Walker emblem on their power-proof vests glistening like the constellation that inspired their name.

"Maribelle and Atlas!" Brighton shouts, pumping his free fist.

What has this woman done that she's got the Spell Walkers chasing her? As her arm lights up again in white flames, I get a clear look at the woman's eyes. There are no astral bodies swirling within like a celestial's. They're dark except for one burning ring of orange. An eclipse—the mark of a specter. Now I know why the Spell Walkers are after her. I don't always agree with their violent, vigilante methods, but the Spell Walkers seem to be the only handful of heroes brave enough to admit that specters need to be stopped before they drive creatures to extinction and ruin the world. I hope every last specter gets locked up. Stealing blood from creatures to hook yourself up with powers, just because you weren't born a celestial, is a heartbreaking crime. Regular fire-casting is scary enough, but we're not about to hang around here if this specter is burning up with phoenix fire. I'm about to drag Brighton away, but I'm haunted by the glint in his eye. We know damn well how risky it is for someone to consume creature blood.

Specters trade their lives for power, and I pray my brother never mistakes this tragedy for a miracle.

TWO

HEROES

EMIL

The specter hurls a stream of white fire through the air, its flames spreading like wings and screeching like a phoenix.

"Bro, she's a specter," Brighton says.

"Probably got her power from a halo phoenix or—"

I shut up as Maribelle Lucero gracefully spins away from the flames and torpedoes directly into the specter. Maribelle's young—I'm going to guess our age, though Brighton can no doubt list off every Spell Walker's age and favorite color—with light brown skin and dark braided hair that whips like a rope as she lays into the specter with right hooks. Atlas Haas's blond hair is windblown as he hovers over the tents, doing his best to keep the fire at bay with gales shooting out of his palms. It's a losing battle. The fire spreads toward apartment buildings on one side and a run-down bar on the other, residents and patrons vacating as quickly as possible.

My heart hammers—*get out of here, get out of here, get out of here, get out of here.*

"Bright, we got to bounce."

"Then go."

I'm a millisecond away from snatching the camera and hurling it like a football when the bar explodes with a deafening roar. The blast catches Atlas off guard, and he flips out of the air and crashes into a parked motorcycle. We take cover under a bodega awning as bricks rain from the sky. The waves of heat remind me of baking flan in our late abuelita's tiny kitchen except magnified by a thousand.

Maribelle rushes to Atlas's aid, and the specter casts white fire again.

"Maribelle, watch out!" Brighton shouts.

She spins, but the fire drives her into a car door with sickening force, as if she's been shoved by someone with powerhouse strength.

"No," Brighton breathes.

Most of the patrons and residents cleared out already, like geniuses with A-plus survival skills. A short woman with stars for eyes busts open a fire hydrant and guides the water into the roaming flames, but the job is too big for her. A crowd cheers on the fight. A few feet away, a pale guy with dark blond hair under his hoodie is recording the whole brawl on a phone that has a yellow wolf on the case. He doesn't look freaked out. Probably not his first time witnessing a battle, but he's also not staring in wide-eyed wonder like Brighton, who catches thrills from filming.

Atlas struggles to his feet. The specter is bent over, taking deep breaths as she charges up another blast of white fire, its screech weaker this time. She extends her arm to attack but stops short when a gem-grenade the size of my fist rolls toward her. The citrine blasts apart in thick shards, and currents of electricity strike the specter. She collapses, writhing in pain.

I might throw up, maybe even piss myself. Seeing people attacked online is one thing, but it's different in person. Maribelle is sweating and limping toward Atlas. She has one hand pressed against the center of her vest, which seems to have absorbed most of the blow.

"That's what I'm talking about!" Brighton shouts, like whenever he gets an aced exam back or wins a game. He rushes off toward Maribelle and Atlas.

I'm dizzy and frozen for seconds that run like minutes before I finally follow Brighton. I try to tune out the specter's screams, but I can't help but wonder about her life and everything that led up to this moment. I snap out of it. Sirens blare through the streets as ambulances, fire trucks, and metallic-gold enforcer tanks seal off the corner of one block. I run to Brighton, my back to the demolished bar still blazing with white and orange fire, casting stretched-out and terrifying shadows across the street.

Brighton is kneeling beside Maribelle and Atlas as they catch their breath. "You guys were amazing," he says, still filming. "I'm a huge fan."

Maribelle pays him no mind, only tensing up as enforcers exit the tanks. "We got to go," she groans.

"Yeah, they're not going to like that you used a grenade," Atlas says.

"I could've thrown snowballs and those bastards would still accuse me of turning the streets into a war zone," Maribelle says.

Brighton's phone is at the ready. "Mind if I get a quick picture with you two?"

"Bright, dude, let them go," I say.

"Right, right."

Four enforcers shout for everyone to freeze as they approach with wands. I don't move a single muscle. It's not uncommon for celestials to sign up to become enforcers, but the majority of people on the force don't have powers of their own, so they're trained to cast attacks at the first sign of danger. Too many celestials have been stunned and met untimely deaths because of hotheaded enforcers.

"Don't move," I tell Brighton.

I watch all the enforcers, wishing I was also geared up in their bronze helmets and sea-green power-proof vests. My breathing speeds up, and my legs tremble, and I'm terrified the enforcers will mistake my shaking for an ability I don't have.

In the middle of the street, an enforcer trains her wand at the specter as another secures her with gauntlets and shackles to render her temporarily powerless.

Atlas's back is turned to the enforcers, and he has a wordless exchange with Maribelle that makes me nervous. She takes a deep breath and nods, and her eyes burn like sailing comets while Atlas's swirl like billions of stars caught in a black hole. Atlas rolls to the side while Maribelle levitates. A gust of wind knocks me and Brighton into a car as spellwork explodes around us, loud like firecrackers. I make sure Brighton is all good before checking out the action from underneath the car. Enforcers are swept off their feet, wands rolling away from them. Strong winds lift Atlas, and he grabs Maribelle out of the air. They fly over an apartment building and out of reach of the spells being shot their way.

"Emil, let's go. Get up. Come on." Brighton crouches as he runs in the opposite direction of the enforcers. Now that the Spell Walkers are gone, he finally wants to leave. Of course.

I was never the sort of kid who ran in the halls, talked during class, or crossed the street when it wasn't my light, because I hate getting in trouble, but right now it's as if I'm possessed by the bravest of ghosts as I pound the pavement, zigzagging away from the enforcers in case they take another shot at me.

If it weren't for Brighton bouncing, I would've hung tight, my face kissing concrete and arms outstretched in the hopes that the enforcers would realize I'm not dangerous. Being associated with the Spell Walkers after the Blackout is a gamble we can't afford to take.

Couple blocks later, we hop on a bus that's headed home. We take advantage of how empty the back is, stretching out. We're drenched in sweat, and I desperately want a gallon of water to drink and pour over myself.

"You okay?" I ask, while massaging the elbow I landed on and trying to breathe past the sharp pain from my rib cage.

Brighton's arms are scraped up from the fall, but he doesn't seem bothered. "That was a rush! We got to meet the ultimate power couple!" He sounds like he's bottled all the joy in the world, and I really wish I had some to drown out my panic. "Atlas even used his winds on us. I hope the camera caught that." He stares at me. "Where's my tripod?"

"Oh, I don't know, I left it behind somewhere between the specter burning the street down and enforcers shooting at us. I can run back and get it."

"Don't worry about it," Brighton says.

"That wasn't a real offer."

Brighton rewinds the footage. "The ad money I should be able to make off this video will pay for another one."

"How can you think about your video right now? Enforcers

shot at us, and Maribelle almost killed someone."

"No one would've blamed her if she had. That specter was raising hell."

I don't know the specter's name or anything about her life to argue that there's a good bone in her body, but I still didn't like seeing her on the ground with a wand aimed at her. Who knows if the enforcers will lock her up in the Bounds with everyone else who has powers or make her disappear completely.

I'm not about where this conversation is headed. This isn't over something stupid, like Brighton wearing my shirt because he needs to rock something new for a video or me borrowing his bike without checking in.

My phone buzzes. It's Prudencia texting to wish us a happy birthday; for the first time ever, we've missed celebrating our midnight minute. Eighteen is off to a rough start. Dad would've been disappointed. I'm so tight that Brighton's not going to catch me throwing out a fist bump and acting like everything's good.

"Why are you mad?" Brighton asks, taking his eyes off his camera. "Because I would've been fine with that specter dying? The Spell Walkers save more lives than they take, but if they have to kill, I trust they're taking the right lives."

I don't want to engage—I'm one of those angry criers, and Brighton is straight pissing me off—but I can't shut up. "We don't get to decide which are the right lives to take."

"Ever since the Blackout, the game isn't what it used to be," Brighton says. "I'm not going to get mad at good people killing bad people."

Truly tempted to get off the bus and walk home alone. "It's not a game."

"You know what I mean. People die in wars, that's inevitable." Brighton leans forward and nudges my knee. "If we had powers, we could've helped them. The Reys of Light, right?"

He's been calling us that since we were ten, right after we found out our last name, Rey, means *king*. You couldn't stop us from fantasizing about how our name was probably some prophetic code that we're destined for greatness—the heroic twins who are doubly strong and can communicate across the city without phones. We're not special at all, but the name stuck, even though our brotherhood seems to be getting dimmer and dimmer by the day.

"Yeah, well, I thank the stars we don't have powers," I say. "Not trying to find blood on my hands."

"Killing to save the world is different, bro."

"Heroes shouldn't have body counts."

For once, he's quiet.

We stare each other down like a game of chess that's hit stalemate. Both kings live but no one wins.

THREE
DREAMER

BRIGHTON

The world's about to find out I'm the real deal.

I struck gold with this video, not even playing. It's not the first time I've seen celestials perform miracles with their powers. One of the craziest was when this Suit fell onto the subway tracks as the train was approaching; kind of cliché, but it happened. Before I could be his hero, this little kid grabbed the man's wrist and lifted him onto the platform as if the Suit were as light as the doll clutched in the boy's other hand. Problem is, moments like that are too quick to catch on camera. That's why the power brawl I've just finished uploading is going to make waves.

I play the video over and over. Right as the enforcers cast

their spellwork for the millionth time, Emil shoots up from bed and tells me to turn it off already, but I just throw on headphones and crank up the volume. I really should get some sleep so I have energy for all the fans I'm meeting tomorrow, but I can't help staying up and refreshing the video every minute to track views and read comments. Half an hour in, the stats are good, but this late-night crowd isn't coming through the way I hoped they would. Still, I know my thirty thousand Brightsiders will do their thing and get this circulating by the time I wake up—it's too irresistible.

I close my laptop and leave it on my desk, which is cluttered with my Nikon camera, candy wrappers, comics, and an ongoing list of videos I'm hoping to film once I get to Los Angeles. In bed and under the covers, I relax on my back because my shoulder is sore. I can't wait to show off the bruise to my fans. This is a war wound I'm wearing with pride because not many people can say they've been thrown by Atlas's winds.

The Crowned Dreamer needs to come through on our birthday and bless us. If our latent powers kick in, I know Emil will change his tune about living out our original fantasy of being the Reys of Light, the people's champions. We grew up on books and movies where ordinary teens discover they're special—chosen ones, long-lost wizards, whatever. It rarely plays out that way in real life, but who knows.

Unlikely but not impossible are the best odds for any dreamer.

Our bedroom door slams against the wall so hard that my childhood drawing of the Spell Walkers falls. Ma is standing in our doorway, breathing in and out as she holds her chest; her heart must be attacking her again. I nearly trip over my covers to get to her.

We're about to watch Ma die, so soon after losing Dad.

"Call 911!" I shout at Emil, who is frozen in bed.

Ma shakes her head. Her eyes are watering. "The block party was attacked, and I have to find out from the news? I thought I was coming into an empty bedroom. . . ."

Emil snaps out of it and comes to hug her. "We're okay, Ma, sorry. We got in late, and I was in shock, I think."

Hold up.

"The news? My video got picked up?"

"You filmed it?!" Ma shouts.

I grab my phone while Emil tells Ma how he tried getting me away from the action last night. Judging by all the notifications on my phone, I'm damn glad I stood my ground. I check YouTube, and my video is coming up on ninety thousand views, which is more than triple what I've ever received but it's not skyrocketing the way I was expecting. It's still early, and I've gotten a few thousand new subscribers too. Everyone's thanking me in the comments for capturing this fight, and I smile when someone calls me a hero in my own right.

I wonder which stations and websites have circulated the video, so I hop on Twitter, where I get all my news. BuzzFeed tweeted out an article titled "Vlogger Films Explosive Battle with Spell Walkers."

"BuzzFeed covered my video!"

I've done hundreds of quizzes on BuzzFeed, and now I'm featured. What is this life?

I open the article, and there are GIFs galore, but they're capturing angles that my video doesn't. I scroll back to the top of the article. They've linked to another YouTuber's account, MinaTriesThis.

"No way."

Her video has hit over one million views.

I press play: it looks like Mina was vlogging, trying out a celestial's homemade moonbeam ice cream right as the first tent lit up in flames. So many people run past her, but she just had to go ahead and keep filming.

To steal my spotlight.

I keep tuning out Emil and Ma as I bounce around online. Screw BuzzFeed for highlighting Mina's video instead of mine, but I must've gotten some love somewhere to reach my stats. The brawl has been covered by the *New York Times*, CNN, *Time* magazine, the Scope Source, and Huffington Post, but Mina's video is embedded in all of them. It's the top trending video on YouTube.

"This isn't fair," I say.

"What's going on?" Emil asks.

"I got screwed. Some other video has gone massively viral."

I work too hard to keep being the runner-up. My motivation for top grades throughout high school was dreaming of the moment when I'd get to walk across that stage while everyone applauded me so I could deliver my valedictorian speech about what it feels like to be a kid from the Bronx who no one is expecting to take the world by storm. The only reason I didn't flip out when the vice principal brought me into her office to congratulate me on becoming salutatorian was because I couldn't risk losing that spotlight, even if it wasn't as bright, to whoever was below me academically; sitting through one speech by someone I know I'm smarter than was bad enough.

Ma sits on Emil's bed. "You hurt my heart, and you're upset over people not watching your video?"

"I'm sorry, okay?" I can't look away from Mina's increasing views.

"Don't take that tone with me, Brighton."

"Ma, you don't get how much money I could've brought in if my video took off."

"No money makes me feel better knowing I could've lost the rest of my world because you're pretending to be grown."

She doesn't look at me as much as she used to. Sometimes I think it hurts her so much since I really take after Dad, green eyes and all. Other times I'm sure it's because she's in denial that when I leave on Saturday afternoon to study film and reset my life, it's only going to be her and Emil, who's staying in the city to attend some third-best community college. No one can pay me enough to stay in this place where I watched Dad suffer for seven months, where I got my hopes up when alchemists called to accept him into a clinical trial to test him with hydra blood. The idea was, their blood contained their essence, so it would transfer all the properties that allow those serpents to heal themselves and regrow their multiple heads.

I was the only one home when my father choked to death on his blood.

I *am* grown.

FOUR

ORDINARY

BRIGHTON

I cage myself in the room until I can trust myself not to go off on anyone. The door is locked, and I ignore Ma when she calls me out for breakfast. I'm starving, but I'm done eating toasted tortillas with refried beans and avocado without Dad. It's an easy enough dish, one that Dad learned to prepare to better connect with Ma's Puerto Rican side, and his were so crispy. I'm just not ready to pretend Ma's are the same. I'm especially not ready to have family breakfast in the living room and talk about how this is our first birthday without him. It's too much.

It's better in here, anyway. Dad once said our bedroom is just a celestial shrine with beds. Years ago, when the Spell Walkers were more embraced by the public, they licensed their image to help bring in money, and I was lucky enough to get my hands on them before manufacturers stopped making them. By the window is a poster of Maribelle and her parents, Aurora and Lestor Lucero. Limited-edition Funko Pops of the original Spell Walkers—Bautista de León, Sera Córdova, the Luceros, Finola Simone-Chambers, and Konrad Chambers. The playing cards I used to bring to school before we graduated. Key chains with the Spell Walker sigil—a constellation of a being who is taking a step, with the brightest of stars lighting up their fists, feet, and heart. There's nothing official for the new wave of Spell Walkers, but I do have these framed art prints of them hanging above my desk, one signed by Wesley Young as a perk for donating to a campaign to fund supplies for one of their hidden havens.

I'm the one who should be famous today. Not some twenty-one-year-old who's probably going to write a memoir about this gap year when she traveled the country taste-testing food.

A few hours later, I drag myself out of bed and get everything ready for the meet-up. I threw down money on custom glow-in-the-dark gel bands for my Brightsiders, notepads with my logo to encourage everyone else to take interest in the celestials around them, and a few T-shirts. There's this local YouTuber, Lore, who always sells out on their swag whenever they host meet-ups. I told Emil I would call the day a win if I make back at least sixty percent of my money this afternoon, but I'm counting on a stronger profit and will hype myself up hard later when I hit it.

I leave the room so Emil can come in and get dressed. He's stretched across the couch and reading a graphic novel, and Ma has the news on, but her eyes are distant.

"We got to go soon," I say.

"You done torturing yourself?" Emil asks.

I scratch my chin, then realize that's what Dad always did with his beard whenever he was upset. I cut it out. I turn to the news.

". . . we're waiting on Senator Iron's statement on the death of an unidentified specter in the middle of the night," the Channel One anchorwoman says.

Emil turns away from his book. "She died?"

Viewer discretion is advised before the clip comes on. It's not the woman from the block party, but instead a man standing on the edge of a roof. This specter also has white phoenix fire, but unlike the woman from last night, *both* his arms are blazing, and the flames stretch like massive wings—wings that are holding their own against the pummeling winds. The man looks hesitant, but he jumps anyway and takes flight, rising higher and higher until one arm snaps clean off his shoulder. He howls in agony and panic while plummeting like a bird shot out of the sky.

The anchorwoman returns before the station can show the impact. "Medical officials arrived to the scene to find the specter near death, expecting a recovery, as his arm was growing back, but he died minutes later."

"He regrew his arm?" Emil stares at the ceiling as if answers can be found there. "Song-rooks are the only phoenixes who can regenerate body parts like that, but it takes hours. And their fire is violet, not white."

"Guess there's another phoenix out there that can," I say. I'm not up on phoenixes like Emil is, but he wasn't exactly acing all his coursework on creatures either. "Not the first time blood alchemy failed someone."

We're quiet.

The alchemists who were working on Dad didn't exactly promise a full recovery, but they sure were arrogant about how brilliant they were for developing a potion with the regenerative properties of a hydra's blood and introducing it into the systems of sick people. I wonder how much more time we would've had with him if we'd let him waste away without their help.

The anchorwoman cuts to Senator Iron, and Ma groans as she raises the volume.

New York's senior senator, Edward Iron, has a full head of dark hair, pale skin that's gone a few rounds with Botox, thick glasses, and a suit that probably costs more than our rent. "Last night's specter incidents, hours apart in our city, are disturbing signals of the crisis our country hasn't escaped. If elected president, Congresswoman Sunstar will create more opportunities and freedom for her people, when we need stricter regulations to avoid the horrors many woke up to this morning. My opponents campaigned against me, claiming this was only a conflict with specters, not celestials, but the Blackout sadly proved me right about how dangerous the Spell Walkers are. . . ." Senator Iron closes his eyes, takes a moment, and nods. "We're working around the clock to locate and apprehend the Spell Walkers."

The station cuts back to the anchorwoman. "As you can see, Senator Iron remains troubled discussing the Blackout after losing his son, Eduardo, who was on a class trip in the Nightlocke Conservatory when the Spell Walkers demolished the building with their powers, taking the lives of six hundred and thirteen people this past January."

I stand by the theories I voiced on YouTube about how someone else must've framed the Spell Walkers for the Blackout to move their own agenda.

But what do I know? Go ask a valedictorian.

As for Eduardo Iron, I'm not dropping tears for him. When he was alive, all he did was bad-mouth and bully celestials and incite more violence. There are better people to mourn.

We get it together and head out. When we reach the park's entrance, Prudencia is waiting for us. This day has finally brought me something good.

Prudencia Mendez is glowing in a knotted T-shirt, navy shorts, boots that make her look like an archaeologist, and her late mother's watch, which doesn't work but never leaves her wrist. Her black hair is pulled up in a long ponytail. When I go in for a hug, her brown eyes narrow and she shoves me.

"I almost didn't come, but then I wouldn't be able to hit you," Prudencia says. "You idiots could've died."

"We were fine," I say.

"We're not fireproof," Emil says.

I glare at that traitor. "Prudencia, even you have to admit I was brave to record that power brawl like a true journalist."

"Not a journalist. You're being a fanboy who doesn't care about his life or his brother's." There's no lightness in her voice. "Your life isn't worth fifteen minutes of fame, Brighton."

"Tell me about it. My video hasn't even reached a hundred thousand views yet."

"That's a new record for you," Emil says. "Wasn't that long ago when you were celebrating one thousand views."

"Dreams grow," I say.

"Last night was a nightmare," Prudencia says. "One I know well. Losing my parents to wand violence was already too much, and if you can't promise me that you'll leave the next time there's chaos, then I don't want you in my life."

I'm not going to be responsible for breaking her heart.

"I promise," I say.

"Same," Emil says.

Prudencia lets out a deep breath and hugs Emil, then me. I relax into her hug, which seems longer than the one she shared with Emil—probably something to do with our whole will-we-or-won't-we thing we've had going on since meeting in high school.

The timing has always sucked. I dated my first and only girlfriend, Nina, through freshman and sophomore year, then broke that up after finally admitting to myself I saw Nina more as a friend and Prudencia as more than that. Before I could express anything, Prudencia started flirting with our classmate Dominic. Definitely didn't help that of all people Prudencia could've dated, she linked up with a celestial who could travel through shadows. For weeks after, I was nonstop calling Dominic a snob for not agreeing to be on my series, and I'll never admit this out loud, not even to Emil, but my recent buzz cut may have had something to do with modeling it after Dominic's hair. Their downfall was a combo of Prudencia's aunt being as intolerant as they come, and Dominic's parents only wanting him dating other celestials to preserve their bloodline, as if he was trying to be some young dad. Secret-keeping got to them, and they broke up.

I've still got a few days before I go; maybe Prudencia and I can click into place before then. Find a way to make it work across the country.

We get deeper into Whisper Fields, named so in honor of Gunnar Whisper, a late-bloomer celestial who took charge in the Undying Battle of Fountain Stone against gangs of necromancers. The textbooks of course credit the win to ordinary soldiers who fought off those ghost-raising maniacs with wands, gem-grenades, and gauntlets—all man-made by celestials, though people are quick to forget that—but I'm not shy about making sure anyone and everyone knows about Gunnar's glory and how proud I am to share Bronx roots with this hero who truly saved the day. The statue is erected by the lake where Gunnar first came into his power of clairvoyance at twenty-three years old, and I always feel this electricity in the air whenever I'm near it, like maybe I'm moments away from discovering I'm a celestial too, who will one day have a park named after me, or that Prudencia and I will take a step into a cooler future together.

But as I approach Gunnar's bronze monument today, there's this dread unlike I've ever had before. I expected to find dozens of Brightsiders waiting for me underneath the shade provided by Gunnar's salute, but I can only make out . . . one, two, three, four, five, six . . . seven. Seven people.

"No one showed," I say.

"There are fans literally waving at you," Emil says.

"Seven people."

"It's still early."

"And train traffic," Prudencia says.

"Got any more excuses?" I point at the blue skies. "Should we blame the weather too?" I put on a smile and wave back at my fans. "Let's knock this out."

I chat with the six Brightsiders—turns out the seventh person is a friend tagging along—about their favorite videos. I grow more and more self-conscious as Emil films, my original vision for the video with big crowds surrounding me completely collapsing. Someone of Lore's caliber—a successful YouTuber—would never have to learn their fans' names or have lengthy conversations outside the comments sections, because of their high demand. I bottle those ugly feelings and put on a grateful face as a couple more people trickle in for quick hellos before the hour is up, and I'm left lounging by the lake with Prudencia and Emil, using the unsold T-shirts as a pillow.

"I know it's not what you wanted," Prudencia says, dipping her feet in the water. "But you made their days."

"I'm a failure on every level. I had the superior video, and it didn't go viral. I mean, come on, I was deep in the action. And now this meet-up was a bust, and . . . whatever."

I shut up because complaining isn't a good look in front of Prudencia; I'll be a punk in front of Emil later. I gather all the swag and beeline toward the exit. Celestials are bravely playing beam-disc, which is basically Frisbee with someone's conjured energy, but I'm not in the mood to watch other people show off their powers, so I keep it moving.

Hours pass, and I become more tightly wound, waiting for something extraordinary to happen. During my shower. When I'm changing. While we eat dinner with Ma at Emil's favorite vegan diner in Brooklyn. After we get home, I spend time alone on the roof, staring up at the faint outline of the

Crowned Dreamer, barely noticing when Emil climbs up the fire escape.

"You good?" Emil asks, tossing me my hoodie.

I'm freezing, but I can't bring myself to put it on. "It's not going to happen, is it?"

"No, but it's okay. You're already a hero because of all the stories you're telling with Celestials of New York."

"More like a sidekick," I say. "Aren't you bummed we're not going to be the people's champions?"

"We don't have to be chosen ones or whatever to do good."

We sit in silence as I pray to the Crowned Dreamer to change my life. But when midnight hits, I turn my back on the stars. We go down the fire escape, through our window, and straight into bed, where we fall asleep, as painfully ordinary as we've been the last eighteen years.

FIVE

A CYCLE OF PHOENIXES

EMIL

The train's air conditioner shutting down sucks in this September heat, but for once the train is getting me to the Museum of Natural Creatures early enough that I can linger a little before my shift begins. My back is sweating by the time I enter the cool indoors. It's all good—my body is hidden thanks to the baggy work polo I ordered one size larger. I check my bag through security and throw on my name tag, stealing a second to marvel at the massive coal-black fossils of a primordial dragon suspended from the starlit ceiling. It sucks that I'll never get to see a dragon in my lifetime, but it's probably for the best they're all extinct so we don't have to worry about alchemists getting their hands on dragon blood. The way people are hunting down living creatures for power, it won't be surprising if they're all history soon.

I cut through the Ever-Changing Chamber, which doesn't live up to its name anymore due to the museum's budget being slashed, so I'm still caught up on July's rotation of shifter art. I completely avoid the dark and chilly Hall of Basilisks, because no thanks. I had to brave it on my first day, and that was enough. I have not been about that serpent life since our sixth-grade field trip to the zoo, when this blind basilisk lunged at the barrier hoping to swallow me whole with its fanged mouth.

I reach the forked path where one stairwell leads down-stairs and the other up, which during orientation I learned was intentional out of respect for the long-standing war between hydras and phoenixes, who seem magnetized to eliminate each other. The Hydra House downstairs starts off pretty innocent, with illustrations of hydras being tamed by fishermen to catch fish and ward off bigger sea animals, but it gets progressively scarier the deeper you venture. The last room shows footage of a territorial fight between a hydra horde and a cycle of phoe-nixes. I was speechless and heartbroken when I first saw the clip of a massive, seven-headed hydra biting phoenixes out of the sky and swallowing them whole.

Another room I haven't returned to since.

I race up the spiral steps to my happy place, the Sunroom. Above the entrance is a stained-glass window of an egg and phoenix connected by a ring of fire. For our thirteenth birthday, Ma brought us to this exhibit. Brighton was into it just fine, but he got impatient quick as I stopped to read every card—I wasn't a fast reader then, and I'm still not today—and I posed for pictures in front of every display in case I never got to come back.

The Sunroom has it all: flutes that mimic the music of a phoenix cry to train and communicate; wooden and iron crossbows shaped like wings; fans made from green and blue feathers; ceremonial candlesticks for believers praying to phoenix fire for renewal when loved ones pass; eggshells ranging in size and color and texture; an hourglass with ashes inside; clay masks with massive beaks and leather jackets with feathered sleeves, close to the ones still worn by the Halo Knights today; dried tears fossilized; a row of ender-blades with bone hilts that are charred black and serrated blades as yellow as the hydra blood they've been cruelly forged from, designed to snuff out a phoenix and keep it from ever resurrecting.

"Excuse me," someone says in an English accent, which is no doubt my favorite accent. My chest tightens. I turn to find a young, beautiful guy with pale and freckled skin, stubble, messy red hair, and the kind of New York T-shirt someone only wears if they're a tourist or lost a bet. He points at my name tag. "You work here, yeah?"

"Yup." My face warms up and I wish I could turn invisible to hide my blushing cheeks. "You need help?"

"What time are the group tours?"

"Start of every hour."

The guy checks his watch. "I have a show to catch at half eleven. Would you mind giving me a brief tour? Promise I won't ask too many questions."

With a voice like that, I want to hear all his questions. I got ten minutes before my shift officially starts, and man, I have no problem working a little earlier to hang out with him. "I could show you around. You with anyone else?"

"No." He extends his hand, which I eagerly shake. "Charlie."

I shouldn't be doing this. I'm far from a know-it-all like Brighton, who always has answers, but this is one of the rare times when I have tons myself. I fight back against the thought that my fitted jeans and favorite brown boots from Goodwill don't make me look as good as I usually swear they do. I don't even care that Charlie doesn't appear to live here—that's what FaceTime is for.

"So what do you want to know?"

"I didn't realize there are so many phoenixes," Charlie says, running his hand through his hair like I've seen countless models do online.

"Tons of phoenixes," I say, while wondering if I would compare the green in Charlie's eyes to emeralds or trees in spring. I'm fantasizing about staying up late with Charlie on the phone to hear more of his voice when I remember I'm supposed to be doing the talking here, like a tour guide who has his act together. "Check this out." I point at the suspended phoenix models above us. "There are dozens of breeds, and the curator, Kirk Bennett, highlighted some of the more popular ones for our guests. Walking through here with the phoenixes above me is one of my favorite things."

"Can you tell me about them?" Charlie asks.

"My favorite things?" I don't know where to start.

"The phoenixes," Charlie says with a smile.

I'm suddenly extra warm, but I'm not standing underneath the sunbeams filtering through the skylight. I recover, pointing at each phoenix like a star and telling their stories like a constellation: the crowned elders, who are born old; sky swimmers, who live underneath water and can set an ocean on fire with their cerulean flames; century phoenixes, who only spawn every hundred years; obsidians with their glittering black feathers and eyes so dark I once thought they'd been hollowed out; breath spawns, who dive into battle like missiles and explode against their enemies, resurrecting moments later in fields of ash; blaze tempests, who conjure the fiercest storms with massive wings, three times as large as their tiny bodies. I stop to catch my breath after telling him about the sun swallowers, who breathe the hottest fire, but also burn out fastest of any breed.

"Amazing," Charlie says. He wanders over to the replica of one of history's most famous phoenixes. The gray sun phoenix is propped on a bronze perch. It has pearl eyes, a gray belly, dark tail, yellow wings, and a gold crown. In front of the model are pictures of the specters Keon Máximo and Bautista de León. "Sort something out for me. I read about the queen slayers that used to claw dragons in the eyes—now that's a real phoenix! Why did these men bother with the gray suns?"

Yo, it's like everything I found attractive about Charlie has been sucked away: his English accent is no longer music to my ears, his green eyes are not worth poetry, and dude needs to make a decision between growing out his beard or shaving because stubble is not the look.

"No one should harm innocent creatures for any reason," I say defensively, but I'm unable to look him in the eye. "You're also super underestimating the gray suns. Every time they're reborn they come back with stronger fire and sharper instincts. Gray suns are good for a fight, but they aren't weapons. They're so . . . good-hearted, and they rescue wounded travelers in the wild and protect all animals and creatures."

"These thugs killed them anyway," Charlie says. "Why?"

I stare at the gritty photo of Keon Máximo, the alchemist who transformed into the very first specter. Keon's piercing slate eyes are gazing to his left as he bites down on his thin bottom lip, and his ashy blond hair flows underneath his hooded cape.

Before I can try to answer, a voice behind me says, "Keon Máximo is responsible for this chaos." Kirk Bennett is in his

39

early thirties, and he's got a brilliant mind. I wish he could take me under his wing. My eyes are drawn to the bright blue sky swimmers tattooed on his pale wrist as he continues to speak emphatically with his hands. "No one knows Keon's motive, but historians believe the explanation to be simple—he wanted power."

"You lot lucked out when this man stepped in," Charlie says.

He points at the picture of Bautista de León: buzz cut, brown eyes, a shadow of a beard, and the original Spell Walker power-proof vest, which has the insignia sprayed on the chest like graffiti.

"His history is complicated because unfortunately we don't possess direct answers," Kirk says. "Some believe Bautista to be a hero, because while he was alive, he kept the threat of specters in check. Others point to the fact that by nature, as a specter himself, he couldn't be a hero and was simply someone eliminating the competition so he could rule the city. Whether or not there's any truth to Bautista sourcing his powers from a gray sun phoenix who had already been cut by a hunter's infinity-ender, communities are still outraged that he perpetuated the cycle of creatures being killed for one person's benefit."

"They don't even get all the powers," Charlie says. "These men were never reborn, yeah?"

Kirk shakes his head. "Thankfully not. Phoenixes resurrect at different rates, of course, but no specter with their blood has ever reappeared. It would be a tragedy for phoenixes everywhere if their resurrection proved successful among humans." He looks up at me with his thick frames. "Shouldn't you be clocking in?"

"I thought you *were* working," Charlie says to me.

"Have a great day," I say, just to be on my professional flow, but I keep my eyes low as I head out.

Working up here in the Sunroom is the dream, but I go down the next set of stairs and walk inside the gift shop, where I actually make my money. One afternoon when I was visiting the Sunroom as a guest, sketching the suspended phoenixes, Kirk complimented my art, and I expressed how much I wanted to be a tour guide here one day. Kirk returned shortly with an application. I thought it was to work with him, but nope, just an opening in the gift shop. Wasn't what I wanted, but it was a foot in the door.

My coworker, Sergei, is working the cash register. My anxiety spikes as he side-eyes me, and I pick at my cuticles before clocking in and taking over the register so he can handle some business in the office. The shop is busier than usual, thanks to some kid's birthday gathering, but I knock out the line in minutes and get everything back in shape.

We only carry phoenix merchandise, and if I was better off, I'd be cashing my checks and giving them right back to the museum to buy these prints all done by local artists. I tidy up the ash-tempest plush dolls and restock the common ivories, which are top sellers even though they're more snow white than they should be. I'm taking inventory with a faux-phoenix feather pen when Kirk walks in.

Kirk is short, with a thick beard that reminds me of Dad, and he's always dressed in an oversized suit. I wonder if he's hiding his body too, or if he doesn't know how to shop for himself. None of it is my business, and this is the same kind of nonsense that invites people to comment on my own body.

You're like a skeleton.

You need to eat more.

You look sick.

You're so gaunt.

Normally whenever Kirk swings through the gift shop, he checks in on how his nonfiction book about one of his expeditions is selling—never well—but I know today is different.

"I'm sorry for giving that guy a tour," I immediately spit out, since he's no doubt here to remind me of my place. "I couldn't beat the combo of him being interested in phoenixes and looking like that. If I'd known he was such an idiot about blood alchemy, I would've backed off."

"Other countries have their own corruptive figures, but nothing in recent memory in the way of Keon, or even devastations like our Blackout, for that matter. They don't understand how tense it's gotten here in the States." Kirk opens his folder, turning past pages of sealed crates and guard services. "I still don't have an opening for you in the Sunroom, but I could use some assistance on a project that might bring in enough money to refresh our exhibits."

"I'm in," I say. "I mean, I don't know what it's for, but I'm game."

"Something extraordinary. The museum will be hosting a gala toward the end of the month, but it has to remain a secret for the next few days. This is going to be the celebration of a lifetime. We'll be witnessing the hatching of a century phoenix."

"Say what?" I never thought I would see a century phoenix at all, let alone the birth of one.

Kirk's eyes gleam. "It gets better, Emil. Century phoenixes are an exceptionally rare breed, as you may know. It certainly doesn't help that they don't often reproduce when they do respawn, but this blue egg was feathered."

I give myself a second to figure out what that means, but nothing. I know I shouldn't compare my knowledge to someone who has a master's degree in Creature Sciences and years of experience raising phoenixes and building habitats, but every time I don't know something, it's hard to appreciate it as something I learned, and instead I feel stupid for not knowing it already. "What does that mean?"

"A century phoenix's egg is only feathered when it's a first-born."

"So this is the phoenix's first cycle of life!"

"The world will be able to witness Gravesend's first breath."

"Where is the egg now?"

"Gravesend is being guarded by Halo Knights in a secure location. She'll remain there until it's time for her birth, to protect her from the traffickers and Blood Casters who will no doubt try to hunt her down once we announce the purpose of the gala. We'll tend to her here for the first month before releasing her into the wild."

I think about the specters with phoenix blood who made headlines this week.

"On the news, they said a specter regrew his arm before he died, but his fire looked like it came from common ivories or crowned elders or halos. The regeneration doesn't make sense, right?"

Kirk looks around the shop, like it's been on his mind too. "Nothing is more important to a specter than power. It doesn't surprise me when anyone works around the clock to make the impossible possible, the way Keon did when he had his first blood alchemy breakthrough. My hunch? Someone has found a way to double their abilities. The world is always changing, and I believe we're about to be audience to a particularly dark turn of history, especially with the Crowned Dreamer rising. Let's brace ourselves and pray no one messes with Gravesend."

It's rare that I keep secrets from Brighton, but I'm holding this one close to my chest. He's bouncing to Cali in two days, and this is my chance to grow. To transform. My own little rebirth as I study hard in school—for real this time, no giving up after a week—and prep for Gravesend and straight wow Brighton when he sees what a phoenix pro I've become. I got to get in good with Kirk, because it'd be a legit dream to hit up Brighton, invite him back to New York, and hook him up with some behind-the-scenes exclusives of Gravesend's journey for his series.

If I can pull this off, maybe, for once, I'll stop feeling like a little brother who is years younger, even though we were born seven minutes apart.

Maybe I'll stop feeling like the sidekick.

SIX

CELESTIALS OF NEW YORK

BRIGHTON

My last full day in New York is off to a rough start.

Today marks six months since Dad died. Ma cold-shouldered me because I chose to keep packing instead of talking about my feelings. Then I tried to distract myself with some instant gratification online, posting a new profile; there's no high like watching comments come in and views increase. But the Brightsiders were underwhelmed, to put it lightly. They don't give a damn about the assistant manager of a travel agency that hires teleporters to transport celestials who've been blacklisted from boarding planes because of powers deemed hazardous. Instead, the Brightsiders flooded me with questions about why I didn't work harder to get an interview with

Atlas and Maribelle, as if the enforcers were going to grab coffee while I handled business.

My fans can be unreasonable.

To top it all off, we're extra late to the Friday Dreamers Festival because of Emil, and wading through the crowds in Central Park is the worst. I want my series to grow beyond YouTube—a prime-time talk show is the dream—but all the incredible content I could've been filming the past couple hours is lost because Emil took his sweet time at work on some project he won't tell me and Prudencia about. Whatever the secret is, I'm not expecting anything too exciting from a failing museum. But because Emil is still freaking out about enforcers since the other night, I promised him we'd all go together.

Dozens of enforcers line one path, and Emil's panicked breaths make him look really suspicious.

"What if they're the same ones who shot at us?" Emil asks.

"I doubt it."

"You don't know that!"

"Do you want to leave?" Prudencia asks.

He turns to me, and I don't know what look I'm giving off, but he shakes his head.

Great.

I get that enforcers casting spellwork and buildings exploding can get any heart racing. But I'm not traumatized over it. My anxiety—if I can even call it that—has always been more academic, though, and never quite blows up the way Emil's does, even when things are troubling me the most. Like when college acceptance letters were coming in, and my top choice wait-listed me.

"Sorry I'm a mess," Emil says as we get past the enforcers.

"You're not a mess, and you're going to be okay," I say. It's the best I can think of, though I'm not sure there are any right words to calm down Emil or heal his emotional scarring.

I love my brother, but we need time apart. Once I move to Los Angeles, I'm only focusing on myself. Emil is going to have to up his game to take better care of himself without me around. It'll be good for us. Brothers shouldn't get in the way of each other's lives.

I'm doing my best to keep it together, especially since Prudencia already saw me get down on myself once this week, but the field is packed with attendees on picnic blankets, and we're so far from the domed stage, and I've lost all natural light out here for filming. I set up my camera anyway. The Crowned Dreamer hasn't cared about me since showing up in the sky, but maybe tonight the constellation will throw me a bone so I can get some halfway decent content.

We've already missed my favorite artist Himalia Lim's first public interview since making it her mission to fly around and paint neighborhoods in the Bronx that get a bad rap, ensuring that people won't dismiss them so easily. It sucks how I'll have to watch that on someone else's YouTube channel and have to sit through Oak's band right now instead. I unfollowed Oak on Instagram a few months back because he stopped posting clips of his blooming power and was only sharing ultra-bait shirtless pictures and asking followers to answer random questions that had nothing to do with the ripped abs on display. I studied his engagement, and I got to give him credit because people care way more about his muscles than using his gleam in gardens. We all got to do what we got to do to make ourselves known.

I'm positioning my camera for the main event when a celestial begins floating in my line of vision. Her fake glow-in-the-dark tattoo is awesome, but it's not going to get me views.

"You okay?" Prudencia asks.

"She's blocking me," I say.

"Let her live. She probably doesn't get to use her power in the open," Prudencia says. She rests her hand on my shoulder and I meet her eyes. "You should put your camera away anyway, Brighton. It's our last night together."

Tonight could've been so different if it were just me and Pru sitting under the stars. If my power brawl video had gone viral so I could take the night off. But I can't level up if I don't put the work in every chance I get. "I'm never going to find myself on that stage if I don't give it my all."

"That's fair," Prudencia says, but in a way that I hear as "Your loss."

Maybe.

The crowd erupts into cheers as Lore appears onstage. Lore has the life I want, and they rose to internet fame pretty quickly: they initially went viral when they campaigned to become their school's first-ever Korean American genderqueer class president, inspiring others to follow in their footsteps; they reached a million subscribers within a year with content that ranges from comedy skits to news about heroic acts from celestials to counter the overwhelming media against them; they even got to sit down with Wesley Young last December on his birthday and chat with him about fat acceptance as he played with puppies; and now they're getting an interview that makes the rest of us look like amateurs.

"Thanks for the love, New York," Lore says into a mic. They're wearing a silver dress that sparkles like stars on the stage. "I can't *even* believe that we're being graced by this inspiring woman's presence, so let's get her out here before she changes her mind. Huge round of applause for the candidate I can't wait to vote for in November—Congresswoman Nicolette Sunstar!"

The roars are thunderous as Nicolette Sunstar appears in a yellow pantsuit and hugs Lore. The two sit down and immediately seem like old friends, when in reality they probably spoke for a few minutes backstage. But the way Congresswoman Sunstar praises Lore for their high school election with the air of it being as significant as her run for president is so genuine.

Lore leads Sunstar into a deeper conversation about what it

means to be the first ever Black celestial on the ticket before she reminds us all what she's fighting for: better job opportunities for gleamcrafters so they don't have to make money by powering wands, gem-grenades, and shackles with their gifts, only for enforcers to use those weapons against them; protecting pregnant celestials who are being killed, and in other cases, being detained by authorities and locked away underground, far away from the stars that give them power, to suppress their children's abilities from reaching their true potential; removing the corrupt enforcers from the force so gleamcrafters can live their lives in peace—and *not* in havens; condemning the alchemists like Luna Marnette, leader of the Blood Casters, who are clearly doing more harm than good, no matter how much money they make for the enforcers.

I've given up catching any of this on camera—everyone's footage and livestreams will have me beat—so I lean forward with everyone else on the field as Sunstar commands our attention.

"Time and time again my opponents—Senator Iron, especially—have put down those with powers as they pursue their own," Sunstar says with the gentleness of a mother telling a bedtime story. "There is no question that the senator has faced tragedy with the loss of his wife and son. But the faults of some do not represent the lives of all. I truly wish I could lead an ordinary life as a mother who is stressed about parent-teacher conferences instead of global affairs. As a wife keeping my love strong instead of a country intact. But as a celestial who wants to see my community safe and nurtured, I can't sit still and expect others to do the work I'm unwilling to do myself."

Sunstar walks to the edge of the stage. "I have felt hopeless—felt that there is no light to be found in the shadows. But even if I can't see the light, I trust it's there because of all of you. Look around at your neighbors. You're not alone in your hope. You're here because you believe." She raises her fist. "We won't let the darkness overtake us. We must keep the stars in the sky!"

Golden light sails from Sunstar's hand and erupts into fireworks under the Crowned Dreamer.

Everyone applauds as Sunstar is joined by her husband, Ash Hyperion, and their daughter, Proxima. It's going to take a miracle to get them into the White House. Tons of people crowd the stage, hoping to get a moment, but when Lore poses with Sunstar's family for a picture, that's when my jealousy peaks and I have to go.

I'm on a mission tonight to become as great and worthy as Lore. If I'm not going to become a celestial, then everyone will remember me as the greatest mortal.

Emil and Prudencia tag along as I chat up people, picking their brains about Sunstar and the world at large. A group of girls are infectious with their chants of "Keep the stars in the sky!" and I get it all on camera. I get an interview with this blue-haired celestial who tells me about how even with her ability to generate a shield around her entire body, she still doesn't feel safe around enforcers. We attract more attention from other celestials, like an older woman who feels confident in saying that enforcer violence these days hasn't felt this regularly heartbreaking since she was a little girl, right when specters first came into existence sixty-something years ago. The most unnerving is from a man with glowing fists that crack with lightning when he knocks them together, and he promises that if an enforcer aims a wand at him, he won't think twice about striking them down first.

"Burn that footage," Emil says as the man storms away with lightning jumping between his palms.

"No kidding."

My videos won't ever be used to build any cases against celestials, I swear my life on it.

Four young men by the lake catch my attention. Two are circling each other with their fists like they're about to fight. Another is filming on his phone while the last is laughing and holding a cooler.

"Check it out."

"I know they're not about to watch these two guys go in on each other," Prudencia says. She charges over. "Hey, enough!"

"I'm going to turn you into ashes," the freckled teen says. Gleamcrafter . . .

I drag Prudencia back before she gets hurt. The Crowned

Dreamer season is truly stirring some trouble if we're about to witness our second power brawl in one week.

"Not if I blow you away first," says the boy whose muscles are flexing out his gym wear.

Freckles opens his mouth and squints his eyes, but no fire appears. I wonder if Gym-Rat is maybe burning from the inside out, but he holds his fist up to the sky and spins it around as if expecting a tornado to swing through. The guy with the cooler holds his stomach, laughing, and I think the only thing funny here is his awful man bun. The young men continuing to battle with no powers isn't hilarious, it's confusing.

Emil cautiously approaches. "What's happening?"

I shrug. "Maybe they're filming some movie and adding effects later?" My favorite indie movies lately have celestial actors using their real powers, but Hollywood largely prefers special effects since it's safer for sets.

"They don't seem to care that we're in their line of vision," Prudencia says.

Freckles and Gym-Rat sweat as they gesture at each other some more. It's one of the most bizarre things I've ever seen. Reminds me of when Emil and I used to wrestle each other with imaginary powers, but we were kids. These two are too old to be playing pretend. They sway back and forth and rapidly blink before steadying themselves.

"You're okay!" Freckles fist-bumps Gym-Rat. "That felt so real!"

"I hurled you over the trees," Gym-Rat says with a laugh.

As they walk away, Man-Bun shouts after them to tell their friends.

"What was that all about?" I ask.

The other guy stops filming and puts away his phone. "Business."

"What business?" Emil asks.

He turns and does a double take at Emil, then stares in silence.

"It's called Brew," Man-Bun says. He reaches into his cooler and pulls out a vial containing a light gold liquid that looks like champagne. I've never heard of it. "We use illusionist blood to create hallucinatory potions so the drinker can experience what it's like to have powers. Not cheap, but it feels extremely real. Helps people blow off steam."

I've done some virtual reality where you can play as a celestial, but I never forget it's a game. This sounds more convincing. "How much for that bottle?" I don't have a lot of cash on me or a lot of money in general, but I have to get in on this.

"Three hundred."

The soaring possibilities in my chest are crashing. I'm still at a loss after not selling my swag at the meet-up, and my videos aren't getting enough traffic to make solid money off my ads. "I could do two hundred if you let me run to an ATM."

"Are we doing discounts, James?" Man-Bun asks.

"No discounts, Orton."

Orton puts the potion back into the cooler.

"Wait."

Emil tries dragging me away. "You don't have the money. We're going home."

I ignore him. "I run an account called Celestials of New York. Have you heard of it?" They're glaring at me like I asked for the meaning of life. "I profile people about their stories and powers, and I can help you spread the word about Brew. We can do a trade. You give me a potion, and I give you publicity. Is this your blood you're using?"

Orton grins. "I'm superior to celestials." His eyes are suddenly consumed by a glowing eclipse before returning to normal. "Superior to other specters too."

This is a rare opportunity. This is what I need to revive my channel—a special kind of profile. "I've never interviewed a specter before," I say.

"Don't give him a voice," Prudencia says. "He's part of our country's problem."

"You don't know my story," Orton says.

I ready my camera. "Tell it to me. I want to know all about what drew you to blood alchemy, how you decided on which creature, where you found a reputable alchemist, and when you got your powers."

"That all?" Orton asks.

"We're not doing interviews," James cuts in. He's shorter

than Orton, and apart from his firm tone, I get sidekick vibes from him.

"Just give me ten minutes. Fifteen tops," I say.

Prudencia gets in my face. "There are so few specters who do good with their powers. Stop trying to shine a light on someone who's clearly corrupt."

"I just want to have a better understanding," I say.

"No, you want guidance on how to pull this off yourself."

I stand tall even though I'm rocked by her accusation. "My father died from blood alchemy. I wouldn't ever do this to myself. Even if I did, though—Bautista was a specter, and he formed our city's greatest group of heroes. Why does everyone conveniently forget that?"

Prudencia points at Orton. "He's a potions dealer, Brighton. Not a hero."

"I have feelings, by the way," Orton says.

"So did the creature you harmed." Emil speaks up with his eyes cast to the ground.

Orton pays him no mind. "I'm making dreams come true."

Prudencia's fist clenches. "You need to get your life straight. Bye."

She storms away, and even though this could be huge for me, I follow.

"You should've had my back, Brighton," she says.

"I wanted an interview."

"You are so obsessed, and—"

"I want to understand the psyche of anyone risking their lives for powers when blood alchemy is such a killer, especially after that happened with my father—"

"Guys, guys," Emil interrupts, looking even more panicked than when he saw the enforcers. "The specter is following us."

SEVEN

GOLD AND GRAY

EMIL

This is one of those rare times I wish I had powers. Instead of rushing down into the subway, I could teleport away with Brighton and Prudencia. I'd even be good with a defensive power like shield generation to protect us. I can't believe there's a chance we're going to be attacked, and we have no clue what powers to expect from Orton. Is he going to strike like a basilisk? Light us up like a phoenix? Paralyze us with illusions like a wraith?

"Let's go, let's go," I say as the train arrives and we squeeze into the packed car.

The doors close behind us before Orton and James can enter. Orton grins as the train begins pulling away.

I catch my breath and stare down Brighton. "Can you not buddy up with the egomaniac next time?"

"He was fine until you both went off on him," Brighton says.

"Don't turn this around on us," Prudencia says.

"I document people's lives, and his story could've been eye-opening!"

Brighton stays shut when he realizes their arguing is catching the attention of other passengers on the train. Someone at the opposite end of the car is standing on the bench with his phone aimed at us. I'm about to tell them to cool it when the connecting doors open and Orton and James walk in.

My heart is pounding. This is impossible, the train was taking off.

"Don't look, but they're here," I say. Like an idiot Brighton turns around. "What did I say?"

"How did he even get here?" Prudencia asks.

"Doesn't matter now," Brighton says. "Stay calm, they can't do anything. Too many people here."

I don't believe that. He's followed us this long—he doesn't care. If we can get off this train and get home, I won't ever leave my bedroom again. I don't want to be some damn statistic of victims killed by chaotic specters. I'm so pissed at Brighton, but as Orton shoves passengers aside, Brighton's hero complex kicks in and he guards me and Prudencia.

"Didn't get a chance to say bye," Orton says.

Prudencia shakes her head. "You feel good about yourself?"

"Prudencia, stop," I say. Sure, there are some people who would rather go down fighting, but I'm in the business of staying alive.

"Your friend wanted to know my story," Orton says. "I was tired of being everyone's punching bag, so I became a god."

"This is not what we're here for." James tugs Orton's arm.

"Celestials are born with the gleam, but taking in power is a truer show of strength. These other punks try and die." Orton's fist tightens. "I'm beyond the others too."

Orton might be running his mouth about how superior he is, but you don't need that much power to take down three teens without any of our own. Passengers clear back as I finally crack into a full panic, begging for help, but only a few people shout at Orton to leave us alone while others get out their phones to record. Maybe if I was their favorite show that was about to get canceled they would care more, but instead I'm about to become a headline they'll glimpse before moving on.

It's wild how even though I've been shot at by enforcers, the terror squeezes harder now. I was a third party to that power brawl, the kind of nameless and faceless person who bleeds into crowds and either becomes a casualty or someone with a story of how he survived. But now I'm a target.

"Back up," Brighton says.

Orton gets in Brighton's face, noses touching.

I split them up because no one steps to my brother like that.

I sucked at biology, but even I know hearts aren't supposed to beat this fast, this hard. "You win. You're a god. We'll shut up."

Orton grins and reaches out for a handshake. "Truce."

I notice two deep, fresh scars around his forearm, almost surgical, even cleaner. I reach out to shake his hand because I'm scared, okay?

Orton withdraws his hand. "You were about to use your powers," he says.

I shake my head. "What, no. We don't have powers, don't worry about—"

I shut up, but the damage is done. The specter's grin is dark, and I screwed up. I should've lied because the truth wasn't doing it for Orton, who swears we should be bowing before him.

Orton grabs my arm and flings me toward the train door, and my head bangs against the pole; that's going to swell in no time. I fall face-first into a puddle of someone's cold coffee, and my spit drips onto the floor. I inhale a deep breath as I try getting up, but the air has been knocked out of me. Everything is spinning as I wheeze, my eyes welling with tears. A hand touches my shoulder, and I flinch, thinking it's Orton grabbing me again, but it's Prudencia asking if I'm okay.

Chaos erupts throughout the train.

Brighton leaps at Orton because that's how stupid we are for each other, but he somehow flies through the specter's body as if he's nothing but a projection. That doesn't make sense. Phasing through solid objects is a celestial's power, and specters haven't been successful with stealing their abilities.

I stand, my back aching, and I wish someone on the train would give more of a damn instead of filming us get tossed around. Prudencia lifts her hand like she's about to backslap Orton, but he kicks her square in the stomach, and she topples into me.

"You okay?" I ask.

Prudencia points at Brighton. He picks himself up, his face red and beat, and he clocks the specter from behind. Orton spins, grabs Brighton by the throat, and drags him. Orton is phasing himself through the door, looking to throw Brighton off the train.

"BRIGHTON!"

I shiver as my temperature is rising, fever-warm. My teeth ache, my head is pounding, my throat is raw, my bloody lip is swelling, and I'm too young for heartburn, but I have no other words to describe this heat in my chest. My vision blurs like I'm walking through a cloud of steam, and a growl within me crescendos into a melodic roar, and then everything clears away. I have no idea how hard I've been hit—maybe adrenaline is preventing me from feeling it in full force. But seeing my brother about to be thrown onto the tracks by that maniac hits me with this fear that if I don't get to him quickly enough, the next time I see him he'll be dead on the train tracks, unrecognizable. It's a fear like never before.

My fist is on fire.

The flames are gold and gray, alive and heavy, and they bite with a heat that puts summer to shame, but my skin isn't melting. I'm okay—somehow. The glow catches everyone's attention, and they freeze in place, even the specter who steps back and stares in awe.

Brighton's breathing is rough, and even with his very life at stake, I catch surprise in his eyes. He snaps out of it and elbows Orton in the stomach, breaking free from his grip. White fire runs up Orton's arm, like we saw on the other specters this week—this is gang work, no doubt—and he lunges. I take a fighter's stance to defend myself. I have to survive long enough for the train to finish pulling into the next station, then we can all run off and find help. Even though I'm scrawny and haven't won many fights, desperation kicks in, and I swing at the specter. Fire flies from my fist, small and fast, six burning darts that screech as they strike the specter in his shoulder and stomach. Orton is blasted off his feet, and just as I think he's going to slam into the door, he phases beyond it and lands flat on the platform.

Passengers cheer, and I'm frozen.

I didn't just . . .

I didn't kill Orton, right?

Bad dude or not, a life is a life, and I'm not about stealing anyone's. That isn't up to me just because I have powers.

How? How the hell do I have powers? Just . . . What? This isn't some trick.

My fist is a torch with gold and gray flames, burning in all its confusing glory. I shake my hand and blow on it like a candle. The flames cool down and vanish.

Everyone is safe. Brighton and Prudencia stare at me like I'm a stranger who fell out of the sky to save the day.

I taste blood again. My body aches like a gang stomped me out, not just a single specter. There's zero joy in cold showers, but I'm ready to sink into one of those steel bathtubs filled to the brim with ice; Brighton probably feels the same. The way my flesh stings reminds me of a few years ago when Brighton and I were cooking up an anniversary breakfast for our parents, and I grabbed the frying pan with my bare hand before it had a chance to cool down.

The doors open. We step off the train while passengers continue filming. They need to stop, because enforcers aren't going to give a damn that this was all self-defense. I don't know how I'm going to live with myself if I killed Orton. Wisps of smoke trail into the air from Orton's chest, which is slowly rising.

He's alive.

I'm so relieved I could cry. But nerves strike again as an enforcer approaches, his metallic wand aimed at my chest.

"Everyone get on the ground." The enforcer's eyes shift between us.

I so badly want to explain that I have no idea how this happened, but instead I sink to my knees with Brighton, Prudencia, and James.

"He attacked us," Prudencia says.

The enforcer hovers over Orton. Just as he reaches for the gauntlet on his belt, Orton's eyes open, flooded by shadow, and he swings up with a fist of phoenix fire and clocks the enforcer in the jaw. The enforcer shoots into the air and crashes back down. A pair of enforcers charge our way, blasting bolts of lightning at Orton from their wands.

I get up and run with Prudencia, Brighton, and James. As we rush up the flight of steps, a phone falls out of James's pocket. I recognize the yellow wolf on the case. Even in the flurry, I remember someone else with the same case recording the power brawl during the awakening of the Crowned Dreamer.

James scoops up his phone and runs away like I'm about to come for his life. I chase him up the steps, just wanting to piece together this puzzle. We reach the turnstile, and James ducks into a crowd, shoving people out of his way. I keep my eyes on the exit, but James doesn't pop back up. Completely out of sight.

That is new. No one has ever been scared of me before. I've never had a fist of fire either.

"I think he was there the night of the block party," I say, catching my breath.

Brighton shakes his head. His eyes are red, like he's about to cry, which I've never been good at handling without being quiet and awkward. "You have powers."

"I guess. I don't know." I lead the way out of the subway before the enforcers or Orton can catch up to us. "Our blood-line came through just in time."

"Don't play games with me. We saw your eyes. You've been holding out on me."

I stop at the corner and turn to my brother. "What about my eyes?"

Brighton stares right back. "They burned like a specter's."

That's impossible. "I don't know what you saw, but I'm not messing with blood alchemy."

"Your eyes were dark," Brighton says.

Prudencia rests her hand on Brighton's shoulder. "Chill out. Some celestial flares are darker than others." She turns to me. "You've never shown any sign of powers before now, right?"

"Can't imagine literally any scenario where I wouldn't have mentioned that."

I don't know how we're going to get home from here, maybe a bus, but we're definitely not hopping back on the train, so I speed-walk forward across the street while the cars wait at the red light. I want to get home, stay low, and figure out what all this means.

"But what about the fire? That was phoenix fire, right?" Brighton asks.

I halt in the middle of the street.

I'm burning up, so hot that I think I'm about to find myself on fire again, maybe my entire body this time. I try reaching for any memory of a celestial who wielded flames like mine, and I come up with nothing. Only specters have that power. That was fire from a gray sun phoenix, no more doubts about it. It's impossible that phoenix blood could've found its way inside of me, but not knowing how I got it is eating me up from the inside like poison. The world is spinning, like days where I don't feed myself right but ten times worse. I'm falling, and my brother and best friend try catching me as cars honk. I'm blacking out, and the only thing on my mind is how quickly those gold and gray flames will burn everything good in my life to ashes.

EIGHT
VIRAL

BRIGHTON

I once pretended I could see the future.

The night before our fourteenth birthday Abuelita put me and Emil to bed and told us stories about her power. Her visions weren't much to brag about, usually only ever taking her a minute or two into the future. Quick warnings to pick up the pace to catch the train or a heads-up that the phone was about to ring. But every few years a notable vision would break through, like how when she met Abuelito on the subway she foresaw their wedding.

Hours after midnight, I woke up Emil and claimed I had a vision about the owner of our favorite corner bodega getting hurt. Emil tried writing it off as a dream, but I doubled down

69

on my lie, saying it felt different, it felt real. That I inherited the power from Abuelita.

We had snuck out through the fire escape because Emil was game for an adventure back then, especially after I told him that if I had power, then it must mean his power would kick in too if we worked together to save William. We did a mini stakeout and even convinced William to close up early. It was a good lie because, for all Emil knew, we prevented disaster. I felt guilty after we got home, though. No matter how happy he was for me, Emil was getting more and more frustrated when his own power wasn't surfacing. I couldn't lead him on like that any longer, so I came clean. He punched me really hard in the arm for waking him up at three in the morning over a fake vision of a fake crime, but then he laughed it off and said it would've been awesome if we really did get powers on our birthday. Better than a chosen one—the chosen two.

Fast-forward to today, and I never saw any of this coming.

This can't be real.

I try shaking Emil awake in the streets, but nothing. He still has a pulse, but between the burning up, bump on his head, and cut lip, I've never seen him in such critical condition, and my own heart is racing harder than when we were fighting for our lives on the train. Drivers are getting out of their cars and pedestrians are calling for help, but we can't waste time waiting around for an ambulance. Prudencia is quick with hailing a cab, and we carry Emil into the backseat.

"Darden Hospital, now!" I shout with my brother's head in my lap.

The driver looks hesitant before taking off. "Make sure he doesn't bleed all over my backseat."

Prudencia is fighting back tears, but her voice is firm. "We should take him to Gleam Care."

I'm still in total shock that my brother even qualifies to receive assistance from gleamcraft practitioners. "No one will take care of Emil like Ma will."

"Emil's blood may need special treatment, Brighton. Let trained celestials revive him."

I nod.

"Take us to the Vega Center on the Concourse," Prudencia instructs.

I'm digging my nails into Emil's arm. I don't care if it hurts him; maybe he'll wake up. "Why didn't he tell me he did this?"

"Emil wouldn't willingly become a specter," Prudencia says. "I don't know what happened. Maybe he drank the potion without realizing what it was. Emil loves phoenixes too much to steal their essence."

I know she has a point, but there's something so off about all of this. And already, I'm struck with how badly I want to talk nonsense with Emil, how stupid I was to think that I won't miss him when I leave for school. We can figure out the phoenix blood business later, but as I'm freaking out over if my brother is going to be okay again, I'm missing when we ask each other questions the world doesn't need answering. Like what I would do if I suddenly grew two extra arms or how Emil would occupy himself if he were stuck in an empty room for a whole week. No one else cares that I would take up wrestling if I had four arms or that Emil would have the time to perfect his cartwheels, but this is the kind of stuff you talk about with someone you've known your entire life. And Emil isn't allowed to die now because we have so much more to chat about as old men on our deathbeds.

I'm shaking too much to call Ma so Prudencia grabs my phone and takes over, giving her the heads-up to meet us at the hospital.

We arrive at the Vega Center for Gleam Care, where we haul Emil through the lobby until nurses place him on a stretcher, wheeling him away to a room where we can't follow. I'm not trying to hang out in the waiting room or pretend a magazine will have the power to distract me. It didn't work the countless hours we waited for Dad, and it won't work for Emil. I pace the halls, feeling Prudencia's eyes on me as I go back and forth between the check-in counter and the gender-neutral bathrooms. Who knows how long later, but I'm rescued from dark thoughts when my mother shouts my name.

"Where is he?" Ma asks with her hand pressed against her heart.

"He's already in the ER."

Ma sees how busted we look and pulls us both into a hug. "Are you okay? Do you need to be seen too?"

"We're fine. Thanks, Carolina," Prudencia says.

Ma runs her fingers over my swollen eye. "What happened?"

"We were headed home when . . ." I shut up. I'm not talking about Emil's powers; that's his call. "A specter jumped us on the train. We were okay until Emil fainted in the middle of the street, so we brought him here in case there was some side effect."

She bursts into tears. "Is he okay? What powers did the specter have?"

"It was strange," Prudencia says. "He could phase through us and the door like a celestial, but he also had phoenix fire."

"Is Emil okay? Was he burned?"

"No, Ma."

She takes a deep breath, but she's shaking. We guide her to the waiting room, and Prudencia keeps her company while I stay by the doors my brother is behind.

I'm getting more and more steps in when my phone goes off and won't chill. There's a stream of notifications that keep coming in, like people asking me *Do you have powers too?* and saying *Upload an interview with your brother!* I finally stop in my tracks.

I've been tagged in several videos where all the thumbnails are cropped pictures of Emil holding phoenix fire. I click the viral video so fast, even though I know the scene firsthand. I watch, getting to see the moment the gray and gold fire first lights up my brother's fist, paying close attention to Emil's reaction—he's just as shocked as anyone.

The video is making serious numbers. Any outsider would assume Emil is extremely popular online and not someone with a near-dead Instagram with posts that never even get a thousand likes. I check out all of Emil's social media accounts. His Twitter of two-hundred-plus followers who hang around for his random musings on video games, nonfiction, and phoenix activism has exploded into six thousand followers; in the same way I feel weird that hundreds of thousands people peripherally know who I am, I can only imagine how Emil will react when he wakes up to this. After staring at a GIF of Emil's flaming fist, I switch over to Instagram, where his following has skyrocketed. Everyone is leaving comments on his latest photo that have nothing to do with his review of some graphic novel, like asking whether he's flying solo or part of a squad.

This isn't something he's going to be able to keep to himself.

For all I know, Emil is near death, and still, I envy everything about my supernova superstar of a brother.

NINE
THE SPELL WALKERS

MARIBELLE

I'm the most hated celestial alive today.

I'm holed up in my room at Nova Grace Elementary, which was once a low-income school for celestials and which we've taken over as a hidden haven for everyone we rescue. There are more people in this building who resent me than I can count, but they know better than to say it to my face as long as we're giving them shelter. Everyone swears my parents are responsible for the Blackout, and even when I finally prove otherwise, the Lucero line will still be blamed for the recent surge of intolerance that marked many celestials as terrorists.

If the world doesn't want to remember my parents as heroes, then maybe I'll stop saving it.

I kill that thought.

When I was little, I was always threatening to run away every time I didn't get my way, and Mama made me promise I would never make any decisions with rage in my heart. If I still wanted to leave whatever haven we were camping out in after I calmed down, she would help me pack my bags, kiss my forehead, and send me on my way.

Deep breaths bring me back to reality. I will continue to protect celestials because it's how I honor my parents' legacy best, even though it feels pointless on most days. Our movement isn't ever going to be a big enough tide to wash out the world that's so ready to set itself on fire. Especially under our team's current leadership. But maybe we can take down Luna Marnette and her Blood Casters since the enforcers never seem to be knocking down their doors.

I'm in the zone on my laptop, reviewing security footage for the millionth time of everything that went down in the Nightlocke Conservatory nine months ago. The only camera in the room was aimed at the students and teachers visiting for their class trip, and on the screen, they're all surrounding a massive bronze telescope. I continue scanning faces in the crowd for one particular girl, but when shards of glass begin raining from above, I brace myself and watch as Mama and Finola crash through the ceiling, my mother's hands wrapped around Iris's mother's neck. Papa and Konrad arrive through the entrance, trying to pry their wives away from each other, but Finola breaks out of the grip with her powerhouse strength and sends all three of them into the air and collapsing around her.

There's no point turning away as Finola pursues Mama. The memory is all burned into my head anyway: Mama slams Senator Iron's son, Eduardo, to the floor, and she pulls out two ruby gem-grenades from inside her power-proof vest. Mama throws one gem-grenade high into the farthest corner of the room, and Papa jumps into flight and soars after it. Then Mama throws another over Finola's head, and Finola and Konrad try to catch it.

Everyone fails.

The end begins with electric red lights flowing through the room like furious waves meeting in the middle, and with one last crash into the telescope, the conservatory becomes nothing but glass and blood and smoke and fire, all in the time it takes to inhale a single deep breath.

All that's left standing is a girl peeking out from the smoke— big eyes, pale skin, tiny frame, and an eerie calmness about her despite the destruction. Then she turns away from the camera and sinks into smoke, vanishing like an illusion. Except I know she's real. There are even message boards devoted to trying to figure out her identity. Is she responsible for the chaos? Was she a student whose power protected her? Does she have any information on what really happened? I need answers.

I could've prevented all of this if I trusted the dream of

where I was underneath the stars and saying goodbye to Mama and Papa. I was used to my parents leaving to fight the good fight, but that morning when they were leaving to investigate a situation near the conservatory, I was unsettled and nervous and light-headed and thought about asking them to sit this one out, but I shrugged it off. That's the last time I ignore my instincts.

There are three quick knocks at my door, and Atlas walks in.

"You decent? I got Wesley out here."

"I'm good."

Two words that are true, and two words that couldn't be further from the truth.

Atlas comes over and kisses me on the top of my head as Wesley enters. They both reek and need showers. Atlas certainly isn't helping the case when he kicks off his sneakers, but there's something odd about how the smell of his sweaty socks brings me comfort. I'm transported back to our training sessions after the Blackout. I would be fine and focused for hours, but eventually I would snap over how much my life had changed. I would throw equipment because I was now an orphan. I would punch walls because Iris and I stopped being best friends. I would howl until Atlas could calm me down, bring me into bed where we would kick off our boots, and I would let him hold me.

I can't sleep without his arms around me anymore.

"How did it go?" I ask as I review my notes.

"Turns out we suck at manual labor," Atlas says.

"Speak for yourself," Wesley says as he plants himself onto the beanbag chair Atlas called dibs on when we all first moved into Nova. "You were slowing me down."

"You run ten times as fast as anyone else," Atlas says.

"Not my fault you were born with the wrong power," Wesley says.

Atlas and Wesley use their downtime to run what they like to call "side quests" to bring in money. We get some cash flow from online donations, but in a post-Blackout world, people aren't as friendly and grateful as they used to be for all our efforts. We need money to pay the illusionists who keep us camouflaged and safe, buy food and beds and clothes for our rescues, and tons of other expenses none of us were prepared for when we suddenly became the new faces of our group.

"I thought we were taking a break from Mystery Girl," Atlas says.

"She's the only survivor."

Atlas crouches beside me, and it's hard to stare too long into his eyes, which are gray as rain clouds. "Have you eaten, Mari?"

After my parents died, I became so gaunt I didn't recognize myself in the mirror. I would ignore my screaming stomach because feeding myself meant living, and I didn't know how to do that in a world that hated my parents and wished I had died with them. Atlas respected my parents, especially Mama,

for giving him and Wesley a chance, and he was always looking after me, even when I said the foulest things to drive him
away. One night I found myself knocking on his door because
crying alone was too suffocating. He distracted me with his
favorite romantic comedies when I needed to space out, and
I eventually started eating all the food he was bringing me.
Being alive and awake stopped feeling so lonely because of
how Atlas cared for me. I even learned how to care for myself
again.

Nine months later, I still slip.

"I'll eat later," I say.

"If I go get you tostones and blaze cake, can we take the
night off and watch a movie?"

I twirl one of his blond curls and nod.

"You in, Wesley?" Atlas asks.

Wesley presses his hand against his heart and throws his
head back with an exaggerated sigh. "You two love me enough
to crash your date night? I'm flattered. But it's been a couple
weeks since I've been able to see my ladies. Maybe I can give
Ruth a break and put Esther to sleep."

"Good call," I say.

Ruth is hiding out in a separate shelter in Philadelphia with
their three-month-old. Cloning comes in handy when you're
raising your daughter alone and taking care of celestials, but
I'm sure her life would feel simpler if Wesley was with her 24-7.

Except none of us will be safe if we can't prove to everyone that Spell Walkers are heroes and that celestials are humans too. That we're more than vessels who are contracted—or forced, in prisons—to power the wands and gem-grenades and shackles they use against us.

Atlas kisses my knuckles after Wesley leaves. "I'll be back in thirty."

There are times I wish we never had to leave this room. Ever since Nova shut down in May because of funding, it's been hard settling in, knowing sooner or later we'll have to relocate when we inevitably get discovered. I was hesitant to ever unpack, but one night I returned to find string lights stretching across the walls and my favorite belongings set up around the room: Papa's binoculars hanging by the window; Mama's reading glasses sitting on top of the Colombian fairy tales she read me when I was young—well, younger—and the bottle of star-touched wine Atlas got me for my eighteenth birthday two months ago, which I'm saving for the day I clear my parents' name. He turned this history classroom into our home and I pray to the stars that enforcers never find us because we won't have time to pack.

"Hurry back," I say.

Before Atlas can leave, our door opens, and Iris lets herself in. Everything good within me vanishes as fast as a blink. This isn't like when we were growing up, and Iris and I shared everything—clothes, toys, beds, secrets. I don't barge into her room, and she sure as hell shouldn't be barging into mine.

"Excuse you," I say.

"Save it," Iris says. "We have an innocent to rescue. Where's Wesley?"

"He just left," Atlas says.

"We need all hands on deck," Iris says. For someone so short, Iris has always done a solid job of making herself appear more powerful, more dominant.

"Why? Who's the celestial?"

"He's a specter," Iris says.

This is the first time I've laughed in weeks. It's great.

Iris glares. "I'm serious, Maribelle. I've been trying to track down more specters with white phoenix fire like we've seen since the Crowned Dreamer woke up, and in a viral video, I found one—attacking another specter with phoenix abilities who seemed surprised. I don't think he's one of Luna's guys, but you can bet that she'll be sending out the Blood Casters to hunt him down."

"Wait. Is this a rescue mission, or are we trying to take down the gang?"

"Two phoenixes, one stone."

I've never met anyone who came to be a specter for under-standable reasons, so I can't believe we're risking our necks for someone who's likely just as power-hungry as all the others. We gear up quickly, hoping this rescue isn't going to screw us over and get us killed, but just in case, Iris is kissing her girl-friend, Eva, at the door.

We know better than anyone that loved ones don't always come home.

TEN

ENIGMA

EMIL

My entire body feels like I've been dropped out of the sky.

I groan as I wake up in a hospital room. Brighton is quick to his feet and looks down at me with eyes redder than whenever he stays up all night editing.

"You're okay," he says. "Don't get up."

The bright ceiling lights hurt my eyes. I take deep breaths, thinking about what makes me happy to try and calm myself down. That very first memory of being in the Sunroom for my thirteenth birthday comes to mind, and just as quickly, the happiness of it all warps. How did that kid who posed in front of gorgeous replicas of phoenixes grow up to find their blood inside of him? "I just don't understand," I say. "I didn't do this to myself—I would never."

"We'll figure that out later," Brighton says. "Right now, we have to deal with Ma. She was losing it when she saw you in this bed, so Prudencia took her to the cafeteria to calm her down."

"Does she know? About me?"

"I told her we got jumped by a specter. She doesn't know anything about your powers, but we can't keep it secret."

He hands me his phone. A video of the subway fight has gone viral. It's weird playing viewer to the moment those gold and gray flames surface for the first time. I can even make out the shape of a phoenix in the fire, flickering in and out. "They're calling me Fire-Wing," I say, reading the top comments. "I'm not some comic book superhero."

"Yeah, and there are better names out there," Brighton says.

"I have no idea how I got us out of there. I wasn't even trying to throw those fire-darts at him."

"However it happened, your hero game is strong."

I struggle with the gratitude. "I'm not a hero for making sure someone didn't kill you two. That's common sense."

"Tons of people disagree with you," Brighton says.

"Like who?"

Brighton hands me my phone. "All your new followers."

I go on Instagram. I've never seen a flurry of notifications like this. My follower count keeps shooting up the couple times I refresh my page. Maybe I can use this new platform for

creature awareness, but everyone would just call me a hypo-
crite since I have phoenix blood in me. Somehow.

There's a missed call from Nicholas and a text letting me
know that if I need to chat with someone who sort of under-
stands what's going on, then he'll be there for me. Knowing
Nicholas cares is a true light in the darkness. Unlike all the
other high school friends who are hitting me up to hang out,
which is interesting since none of them seemed to have my
number on my birthday but suddenly found it again today.
Imagine that. There are two missed calls from the museum.
One from Kirk saying he wants to speak with me, probably
to curse me out for stealing phoenix blood, and another from
Sergei who's annoyed at how my newfound fame is going to
make his life hell at the gift shop. As if I'm actually going to be
able to go back to work this week. Or ever.

"Do you think this will blow over?" I ask.

"Honestly?" Brighton shakes his head. "I've seen every
video out there where people come into their powers, and the
attention you're getting is spectacular. Phoenix fire like that?
You're going to need someone with the power to bring back
the dead to take their eyes off you."

Great, just great.

"I guess we should tell Ma before she finds out some other
way."

"You sure you're ready?" Brighton asks.

"No, but I'd rather it come from me."

"I'll be by your side the entire time," Brighton promises.

Back when I was a kid, oblivious to the world's ugliness, I always imagined myself marrying princes, and Brighton only expressed interest in a princess sitting on the throne beside him. We never questioned this, and the same went for our parents. I had been talking about beautiful princes for so long that I never had to come out to my family, but when I got older and found the word that best fit my romantic worldview—*gay* for the win—it was awesome for telling new people in my life, and most important, how comfortable the word felt on my tongue. It's as normal as my hazel eyes and constant bedhead. I grew to understand that acceptance like that was a miracle.

But the word *specter* doesn't feel good in my heart, and building the nerve to tell Ma I somehow am one is far scarier. Will she ever talk to me again? Kick me out? I won't be able to stay with Prudencia since her aunt is painfully monstrous about all gleamcraft. Maybe I'll move with Brighton to Los Angeles and sleep in his dorm room on an air mattress, but it breaks my heart to even think about leaving Ma behind all alone. I hope I don't lose her love.

Ma and Prudencia return, and my chest tightens as they hug me.

Ma strokes my hair. "How are you feeling, my Emilio?"

I'm freaking out and confused, but I simply tell her that I'm sore while massaging the bruise on my head.

"The police are going to find the monsters who did this to

you," Ma says, and even though there's a comforting reassurance in her voice, I can see this helplessness in her eyes. "I'll call for someone now."

"Don't!" If the police officer who shows up doesn't like specters, they will stop seeing me as a victim and treat me as nothing but a walking weapon. They might even get enforcers involved. "I just want to be done with this."

"You have nothing to be embarrassed about," Ma says. "Speaking to the police will be good so we can get your attacker off the streets."

I have no intention of letting Orton actually roam wild. I just needed to catch my breath before everything comes out, but the sucker-punching guilt makes me want to spit it out. "I get it, I—"

"Let him breathe, Ma," Brighton interrupts. "You can't force him to speak up before he's ready."

"It's okay," I cut in. I look up at Brighton. "Enforcers are going to find out anyway."

"What enforcers?" Ma asks.

I sit up in bed with Prudencia's assistance. "This dealer at the park was selling some new drug, and things got out of hand. He and his partner followed us onto the train and came at us with his powers. And I . . ." Everything feels so chaotic in my head. "I defended us with my own."

These powers are mysterious and terrifying, and I don't know how I'm going to bounce back from this.

Ma holds herself up by the wall as she walks to the chair, but can't make it before her knees give up on her. I throw the blanket off and shoot to her side, taking her hand in mine.

"You okay, Ma?"

There are tears in her eyes. "Are *you* okay?"

I don't feel okay, inside or out.

"Emil saved us," Prudencia says. "He's a hero."

"You could've told me you had powers," Ma says with a crack in her voice.

"Today was the first time. The dealer tried throwing Brighton onto the tracks, and I panicked and got really hot, and suddenly my fist was on fire."

Ma takes my hand and inspects it, but there's no marking. "Fire-casting wasn't part of our bloodline."

We're all quiet. Brighton is staring at me like I'm some stranger who needs to spit it out.

"Please believe me, Ma, but . . . I think it's phoenix fire. I didn't do this to myself—"

"No one wakes up with phoenix blood inside of them, Emil!" This is the second time this week Ma is shouting, but she's even more consumed in fury and disappointment now. I feel like a kid all over again. "You know what I've seen patients go through, what we saw your father suffer through, and you got involved with blood alchemy anyway?" She turns to Brighton. "I take it you have powers of your own too, huh?"

"I don't have powers," Brighton says. "Emil didn't do this

89

to himself. If you watch the video—"

"What video?!"

"Someone recorded the fight," Brighton says. "Watch and you'll see that Emil is just as surprised as anyone else."

The chaos of the video begins, and I force myself to look after seeing the horror and heartbreak on my mother's face as she watches us get rattled around by Orton. I feel guilty for a fight I didn't start. I hear the burst of fire, followed by the stillness of the quiet car, and from the corner of my eye I see Ma shaking, well past the video's ending.

"I'm so sorry, my Emilio, I'm sorry for not believing you," Ma says. "But now I don't know how to protect you. What if that man hunts you down to retaliate? What if the enforcers find us at home? I cannot lose you too. . . ."

I was counting on my mother to reassure me that everything will be okay, even if it was an empty promise, but she's already so defeated, and my panicking keeps increasing and increasing, screaming at me to do the only thing that feels right.

"I need a second by myself."

"I'm going with you," Brighton says. "Alone together."

It's been a while since we've joked about being alone together. Whether it was in our bedroom or riding the train together, we could always go into Alone Mode. And no one disturbs Alone Mode. But this is different.

"Alone-alone. Sorry, I need to wrap my head around all of this."

"I'm here if you need me," Brighton says.

"Me too," Prudencia says.

I leave the room and rush toward the nearest exit. I assumed I was at Ma's hospital, but several practitioners here are all dressed in midnight-blue cloaks with speckled stars. I can't believe I ended up in Gleam Care, but I'm getting out. Between my long legs and New York speed, I'm already such a fast walker, powering through all soreness, and I don't stop until I'm a couple blocks away from the hospital.

I'll go back home, pack a bag, and come up with a battle plan. I'm praying some shelter for celestials will take me in, even though I'm a specter. Someone's got to help the famous Fire-Wing on his life-changing, life-ending day, right?

ELEVEN

THE BLOOD CASTERS

NESS

I've been role-playing my entire life. Too bad my line of work won't ever get me the audience I once dreamed about.

Times Square is extra hellish this evening. Tourists are lining up around the block to see some show about a historical privateer. Casting sheets were circulating in sophomore year, and I didn't bother auditioning because I swore it wouldn't grow beyond whatever small theater hosted the show. Going ahead and blaming my inherited arrogance for that error. That could've been my face lighting up on the Broadway marquees. I always imagined my acting career would involve action blockbuster movies and award-winning indie roles and musicals that get all the love on Tumblr. Instead I'm shape-shifting into whoever the Blood Casters need me to become.

Life's funny that way.

I'm making my way back to base when I catch the reflection of the disguise I'm currently wearing. Dark blond hair, pretty enough, and most important, the pale skin that lets me coast by during charged moments. The impression is not a perfect match, but it doesn't have to be. I can get by with a misshapen nose, shorter eyelashes, hazel eyes instead of brown. It's the key targets that have to be studied carefully. The crow's-feet, the gnawed-on nails, the birthmark on the neck, everything in place so loved ones don't ever second-guess me. Tonight didn't require a deep morph, so I lifted the look from someone swiping his way into the train station while I was on my way out. I needed to get far away from those enforcers after Orton broke code.

Luna is going to have his head if he's still out there.

Mine too, maybe.

I'm not unfamiliar with great housing, but our current stay in lower Manhattan's Light Sky Tower with the other Blood Casters is something else. Security for the city's tallest building is intense, but as long as I have my password, they're instructed to let me in at the back entrance, no matter what I look like. "Breath of wraith," I say. The guard eyes me like he'll be able to see past my disguise if he squints hard enough before letting me into the elevator that shoots me up to the one-hundred-and-tenth floor.

The penthouse is the only place in this skyscraper where I'm allowed to drop my morph. Only the gang knows who I am; the rest of the world can't find out. Blessing and a curse. It's worth it if it means the people I'm hiding from won't ever find me, but it also guarantees no one will ever know the real me. Whoever that is these days.

I wish morphing were as effortless for me as it was for the shifter whose blood Luna stole to give me these powers, but unfortunately, holding a shape weighs on me. It's tougher than holding in a piss on a full bladder. I feel lighter as my disguise falls. The pale skin finds its natural brown complexion. Hair turns dark and shrinks on the sides and curls on the top. My mother's amber eyes are restored; I miss her, but I'm relieved she's not around to see who I've become.

Blessing. Curse.

I cross the empty living space. Dione has been out for days gathering intel on the hydra shipment, but I don't know how Stanton is keeping busy tonight. I go to the balcony, expecting to find Luna gazing at the Crowned Dreamer through the massive telescope. But the only ones out here are June and that awful alchemist, Anklin, who reeks of days-old corpses. I was raised to maintain straight posture whenever I'm in the presence of people I should respect, but I relax my shoulders now because I wouldn't move a muscle if Anklin or June fell over the railing. Luna swears June is a miracle, but I believe she's the end of everything we know. Still not sure if that's a good thing or not.

"Good evening," Anklin says to me as he studies June.

"I wouldn't call it that," I say. "Would you, June?"

June is still as a mannequin. She doesn't answer, of course. She never speaks. Luna is probably the only one who has ever heard her voice. She's short like the first girl I kissed and has the same dead-eyed stare as the first boy I admitted having a crush on. It's chilly tonight, especially way up here, but June isn't shivering, even with all the goose bumps running along her white arms. None of the Blood Casters are natural, but June is the strangest of all. Maybe she'll be the one tasked with taking out the Senator before November.

"Ness," a deep voice says from behind me, with a hint of a hiss.

Stanton is as stealthy as the basilisk he personally hunted to steal its blood. Well, stealthier since he beat it. Before his days of oily blond hair, yellow eclipse eyes that narrow like a serpent's, and dark green veins glowing beneath his white skin like poison, he charmed tons of people into following him home so he could kill them. A little harder these days.

"What's up?" I ask.

Between his muscles, his powers, and his past, I try to stay on his good side.

"Luna wants to see you in her quarters," Stanton says.

I'm quick, because you don't keep Luna waiting.

The room is dim, and the glowing tablet lights up Luna's features—tired green eyes, wrinkled moon-white skin, long silver hair. "I am designing new life from which we all stand to benefit, but that's only if I live," she says. "Do you understand?"

"Yes, my queen."

One day I better be able to serve myself instead of others.

"I want the boy from the train."

I tense up. Has she had me followed? I'm the one tasked with following her targets.

"You understand you were being recorded, yes?" Luna flips her tablet toward me, and there's a video of Orton's fight.

"I'm sorry, I—"

"I don't care if there are eyes on you as long as you are aware of them. It would be a great loss should you become exposed. . . ." Luna coughs violently and wipes her lip with a silk handkerchief.

"No one will ever know who I am," I say.

Fusing someone with shifter blood is complex, and she worked extra hard to make sure I didn't lose myself to the powers—or die—but if I want to live past the average curtain call of a Caster, I have to step up my game.

Everything about this objective is the oddest coincidence considering I'm in the business of never being seen as the same person more than once. I'm uneasy running into the same stranger twice in a gigantic city. But all that matters now is finding and delivering him to Luna to save my own neck.

TWELVE
FIRE-WING

EMIL

Ten minutes into my journey, I ignore everyone's calls and speed up before they figure out what I'm up to. I'll reach out later when I'm somewhere safe. I round the corner to my building and rush up the steps. I bump into my fifteen-year-old neighbor and knock the trash bag out of her hand.

"Watch it, you—" Her eyes widen.

"Sorry," I say, picking up her trash bag.

"Hi." That's a first. "I need a picture with you!"

"I have to go, sorry."

Everyone thinks my life is so damn cool right now. They don't have to live it.

I'm nervous when I enter the apartment. Whenever someone

finds out they're special in movies, they return home and find upturned furniture, scattered papers, and broken glass. But all is good up in here. I'm the only piece that feels out of place. I grab a duffel bag and resist throwing any mementos inside, just clothes. I cast one last look at the bedroom where I grew up and wonder if anywhere else will ever feel like home again. I fight back tears and leave my bedroom before I talk myself into staying and endangering everyone.

The door opens, and I freeze, expecting the worst. Brighton walks in, panting, and locks the door behind him.

"You ran," Brighton says, setting down his backpack.

"You left Ma and Prudencia?"

"To rent a death-trap scooter and chase you down. Where do you think you're going?"

"If enforcers swing through, I can't be here. I don't know what's happening to me, but this phoenix fire business is my mystery to solve, and I can't risk you getting hurt while I figure it out."

Brighton shakes his head. "Too damn bad. Wherever you go, I go. It's us against the world. The Reys of Light."

"You have to protect Ma," I say. "You're all she's going to have left."

Someone knocks on the door.

"Probably the neighbor," I say.

"Stay back." Brighton looks through the peephole.

I stay put even though I'm the one who can set someone on

fire, but fear strikes hard at the possibility of enforcers waiting for me in the hallway for damaging public property and endangering passengers during the brawl.

"No way," Brighton says.

My heart races. I'm about to make a run for it to the fire escape until Brighton smiles.

"It's Atlas."

"I can hear you talking. Open up, it's urgent," Atlas calls from the hallway.

A Spell Walker is here—this unreal day keeps topping itself.

Brighton opens up, and Atlas lets himself in. He's wearing his power-proof vest again and appears incredibly nervous. He looks over Brighton's shoulder and locks eyes with me. "You already packed a bag. Great. We have to get out of here now," Atlas says. "People are coming for you."

"Go where? Who's coming?" I ask.

"Taking you to base."

"I'm going with him," Brighton says.

"Absolutely not," Atlas says.

"Then I'm not going with you." If the Spell Walkers are offering me refuge, I want protection for my people too. If not, maybe we can all escape to another country where specters aren't public enemy number one.

"Do you have powers?" Atlas asks Brighton.

"No. I would've totally helped you the other night if I did," Brighton says.

"What?"

"When you fought off that specter. Remember? I was the one who asked to take a photo with you," Brighton says, though Atlas cocks his head in confusion. "It's okay. There was a lot going on, and you meet a lot of people. I'm a huge fan. I loved when you fought off those traffickers and rescued that psychic from her father. I have your Funko Pop and—"

"Stay here and play with your toys," Atlas says. "Emil, come with me. Leave your brother out of this."

I stare at Brighton. It's his call if he wants to follow me or not. Brighton holds out his fist, and I do the same, fist-bumping and whistling. We stand together.

"Don't say I didn't warn you," Atlas says. "There's no time to pack. Let's go." He rushes out the apartment, immediately returning and locking the door behind him. "Blood Caster is outside. Is there another exit?"

"Blood Caster?"

"Another exit! Come on!"

"Fire escape."

I lead the way as the front door flies off its hinges and in walks Atlas. Again. The Atlases stare at each other. The new one is wearing a solid black T-shirt underneath his power-proof vest, and a scar peeks out of his sleeve. The shadows under his eyes are darker than I remember.

The new Atlas stares at the other. "What the hell?"

"That's an imposter," the first says. "Probably has shifter blood."

"That's you and you know it!" The new Atlas stares at his twin. "You got my freckles all wrong. Not enough on the forehead and none on the neck." He smiles. "You also can't do this." He lifts his hand, and a funnel of high-pressured wind blasts into the first Atlas's chest, flipping him over the couch. "Come with me," he says to us.

There's a grunt from behind the couch and up comes someone else—a boy whose face and body keep stretching and shrinking and changing skin tones. The Spell Walker gear fades in a dull gray light, replaced with a basic tee and jeans. In seconds the shape-shifter has a new face—still pale but longer, with a crooked nose and one eye that's twice as large as the other. I don't know if this is who he is or another impersonation, but my stomach tightens as he withdraws a wand from his waistband and shoots a black light at Atlas.

Atlas rolls out of harm's way, and the black light explodes against a family photo, leaving nothing but ash. I've heard wands are only as powerful as the celestials who gave their blood to make them. I don't ever want to cross paths with the celestial who is walking around with that kind of power—or with the alchemist who was willing to weaponize it for others. The shape-shifter blasts the window open, and the bang and shattering shock my senses as he takes off down the fire escape.

"We're here to take you to our haven," Atlas says.

"Who's we?" I ask.

"Maribelle is in the car, and Iris is guarding the entrance."

"It's actually you!" Brighton says. "We met the other night."

"You asked for a picture." Atlas nods. "In the middle of a fight, Brighton," he adds with a grin.

"You know my name?"

"We did our research after that brawl went viral. Cool You-Tube videos."

"Shut up," Brighton says with wide eyes, and I know he's breaths away from asking Atlas which videos are his favorite.

Atlas claps his hands. "If the shape-shifter made a move for you, there's a chance that other Blood Casters won't be far off either. You won't be able to come back here, so pack whatever valuables you can in the next minute."

I stand still as Brighton rushes to our room.

I can't believe the impostor was a Blood Caster—a specter with shifter blood. He must've been trying to recruit me. Nah, he would've worn his face if this was a recruiting mission. This was tricking and kidnapping. Who knows what would've happened to Brighton if we had followed him. Maybe he would've been turned into a specter too, or held hostage unless I agreed to become a Blood Caster. Or worse.

Brighton returns with one of his rolling suitcases for his flight tomorrow and a duffel bag of his own, the sleeve of a hoodie falling out as he shoves his laptop and chargers inside. "I'm good, I think."

What's going to happen to the rest of our stuff? Will enforcers storm in? It's wild how much money got dropped on collectible figurines and video games and books, and how none of that matters now that our safety has been threatened. Atlas leads the way out of the apartment and down the stairs, with Brighton keeping close like a second shadow. I'm the last to leave the apartment, and I lock the door behind me. I run down the stairs, reliving these fond memories of going outside to play and hanging out with friends. Now I'm running away from home with my brother and one of the most powerful Spell Walkers.

Guarding the lobby door is a short young woman with dark brown skin, shaved hair that's dyed bright green, and a power-proof vest—Iris Simone-Chambers, the small but mighty leader of the Spell Walkers. "What took so long?"

"The shape-shifting Blood Caster interfered," Atlas says. "He fled."

Before I can introduce myself, I spot a crowd outside the building. There are half a dozen signs, but I can only make out two:

Move over, Spell Walkers! Fire-Wing is here!
Burn yourself with that phoenix fire!

"You're going to be okay," Iris says.

I feel like a celebrity as I step outside the building with

Iris and Atlas acting as my bodyguards. I've never wanted to be famous; that's Brighton's dream. I'm the guy behind the camera, and I'm down with that anonymity. Some people in the crowd are chanting "Fire-Wing!" and want pictures while others are calling me an abomination. I don't get how it's possible to feel like my life is in danger when I'm being protected by Iris, who can lift a car over her head and whose skin is spellwork-resistant, and Atlas, who can suspend people with his winds, but I don't feel safe at all.

A car horn honks, and Maribelle Lucero leans out of the driver's-side window of the Jeep, yelling at us to hurry up.

When we move for the car, a figure I'd hoped I'd never see in person slides out of a sewer grate on his stomach and slithers onto the street with the smoothness of a water snake. His blond hair and clothes are dripping wet, and he smells of waste. Dark green veins branch across his pale skin. His eyes are burning eclipses before shifting to yellow pupils that shrink into slits. I nearly trip over myself trying to get away from Stanton, the Blood Caster with basilisk blood whose face can be found on so many Wanted posters for his gang-related crimes. Stanton opens his mouth and emits a spray that smells like rotted animal carcass. Blood rushes to my head and I'm so dizzy and we all fall to our knees. My heart is beating slowly. I'm nothing but prey as Stanton grips my throat and drags me through the street.

Fighting Stanton at the top of my game would've been

impossible enough, and all I can do now is kick at the air and tap Stanton's wrist for mercy. I have no idea where he's taking me. I try casting fire, but nothing. Just as I'm ready to give up, Stanton roars in pain and releases his hold. He rips a dagger out from his stomach and drops it on the ground while applying pressure to his wound. Through the haze I see Maribelle floating toward Stanton. When she reaches him, she unleashes a furious cycle of kicks against his chest until he falls.

She scoops up her dagger by its pearl handle and eyes the bloody blade that is bubbling in red acid. "You ruined my father's blade," Maribelle tells Stanton, as if he threw it at himself. She helps me to my feet as Iris approaches.

Iris sways and rights herself. "Get him in the car."

"Ace idea, Captain. What would we do without your brilliant commands?"

"Now's not the time—*get out of the way!*"

Iris shoves us, and we fly a foot into the air, slam down, and roll against the curb. I pay no mind to the scrapes and aches when I see Iris is bent over as acid eats away at her shoulder—she took the hit for us. Stanton pounces, scoring punches and kicks on Iris. She tries fighting back with her good arm, but his reflexes are swift.

"Get to the car," Maribelle says as she runs over to fight Stanton.

Atlas assists Brighton into the back of the Jeep with our luggage before flying over to us. Gusts of wind carry Stanton into the air as Atlas pins him against the wall, shouting for everyone to escape. I stay to help Iris.

"I said get to the car," Maribelle snaps.

"I'm here to save *you*, Emil," Iris groans.

"You did, you did."

We get to the car, and Brighton and I sit in the far back behind Maribelle and Iris. Maribelle reaches over and slams on the horn. Atlas releases his hold on Stanton, letting him crash to the ground, and glides over and jumps straight into the driver's seat. I can't believe we're moments away from escape.

"Hang tight, Iris. We'll get you to Eva," Atlas says as he starts the car. "What the . . ."

A girl with big eyes and dark silver hair and moon-white skin is rising out of the ground. She's barefoot, drenched in sweat, and wearing a heavy sweater that trails above her knees, nearly concealing her black shorts.

"Move out of the way," Atlas shouts out the window. The girl doesn't budge. "Fine." He steps out of the car, and wind picks up around her. Trash swirls through her. She's untouchable.

"It's her," Maribelle whispers. "It's her! It's her!"

"Who?" Brighton asks.

"The celestial from the Blackout, the one from the surveillance tape." Maribelle grabs Iris's knee. "The one who must know what really happened to our parents!" She goes for the door, but Iris binds her with her unaffected arm. Even though it doesn't look as if Iris is placing a lot of effort into restraining Maribelle, she can't escape. "What are you doing? Let me go!"

"Drive!" Iris shouts.

"Don't you dare, Atlas!"

Atlas is torn, then looks out the window before kicking into gear and speeding off. "Stanton is recovering, Mari, I'm sorry."

The girl doesn't move out of the way, and she phases through the car as if she's nothing but wind.

"Please, please, this might be our only chance to see what she knows!" Maribelle's eyes fill with more and more tears the farther we get from the block. "She could clear our parents' names!"

Iris groans in pain. "I know you have no problem watching me die, but we have two rescues who've survived not one but two fights against specters today. It's imperative that we get them to Nova."

"What's Nova?" Brighton asks.

"Our headquarters," Iris says. "We have a lot to catch you up on, Emil."

THIRTEEN
NOVA

EMIL

The world passes by in blurs as we drive to Nova. My nausea is next level with Atlas driving like enforcers are tailing us. If Iris wasn't so obviously doing her best to not howl in agony, I would've begged to pull over to force myself to throw up. I need this painful stretch of a day to be over already. But even as we get closer to Nova, I have a feeling the Spell Walkers are pushing me deeper into the chaos, not protecting me from it.

Maribelle is wrapping up a call with Wesley Young as we enter Brooklyn, going in on him for not making it to the mission to retrieve me on time. She instructs him to pick up Ma from the hospital and get back quickly before hanging up to make another call. She lets someone at the haven know that

Iris was wounded by Stanton's basilisk acid and will be in serious need of healing. If someone as powerful as Iris is fading in and out like this with her spell-proof skin, I would've been a goner. It's hard to stomach a stranger getting hurt for me.

We pull into the parking lot of a lively gas station in Bed-Stuy. Just as I'm starting to feel nervous someone will recognize me, a massive flash swallows us whole. I shout and shield my eyes, bracing for an explosion.

"It was only an illusion," Atlas says.

I open my eyes, and the gas station behind us is now abandoned and run-down with shattered doors, as if it's been looted. "So it's safe?"

"To the best of our available abilities," Atlas says.

"One day we'll find a solution where we don't have to worry about sellouts," Maribelle says.

Iris groans as she presses her jacket against her wound. "Don't restart this fight when my shoulder is literally melting, Maribelle."

"I'm not going to let you forget how three of our people died because you swore a superintendent would rather do the right thing than be rich," Maribelle says. "That wouldn't have happened if I was in charge."

"But you're not, and everyone is thanking all the stars for that one."

I don't know a damn thing about the history between Maribelle and Iris, but I would've expected the daughters of

Spell Walkers to be there for each other during their time of
grief. Not going to lie, it's hard holding hope in a team with
this kind of energy.

We drive up a hill and park in front of a two-story building where there's a dangling sign for Nova Grace Elementary
School for Celestials. I've long outgrown expecting the Spell
Walkers' hiding spot to be a floating structure, but I still
expected it to have a little more style, like some astronomy
skyscraper with all the latest tech. It's all good; a school where
celestials are able to practice their gleamcraft a little more
freely is going to be its own sight to behold.

Everyone gets out of the car, and as I enter Nova, I truly
feel like a character straight out of a fantasy book who discovers he's special and is now going to attend a school to hone his
powers. Except there's nothing remarkably fantastical such as
moving staircases or glowing wells to greet me. The hallway
appears to be like any other school with a little celestial flair:
posters on mindfulness when it comes to using gleamcraft in
public, reminders on when to wear half capes, sign-up sheets
for after-school training with savants, and more of that nature.

A young woman with brown skin and shoulder-length
black hair runs out of the auditorium aiming a wand that glistens with the same rose quartz gems found in her necklace.
"Password."

Atlas turns to Maribelle. "You have it, right?"

"No, we were all in a rush to save Emil," Maribelle says.

She points at Iris. "Your girlfriend is in pain, Eva. You might want to get to work."

"Password," Eva says again as the tip of the wand glows. Her hand is shaking, and she doesn't take her teary eyes off Iris. "Give me the password. Come on, this is serious."

"Feather of fire," Iris breathes as she sinks to her knees.

Eva throws down her wand and is immediately at Iris's side, inspecting her wound.

"Maybe take them to their room?" Atlas asks.

"Good call," Maribelle says before instructing us to follow her, but we continue to stare in wonder. "Trust me. You don't want to stick around. Healing isn't pretty."

We keep peeking over our shoulders and can only make out Eva leaning over Iris with her hands pressed against the wound. As we head up the steps, screams echo through the hall. It reminds me of Ma's cries when she learned Abuelita passed; I've never been able to get that out of my head. "Is Iris okay?"

"Iris will be," Maribelle says.

"What was the holdup with the passwords?" Brighton asks.

"Precaution. We've been betrayed a couple of times."

As we walk down the hall, Maribelle tells us the story of how their West Harlem haven was infiltrated because of a trio of celestials who were in their care. They were so paranoid about getting caught and detained that they signed up to become enforcers instead who were rewarded with high salaries and health insurance. To prove their loyalty, they exposed the haven. I don't understand celestials who become bodyguards for politicians who are campaigning against their existence.

Maribelle leads us into a room decorated with star charts and posters of children's songs about prime constellations. Brass planets hang from a steel track in the ceiling, slowly orbiting and casting dizzying lights and shadows in the small space until she switches it off. "Tight squeeze, but it's the best we can offer."

"We'll take it," Brighton says as he gazes out the window through a silver telescope.

"What's the plan?" I ask. "Is Eva healing us too when she's finished with Iris?"

Maribelle runs her hands through her dark hair and lets out a deep sigh before pulling out her phone. "Luckily for Eva, neither of you are in critical condition. She's going to need a break." Maribelle's typing away while she heads for the door. "I need to keep digging online for that celestial girl, but I'll send someone over with aspirin and snacks, and we can all circle back in a bit."

Before I can ask for a game plan, she's gone.

"Pretty cool setup," Brighton says, inspecting more of the room. I'm sure that he's itching to run around this building. "I wonder how long they've been hiding here."

I sit on a rug shaped like a comet. "What do they want with me?"

Brighton joins me. "The Spell Walkers?"

"The Spell Walkers and the Blood Casters."

"To join a side, I bet."

When we were kids, we would draw ourselves in the power-proof vests Spell Walkers wear. In Brighton's pictures, he was always flying from one mission to the next. In mine I was teleporting, but I wasn't thinking about using the power to escape danger the way I do now. I dreamed of teleporting onto mountains and sleeping under the stars and sailing in the middle of nowhere with my family and preserving nests for phoenixes.

"I'll never be a Blood Caster, but I don't want to be a Spell Walker either," I say with a crack in my voice. I'm exhausted and starving and scared. "And I don't like the odds of hiding here as a rescue, since two of their havens have been exposed."

"You heard Maribelle in the car—they're learning from their mistakes," Brighton says. "Someone would have to be self-destructive to charge into the spot where the Spell Walkers have home field advantage. We don't even know about the other celestials here and what powers they're packing. I wonder if we'll get to meet them. . . ." He has this faraway look.

This isn't how anyone should be living their lives. Hiding out in some school while being hunted down by enforcers and gangs. My panicked breaths increase, and a phoenix's cry is roaring to life inside my head as I warm up. "I shouldn't have these powers," I say, shaking my head vigorously. "What's to stop me from burning this place down?"

"I will," Brighton says, grabbing my shoulder.

I can't believe I tried running away alone.

Atlas pops in shortly after with bottles of water, protein bars, and a medical kit. I throw back aspirin while Brighton bandages my scraped arm.

The door opens, and I'm expecting Maribelle or Atlas again, but it's Wesley. He's a white dude about our age and height. He's got strong curves, like a linebacker who takes no prisoners, and he's rocking a football jersey that has the Spell Walker insignia—probably custom made but looks legit. In the poster Brighton has in our room, Wesley has a military buzz cut, but now his brown hair is grown out and pulled back into an absolutely hipster man bun that makes him even handsomer than I thought before.

"There you go!" Wesley says. He steps into the hallway and shouts, "They're in here!" He smiles my way and reaches out a hand to shake, but Brighton pops up and beats me to it.

"Huge fan," Brighton says. "I've lost count of how many times I watched that video where you ran up the plaza's wall and stopped those jewel thieves."

"That was supposed to be a personal shopping day," Wesley says with a chuckle before returning his attention to me. "I'm sorry I wasn't there to back up my crew. I was on my way to Philadelphia to see my family, but I did manage to collect yours."

Before I can say anything, Ma rushes in with Prudencia right behind her. After the ten thousand times it's felt like my heart has fallen out of place today, I'm shocked at how good and secure it feels after seeing my people, like I'm not as fragile as I thought. Ma hugs me so hard that my entire body doubles down in pain, but I don't care. She's nonstop telling me how relieved she is that I'm alive without taking breaths.

"You came too?" Brighton asks Prudencia as he pulls her into a hug.

"I'm surprised you survived without me," Prudencia says.

"But what about your aunt?" I ask.

"She's someone else's problem," Prudencia says. "I'm here for you."

I hug the hell out of her.

"You can't run away like that, Emilio," Ma says.

"I don't belong at home," I say. "Everyone thinks I'm a hero. What kind of hero puts his family's life at risk? I had to get out of there and figure out why this is happening to me."

"We are your home," Ma says. "You belong with us."

Brighton claps his hands. "Great. Now that everyone is here, we can figure out our next move. Iris has hinted at some deeper meaning behind Emil's powers. Maybe this is some big chosen one destiny business where we can all help out."

Ma shakes her head and squeezes my hand. "No. Brighton, you're leaving for college tomorrow."

"No I'm not! We can't sweep Emil's phoenix fire under the rug."

"We also won't run straight into the cross fire!" Ma's face is red, and I don't want her getting worked up like this.

There's a hard knock on the door, and Iris lets herself in. She's no longer in her power-proof vest. There's a gaping hole in her shirt, but there's only light scarring where her skin had been bubbling before. She greets Ma and Prudencia with a nod. "How's everyone feeling?"

"We're good!" Brighton says. "Good enough. You?"

"I'll live, thanks to Eva," Iris says. "Emil, it's time to talk."

"Talk about what?" Ma asks.

"How your son has powers he shouldn't possess," Iris says. She catches her breath. She's not standing tall like she was when I met her. She's battered and tired. I guess Eva can't heal someone completely. "There have been a lot of moving pieces in this war, and we have theories and intel to support Emil shaping up to become a major player."

"A soldier," I say.

One stare says everything.

FOURTEEN
INFINITY SON

EMIL

It's time to connect the stars in my constellation.

Iris escorts us to what appears to be a brewing chamber
converted into a boardroom. Steel cauldrons are stacked
between two cabinets loaded with ingredients for potions.
On a dry-erase board is my name in bright blue marker
with arrows pointing to Brighton and my parents. The Spell
Walkers have logged our social media accounts, colleges, my
museum gig, and Brighton's YouTube channel. Maribelle
is seated at a glossy crescent table and flipping through the
pages of a massive textbook. On the other end, Eva looks
hungover as she finishes chugging a gallon of water before
offering a quick wave. Atlas is typing away at a laptop with

the speed of a hacker while Wesley watches on.

"Can we get you anything?" Wesley asks.

"My regular life back," I say. Atlas and Wesley offer sympathetic looks. I sit at the center of the crescent table between Brighton, Prudencia, and Ma. "Why are the Blood Casters after me?"

"We've been keeping track of all the increased specter activity since the Crowned Dreamer surfaced," Iris says from the dry-erase board. "The fight we saw online between you and that specter was horrific, but my mother confided in me to keep an eye out for any specters with gray or gold flames. You exhibited both, Emil."

Maribelle finally looks up. "Wait. You didn't tell us about this."

"It was a secret," Iris says.

Maribelle slams the textbook shut. "What kind of leader is trusted with some piece to the puzzle and doesn't trust her team? Stars forbid something happened to you in our dangerous line of work. The secret would've died with you."

"I knew, just in case," Eva says, standing beside Iris and grabbing her hand. "I found out a month after the Blackout. This is only a working theory, and it could've been a distraction from everything we've had on our plates since January."

"We're not allowed to have secrets," Maribelle says. "This is life or death."

"That was the only secret," Iris says. "I'm walking in the

dark here on everything else."

Before Maribelle can counter, I speak up. "Can you please tell me what's going on?"

"You have the blood of a gray sun phoenix within you," Iris says.

"I cracked that code."

"So did Bautista de León. He never sought out blood alchemy, and his powers surprised him too. The only people who knew that were the Spell Walkers he first assembled, and they all reached the same conclusion. Bautista was a specter with phoenix blood in a past life, successfully reborn in this one."

Brighton inhales a deep breath. "Do you think Bautista is Emil's past life?"

"That's impossi—"

I shut up.

Everything that should've been impossible today is proving itself extra possible.

"The timeline adds up," Iris says. "Bautista died, and you were born days later."

"Reborn," Maribelle breathes as she stares at me in awe.

"It can't be me! It can't. Phoenixes are reborn as they were, and I look nothing like him!"

"It's Bautista's essence reborn," Iris says. "Powers and spirit."

Hours ago, I was a kid having a panic attack at the park, and now I'm the founding Spell Walker reincarnated. Enough already. The world needs to pick on someone else. I've got a good handle on history concerning specters carrying blood from gray sun phoenixes and it's got me thinking. "Please don't tell me . . ."

Iris is quiet, as if she senses the dread in my question. "Bautista believed he was reincarnated from Keon Máximo."

I'm numb as I try to think of something that can disprove this. But there's no known date for when Keon actually died. We only know that it was at the hands of the Halo Knights for his crimes against phoenixes.

"Why did Bautista think that?" I ask.

"Growing up, Bautista apparently had flashes of memories from a life he hadn't lived, and he connected the dots himself. When he realized his past life was responsible for the existence of all specters, he created the Spell Walkers with the psychic alchemist Sera Córdova. He wanted to do good with the stolen powers he was reborn with against his will."

I hop out of my seat, nearly banging into Ma, and I stand by the window to cool down. "But this doesn't make sense. I don't remember anything out of the ordinary. And phoenixes have accelerated aging! I'm eighteen."

"The phoenix blood doesn't make you a phoenix," Maribelle says. "You're still human, so you're aging like a regular human . . . who happens to be the scion of history's greatest and worst specters. Tough break."

If I could transform into a phoenix and fly out this window

before they can guilt me into fighting a war that my past life started, I would be gone in a millisecond.

"Does this mean any other specter with phoenix blood can be reborn?" Brighton asks.

"Possibly," Iris says. "Specters make up a tiny fraction of our gleamcraft community. There's no way for us to know their limits. The specter you fought on the train phased through the doors, which isn't any phoenix or creature's power. It's possible he was a specter in a past life and his essence was reborn into a celestial host. We're only speculating at this point."

Maribelle lets out a laugh. "If only we just found ourselves engaging with a celestial with the same power. We could've asked her all about her powers and what she witnessed at the Blackout. Oh, wait!"

These are all theories, I keep reminding myself. No one can be sure of anything. "Let's say this rebirth business is legit. Why did it take so long for my powers to kick in? Brighton and I are twins. Shouldn't it have split between us in the womb?"

Brighton shrugs. "I have no idea how phoenix essence works, but maybe because we were born together, it messed with the powers?"

"Could be," Iris says. "Again, there's a lot we don't know."

Ma is looking back and forth between me and Brighton. "Boys, can we talk outside?"

On the verge of tears, I ask, "Did you know about my powers all along?" She doesn't say anything. "If this involves what's happening, you have to clue me in right now."

Prudencia stands and addresses the Spell Walkers. "Maybe we should give them some privacy."

No one moves. All eyes are on Ma. She's flicking at her palm, which she does whenever she's nervous.

"Ma, please tell me what you did to me, or I might blow up."

"We saved you," Ma says. "Your father and I, we saved you. You were abandoned, and we brought you in."

"I don't get it."

Brighton stands by me and looks like he can barely hold his head up. "I think she's saying that you . . . that you're adopted, Emil."

I have ten thousand thoughts and no words.

This world doesn't make sense. It's not even about the powers anymore. I don't know who I am. My name is Emil. My middle name is Donato, which means gift from the gods. My last name is Rey. But even those basics being called into question make me feel hard lumps in my throat, blocking all air. Was I actually named after a man who isn't even my grandfather? Am I actually a gift from the gods? Do I still get to be a Rey of Light if I'm not a Rey?

Why didn't my biological parents want me?

I lived in someone else's womb for nine months, and I have no idea who they are. I've grown up reading so many stories about orphans in books, and I was always so grateful to be raised by a family that wanted me. Parents who fed me and rocked me and took care of me and taught me how to talk and how to read and how to love. How could something so real now feel like an illusion?

I'm consumed in dark thoughts as I rewrite my history. I don't belong with the Reys, and every family photo I'm in is a lie, like someone photoshopped me in out of pity.

I can't breathe.

Brighton isn't my brother anymore, and even though we aren't twins and never shared a womb or the same blood, one look at his face, and I know we've at least been lied to together.

I struggle to find a word, any word. All I can manage is: "What?"

"We should've told you," Ma says.

"So who . . . ? And how . . . ?"

"We don't know who your biological parents are," she says.

"Of course you don't, wow. If you were going to kick me out the family like this, you could've gotten an address to send me to."

How is this not a nightmare?

When someone discovers they're special in a story, there's usually some wise adult who tells the hero what's what about their new life. But all I have is a group of young people who are wading through their own uncertainties. Everyone is throwing darts at a board and praying to the stars they hit their target.

"I don't get it," Brighton says. "If Emil wasn't born with me, then when?"

"The same day you were born," Ma says.

"My birthday isn't a lie, phew. All good now." I fake a fist bump with Brighton.

"As far as the doctors could tell, you were a newborn too."

I picture Brighton being born without me and realize that my own birth certificate must've been forged; I would've never known the difference or questioned my parents.

I want to run a flaming fist straight through the wall.

"So what happened? Someone leave me in a basket and knock on your door?"

Every time Ma cries, Brighton and I drop everything we're doing to keep her company. If she wants privacy, she cries alone in the bathroom with the shower running or locks herself in her bedroom. But usually she lets us hug her and remind her what an incredible mother she is, and how we're the young men we are today because of her heart.

Tonight, we keep our distance.

"After I gave birth, Leonardo wanted to get me balloons, but the helium tank in the hospital's gift shop was empty, so he went out to find some." Ma wipes her tears on the back of her hand. "I always pictured myself holding my child in a room with yellow daffodils and balloons, and your father wanted to make that dream come true. He left the hospital, and you were crying on a street corner two blocks away, baking under the sun. No one was around. No note or blanket. Your father never hated a stranger the way he did whoever abandoned you. He carried you back into the hospital and doctors and nurses were all over you. So was he. He was so immediately protective of you, just like he was when he held Brighton for the first time. He kept running back and forth between checking on Brighton and you."

The Spell Walkers and Prudencia are dead silent.

Here's this absolutely wonderful memory of our father that our mother might have taken to her grave. Brighton looks like he may cry any second.

"I didn't get to meet you until that evening," Ma says. "The police arrived to investigate, but when I saw how innocent you were, my heart broke even more. We don't know if your biological parents couldn't afford to take care of you or what darkness possessed them to abandon you in the manner they did. But we knew you were coming home with us. Your father looked at you like he didn't trust a single other person to take care of you."

"Why didn't you tell me?"

"We wanted to give you an easy life and make sure you never felt out of place."

The silence in the room is broken by a "Whoa" from Wesley.

Iris is typing away on her laptop. "Mrs. Rey, where did your husband find Emil?"

"A couple blocks behind the Grand Gibbous Stadium in the Bronx," Ma says.

"That's a few avenues from where Bautista died," Iris says, staring at the map on her screen. "Doesn't line up."

No one here knows phoenixes like I do. "Gray suns never resurrect in the same spot where they died," I say with no life in my voice. "Defense tactic. Their ashes float away and rebuild elsewhere so they're not attacked upon returning."

Eva's head is sinking, and she snaps up. "Maybe our theory about the essence being reborn in a host is all wrong. Your mother said you were burning up. It's possible it's not because your father found you outside, but because . . ."

"I was born in fire," I say.

"Reborn," Maribelle corrects again.

"What are you going to tell me next, that this marks me as some chosen one who has to win this war?" I wait for an answer, but nothing. "Oh, come on."

"There are no chosen ones, necessarily," Maribelle says. "We choose to fight. But you do seem to belong in this battle more than most."

"If you join us, we'll train you to become a formidable weapon," Iris says. "Like Bautista was."

Throwing flames isn't some passive power; I get that I can make a difference in any fight. But I don't want to become some dagger to sharpen or wand to load. "This Bautista business doesn't mean anything, okay? It's a past life that I don't remember. It's great that he was a hero, but that doesn't mean that I have to be."

The Spell Walkers look like they disagree.

Iris lets out a deep breath. "Unless there's a new alchemist out there who's responsible for this wave of stronger specters, Luna Marnette and the Blood Casters are the safe bet. We have been trying to take down Luna for years, and ever since the Blackout, the government is focused on making celestial lives a living hell while she builds her army. It looks as if she's even recruiting celestials to advance her causes. We need all hands on deck, Emil. We can relocate you and your family, but if the Blood Casters are after you, you're going to be running for the rest of your life."

"She's right, for once," Maribelle says. "Become a Spell Walker. Get your strength up and make them regret painting a target on your back."

These can't be my choices. I'm shaking. "I don't want these powers."

"Then stay here and figure out how to undo them," Maribelle says, like she has no time for my resistance, as if we're moments away from entering battle. "Bautista and Sera were working on a cure to expel a specter's power, but Emil, you will never be able to save yourself from this cycle of war unless you help end the Blood Casters once and for all. It's the least you can do since you technically created this evil."

"I didn't do this!"

ADAM SILVERA

I shoot for the door, and once I'm out in the hallway, I'm tempted to escape back onto the streets. But then what? I find the staircase that leads to the roof, where I press down onto the ledge so hard my wrists might snap. There aren't enough deep breaths to escape the weight of the world crushing me, so I scream at the Crowned Dreamer as if the constellation is to blame for all of this misery.

"Hey," Brighton calls from behind.

I hop onto a generator and stare out into the city, and Brighton joins me.

"Your powers can make a difference," Brighton says after a stretch of silence. "This was Little Emil's dream."

"I didn't know any better back then."

"You don't have to fight if you don't want to."

"Of course I don't want to, but they're basically calling me responsible because two lifetimes ago I started this war. I'm not Bautista, I don't know how to clean up this mess. If he and Sera couldn't figure out how to end specters, what makes them think I can? I'm not trying to get involved in this business so I can die like the others, Brighton."

"That's the best part—you'll come back! Your power allows you to go on and on." Brighton snaps his fingers. "Your superhero name could be something cool like Unkillable King or Infinity Son!"

"I don't want to fight for my life for all of infinity."

Brighton apologizes, then is quiet for a beat. "You're not

indebted to the Spell Walkers just because they saved us. But Emil? Sleep on this. Today was a roller coaster with no seat belt. I know you, and you'll regret walking away from all the good you could do."

It doesn't seem possible anyone could know me well when I'm a stranger to myself.

"You really aren't going to Los Angeles tomorrow?"

"No. I'm staying by your side to see this through."

"You'll be disappointed if I turn my back on the Spell Walkers and Nova, right?"

Brighton lets out a deep sigh. "I obviously wish we could've had powers together. The Reys of Light—Firelight. But I'll be your sidekick and keep you alive while we figure out this cure."

I start crying as we fist-bump and whistle, because there's one light that this storm of a day hasn't managed to blow out. "You're not my sidekick. You're my brother."

FIFTEEN

INFINITY SON'S BROTHER

BRIGHTON

No one believed me. I knew we weren't going to be screwed with some normal life. I called it.

I had that blood-and-bones feeling Emil is always making fun of, but I was right, we're supposed to be part of this epic fight. Right now, Emil is the only soldier the Spell Walkers are interested in, but I'll prove to them that I can be a weapon too.

End of the day, everyone knows it should've been me—the powers, the past lives. All of it. I'm built for the Spell Walker life, and Emil isn't. I'm not knocking him. He would also tell anyone that I would pull off gleamcraft better than he ever will.

I'll prove it when the Crowned Dreamer finally turns me into a celestial.

In the meantime, I really hope we get to stay, but that's riding on Emil's decision. But going to Los Angeles for college seems so small now. There's a country of celestials to save. We can't turn our backs on them.

I'm not waiting around for Emil and Prudencia to wake up, so I get off my air mattress to walk around Nova and get my mind off the family bombshell. Last night, when Emil and I came down from the roof, we returned to our room and told Ma we needed space because we weren't ready to talk yet. I don't think today is the day either, if I'm being honest.

Outside our room is a group of kids who bounce in glee before running off. Word's out we're here. In other classrooms and offices, people are waking up, folding away their cots and sleeping bags. I pass a computer lab where a child is crying into a woman's arms, and I want to know their story. In a Spanish class, there's a group of girls reading books, and one is hovering several feet in the air, positioned as if she's lying on the floor. Levitation is obviously a common ability among celestials, but I'm still usually impressed, no different than watching someone bench-press hundreds of pounds without powerhouse strength.

The gym is busy with celestials playing basketball with their powers. A girl dribbles the basketball with no hands. I'm guessing she's telekinetic, but maybe it's something else, like an affinity with rubber or air that's allowing her to control the ball as she bounces it between the legs of her opponent and tries passing it to her partner, only for another girl to appear out of nowhere, intercept the basketball, and disappear as quickly as she came. The teleporter makes her way through the court, several feet at a time, and no one stops her from reaching the hoop and dunking.

These celestials make gleamcraft look like it's all fun and games. I don't know what they went through so that they found themselves under Spell Walker protection, but whatever it is, I'd use it as fuel to get out on the streets and create a better world. If my brother has to fight, so should they.

The teleporter spots me. "He's here!"

The way she disappears and reappears repeatedly reminds me of a video game lagging. Everyone else on the court and bleachers surrounds me too, with wide eyes, talking over each other.

"I can't believe you fought a specter!"

"You should help us train!"

"I can conjure water. We should be partners!"

"You're so brave! What was going through your mind?"

Before I can speak, one boy's eyes narrow. "He doesn't have powers. He's just the brother." He walks away.

"Oh," the water conjurer says, but he's nice enough to stay put.

These celestials should recognize me for who I am because I'm not just the brother, I was also out on the front lines fighting specters, and I did it without powers. That was beyond brave. It was one thing for my own subscribers not to hang out with me at Whisper Fields, but being mistaken for Emil is a roller coaster I hope I never have to ride again. People know and love me—check any of my accounts, which I built from the ground up.

"Do you know where I can find Wesley?" I ask.

"Probably the professors' lounge," the telekinetic girl says.

The idea that Wesley, who's one year older than me, would be in a professors' lounge is hilarious, but I go downstairs and check it out anyway. There are blankets thrown across the couches, but no one underneath. No idea who sleeps in here. I go down the hall, following music, and enter the room to find Wesley poorly playing the flute on a cot, Eva writing in a journal on a piano bench, and Atlas sitting by an outlet while his phone is charging.

Wesley lowers the flute when he sees me. "I swear we're working."

"Every revolution needs a soundtrack," Eva says.

"Every hero needs a break from their warring girlfriends," Atlas adds.

Eva raises a water bottle like it's a glass of champagne. "Maybe if Iris and Maribelle hit each other around, they'll finally stop fighting."

"You're the worst pacifist," Wesley says, and I have to agree. There was nothing peaceful about the way Eva pointed that wand at us. "If I still gambled, my money is on Iris," he adds.

"No comment," Atlas says.

"You're betting on Iris too?" Wesley pushes, but he doesn't say anything. "Brighton, grab a seat."

I already feel like the Spell Walkers are treating me like a friend. I belong here. "Where are Maribelle and Iris? I was walking around and didn't see them."

"Maribelle is holed up in our room, trying to track down that mystery celestial," Atlas says.

Eva lets out a deep sigh as she closes her journal, and I feel bad for disturbing the peace. "Iris is sacrificing another morning of cuddles to coach some celestial who isn't ever going to find themselves doing fieldwork with the rest of the team."

"So you don't go out and fight because you're a pacifist?"

Eva claws at her dark hair and plucks strands from her scalp. "Every time Iris leaves is the worst moment of my life. She thinks she's so indestructible, and one day someone is going to prove her wrong. But she doesn't want me out in the field because my power makes me too valuable. If I end up in the wrong hands, my healing could be used on some serious monstrosities. She would rather die than live knowing I'm being tortured every time I heal."

"Why would someone torture you if you're healing them?"

Everyone is quiet, and it's awkward, and I'm the only one who doesn't know why.

Eva twists and pulls her hair before sitting on her hands to stop herself. "The only way I can heal someone's wounds is by first absorbing their pain. I recover faster than they do, but I still suffer like I might break beyond repair. Imagine what would happen if Blood Casters or alchemists or enforcers got hold of me. I could spend the rest of my life healing criminals and officers who hate our kind."

I never would've thought healing could be so nightmarish. That means yesterday, when we heard screams in the hallway, they weren't coming from Iris, but Eva as she endured Stanton's basilisk acid. I don't know what to say, and I don't want to press Eva any more than I already have, so I turn to Wesley to change the subject. "Thanks for giving my mother your room last night."

"Don't sweat it. It got a little cold, but I might keep camping out here so I can be the first one out the door next time someone betrays us," Wesley says with a forced laugh to lighten the mood.

"Wouldn't you be the first one out anyway with your swift-speed?" I ask.

"That's the joke," Atlas says. "Or what Wesley considers a joke."

I force a laugh too. "Aren't we going to have to relocate anyway when school starts up next week?"

"Dude, Nova didn't receive any government funding. They were forced to shut down," Wesley says, and someone needs to shut me up at this point because nothing I say is good. I haven't felt this idiotic since the first few exams I took after Dad passed.

"Same thing happened in my freshman year. I got moved to some basic public school and dropped out when I realized the teachers didn't give a ghost's cry about my powers."

"Do you guys do lessons here?"

"We do some coaching," Eva says with more energy than before. "But we're not teachers."

"What's everyone's role?" I ask. "I'm ready to help any way I can."

The Spell Walkers have divided up duties. Iris gets the least sleep as the commander for all missions and recruiter for the team. Wesley is the direct correspondent with other rescue groups across the country to coordinate celestials seeking shelter elsewhere. Atlas manages requests for side gigs to bring in money. Eva is the resident healer, which apparently isn't just physical but also mental; she runs therapy groups for struggling celestials and has one this morning. Maribelle is supposed to be training newbies for combat, but she's been occupying herself with clearing her parents' names.

"I can help with fixing your image," I say. This is my calling. I was made for this. Blood and bones. "All eyes are on Emil, right? Let's keep the focus on him. I'll record his journey as a new Spell Walker and give the world his history and updates. They'll see that everything we do and represent is heroic. We'll prove everyone wrong."

"It's a good idea, but also an impossible task," Atlas says. "Plus, some people are happy living in the past. But if we stop the Blood Casters, we can win back a lot of trust that way. One fight at a time. You got to let Emil know we're not expecting him to save the world all on his own."

"Maribelle needs to hear this too, man," Wesley says.

"She went too hard on him," Atlas agrees. "Brighton, if Emil helps us take down the Blood Casters, we'll stop the prime source of violence that's painting anyone with powers as villains."

"We want your brother's help," Eva says. "But we understand what we're asking of him."

"I'll talk to him. Emil isn't going to want to hide for the rest of his life."

I've been given my first mission from the Spell Walkers—purpose. I will do what it takes to protect my brother, and that means encouraging him to join this fight instead of waiting around for someone to track him down and kill him. Emil will know how to defend himself if the Spell Walkers coach him through his powers. Ideas are furiously spinning around my head.

"What time is the group therapy session?"

"Forty minutes," Eva says.

"We'll be there."

I head back to our room.

Prudencia is in the hallway outside our door. She's on the phone with her head hung low and one arm across her chest like she's hugging herself.

"You better not throw away my stuff!" Prudencia is shaking. "Do you hear yourself? No one is threatening you. I'm taking care of a friend who needs me. No one is coming for you! I—" She looks at the phone and sinks against the locker. "She hung up. Why isn't it easier to be happy that I don't live with her anymore? It's not like I ever thought I would keep in touch with her once I moved out."

"She was the only family you had left after your parents died."

Prudencia stares at our door. "I don't know what Emil is feeling right now, but he was lucky to have grown up with a family that loved him so fiercely that he never suspected he was adopted. Is it horrible that I wish the same thing for myself instead of ending up with my aunt?"

"You deserved better," I say. "We'll take care of you."

"It's not about me. We should be more worried about Emil. He's awake."

We knock before entering, but still find Emil fully under the sheet. If it wasn't for his phone screen shining through, I wouldn't know if he was awake or not, because that's how he sleeps and that's how he hides from whatever is bothering him.

"Bro. You want to get up?"

"I'm trying to find info on how to break the cycle," he says.

"Maribelle can get you Bautista and Sera's notes on a potential cure," I say.

"Only if I fight for them first. No. I got to figure out my

own way to end infinity."

"Let's check the library," I say. When he doesn't budge, I pull the sheet off him. "Come on. You're not going to escape this misery unless we do something about it."

It takes a minute to get Emil out of bed, but in no time, I'm picking out a new shirt for him, shoving him into the bathroom to brush his teeth, and leading him to therapy. We're walking side by side, saying nothing, like we've spent our entire lives talking and finally run out of things to say. The library is an absolute mess. I'm guessing there's no librarian in here to stop everyone from completely disrespecting the books. It's an elementary school library, so who knows how many texts they're carrying that might actually spark an idea for how to free Emil from this cycle that Keon started, but I'm feeling doubtful right now judging by the *Basilisks for Beginners* picture book in the Prime Constellation section. Doesn't matter. We're not here for books.

"What's going on here?" I point out the group of celestials sitting underneath a domed ceiling lamp that resembles the sun. "Come on."

Emil doesn't budge. "We should find the books."

"We will after," I say.

"Brighton, let's do what we came to do," Prudencia says.

"It'll be quick," I say.

I guide Emil by the shoulders. I know my brother better than he knows himself right now. This is the right choice, blood and bones. The younger celestials are excited as we approach, and they're staring at Emil like he's a god, but they have no idea how special he actually is. No idea how his first life is one of the reasons they're all in hiding today.

"Morning," Eva says. She's the only Spell Walker present. "Come join us."

"What is this?" Emil asks.

"Therapy. We get together every few days to check in."

Emil glares at me as we join the circle.

Apparently, there have been new faces besides ours the past couple weeks, so some celestials are speaking up on how they got here. There's Grace, whose voice can become as loud as a bullhorn, and she's had a couple training sessions with Maribelle to act as security for the haven. Flynn can speak any language for every living being and was hunted by the Blood Casters, who wanted his talents to track down healthier creatures. Twelve-year-old Alberta can create earthquakes, and she and her family almost died when her power surprised them in New Jersey; she still doesn't have a very good handle on it. Noted. This dude Zachary was cornered in the streets by someone trying to rob him, and when the robber pulled a knife on him, Zachary's power to put someone to sleep surfaced for the first time, and he was accused of attacking the man. Then there's Sapphire, who can create ropes of energy, but she's not very good at it yet.

I raise my hand.

"You can just speak," Eva says.

"How did you end up here?"

Emil needs to hear from active Spell Walkers.

"I've been hunted for years," Eva says. "Two years ago, I was with my best friend when four men hopped out of a van and tried to kidnap me. I'd been terrified before, but that night still haunts me. We only got away because a celestial appeared and hit them all with her sleeper spell. My best friend and I escaped, but . . ."

My heart hammers. This is one of those stories where I know Eva is alive because she's standing right in front of me, but I'm still so scared for her. "Is your friend here too?"

"That afternoon tore us apart," Eva says. "She felt power-less, and . . . she sought out power." She looks like she wants to say more, but unlike when she told me about the consequences of her healing, she doesn't go on. "Emil?"

Emil's head is hanging low.

I wrap my arm around his shoulder. I know he's scared, but if I can't be the greatest hero this city has ever seen, I'll make sure my brother will. "Bro, you're in a ring of people who have been affected by this war. Who do you want to be?"

SIXTEEN

ASSEMBLE

EMIL

They're kidding me.

I can't know who I want to be when I'm still struggling with who I am. It's been twelve hours since my life completely blew up. Some celestials in this circle have always known they were going to come into powers, others were surprised like me, but how many found out they were adopted and are now expected to become a Spell Walker because it's what their latest past life did? Because it's what their first past life caused?

Just me.

I stay shut, and when the group breaks up, I keep my distance from everyone—especially Brighton, who set me up—in a corner of the library. I'm going to look through all these damn books myself and hope to find some way out of this. Before the hour is up, I know I'm kidding myself. I sucked at basic chemistry; I don't stand a chance at alchemy.

I stick to my strengths, reviewing an old textbook on phoenixes, but there's only one page on gray suns. It doesn't tell me anything new. I know they come back stronger every time, which is probably how I'm wielding both Keon's gold flames and Bautista's gray flames, but I don't know if my powers will keep growing or if I hit my limit. Resurrection is clearly a thing, except I won't come back as me when I die. I wasn't even reborn with any of Bautista's or Keon's memories. Were Keon or Bautista self-healing? I never saw any footage of them flying. Some scientists have tried proving a phoenix's ability to move through their past lives, but nothing solid has ever come from those theories. That's the power I would want the most, so I could go back and stop Keon from creating specters in the first place, just like some mission in my favorite science fiction movies.

I spend the next couple hours in the library before hunger gets the best of me. I link up with Brighton and Prudencia to feel a little less alone, and when we get to the cafeteria, Ma is eating by herself. Her back is turned to me; I could walk away and not hurt her feelings. Seeing her hunched over whatever the hell she's eating reminds me so much of when Dad passed, and she would have to force-feed herself.

Everything is terrifying, so I go straight to my mother like

I always have in the home she didn't have to invite me into.

She looks up at me with the reddest of eyes. "Emil."

There's that part of me that's aching to hug her, to forgive her, but I'm frozen.

"My Emilio, I'm so sorry. My heart has never hurt more than seeing that look on your face. . . . I never wanted to put you through that."

"You should've told me," I say.

"Us," Brighton says.

"Of course," Ma says. "We took too long to tell you boys the truth. Part of me wishes I'd kept up the lie, so I wouldn't have the memory of your betrayed faces. But it seemed too important. I will tell you anything you want to know."

I have so many questions, but I've lived through enough truth with my family that it can wait. "I need some real talk first. I know everyone is counting on me becoming a soldier. It's been really impossible to hype myself up enough to fill Bautista's shoes, even though I want to live in a better world like everyone else here. But I know I'm not strong enough to create it."

"You've done it before!" Brighton says. "Sort of."

I'm not Keon or Bautista, and I don't know them any better than anyone else who's researched them online. "They both got killed, Bright. This isn't some video game where I'll respawn as your brother if I die. Are you going to feel good about pushing me into this fight if I end up dying?"

Brighton doesn't hesitate. "I would hate myself forever. But are you going to feel good about walking away from all of this?"

"I would hate myself forever," I echo. "I know too many names and faces and stories to not help. I might be a specter, but I'm a lot like the celestials who also didn't choose to have powers. I want to focus on this cure and reverse the damage Keon and the Blood Casters have created."

Brighton grins. "We're going to get you through this. I'll film your training so we can review everything together. I'll tell you when you're not giving it your all so you don't get wrecked on the battlefield."

"Battlefield," Prudencia breathes. "Hell of a word."

"Different times," Brighton says.

"Ma?" She's been quiet.

"No parent wants to watch their child walk into battle," Ma says with my hand in hers, and I fight the impulse to rip it away. "I wish I could lift the world off your shoulders, Emilio, but I will support you however I can. If you want to stay, we stay. If you want to leave, we leave."

No one can make this decision for me. We hang tight in silence for a little while longer so I can give myself a few more breaths before I change my life even more. We assemble together and march to the brewing chamber. The Spell

Walkers are gathered, and all eyes are on us. My phoenix fire has nothing to do with how powerful I feel in this moment. All credit goes to my own little army standing with me.

"I'll become one of you."

SEVENTEEN
TRAINING

EMIL

The Spell Walkers are no joke when it comes to getting me in shape for the streets.

Atlas coaches me on how to call for my power, and it's harder than the pull-ups Iris has me doing with my scrawny arms during our intense workouts. Whenever I manage to summon the heavy phoenix fire, I'm supposed to try and get some hits on Wesley, which—come on—hitting a regular moving target is hard enough. Learning how to swing bones with Maribelle is off to a rough start when she has to readjust my thumb so I form a proper fist. Brighton is hyping me up from behind the camera, but there's no way this footage will make me look like a hero to anyone.

Day by day, the Spell Walkers have got to realize they're investing in the wrong person. But they're not giving up on me. The bruises are building up after three days of Maribelle going in on me, and I avoid Ma whenever I have to ice them so she doesn't know how much pain I'm in. On our fifth day of training I'm just as stunned as anyone when my balance improves, my focus tightens, and the flames feel lighter. Throwing projectile shots is so much more complicated than hitting targets in video games, and when I stop aiming for where Wesley is and start anticipating where he'll be next, I finally hit him in his power-proof vest.

On our seventh day of training, the Spell Walkers prepare a trial run for me. All our sessions have been private, but this time Iris has invited everyone in the building to spectate, and man, there must be sixty people here who are counting on me to help save them.

"Your objective is to rescue the fallen celestial," Iris says. There's a dummy on the other side of the gym. "And bring them home."

"That's it?"

"Let the trial begin," Iris says, and the lights dim.

All eyes are on me as I fight through Atlas's winds to reach the dummy, like I'm caught in a storm. I've never stopped to think about what weather conditions I might have to face when I'm out on a mission, and it's a new element of fear that strikes me. Right before I reach the dummy, a strong breeze starts whizzing past me, over and over. Wesley is running circles around me, and before I can stop him, he barrels into me with his shoulder. I'm knocked back into the wall with no mat to catch me. Everyone in the bleachers groans as I try picking myself up. Wesley charges again, and I cross my arms over my chest, bracing myself for another hit as my phoenix fire ignites and forms wings. He crashes into me, but this time he's the one propelled backward. He rolls across the floor, and the crowd cheers.

I stare at my hands—my fiery wings don't fly, but they work as a shield.

I need all this to end, so I grab the dummy's leg before Wesley recovers. The dummy is heavier than I expected, and my arms and sides are still beyond sore from all the training. Maribelle floats out of the shadows and kicks me dead in the chin; I have no idea how my teeth aren't raining out of my mouth. She lands and kicks me in the rib cage so hard, like I owe her money or something.

"I quit, I quit," I cough out.

I'm not a fighter, I'm owning that.

Maribelle helps me up, and her head tilts. "We don't get to quit."

She twists my arm and flips me over her shoulder. The air is knocked out of me so hard I fight for my next breath. No matter how many times I've seen that move done in action movies, I wasn't prepared for how much it would feel like my arm was almost ripped out of its socket or how my back feels like it could've been shattered.

I crouch on one knee and gesture for a time-out. "I need two minutes."

"Not a chance in hell," Maribelle says.

"Give me a break!"

"Would you ask the Blood Casters for a time-out? Do you think the enforcers will give you a chance to recover? Your opponents want you weak. Prove them wrong."

Maribelle levitates and torpedoes toward me. I avoid her with a shoulder roll like she taught me. I crouch on one knee and cast fire, knocking her out of the air. She's groaning, but I can't check up on her; I have to focus on the mission. I'm dragging the dummy across the floor when dodgeballs throw me off my feet. Iris launches another dodgeball, and I hurl fire-darts until I've blasted them all apart, shreds of rubber falling between us. I drag the dummy by its legs and collapse when I cross the finish line, panting hard as people shout "Fire-Wing!" over and over.

Everyone in this room is counting on me to be this hero. Fire-Wing.

I hope they never find out that my past life is the reason they all need rescuing.

It's been odd as all hell watching Brighton edit clips of me, but the next afternoon, the Spell Walkers have approved of what he's calling his masterpiece, and it goes live on Celestials of New York. It's basically a two-minute montage of everything I've been up to lately. There's an epic score that crescendos during the original clip of me on the train when my power first surfaced, then slows down when I'm getting my ass kicked during training, and picks up again as I pass my trial. It's cool, yeah, but I doubt people will have sympathy for a specter since I can't exactly prove to the world that I was reborn into all of this. Everyone will accuse me of bringing this onto myself.

Brighton is hyped as the views skyrocket. For every ten good comments, there's someone hoping I'm set on fire and fed to a hydra. I have to stop reading—even the supportive ones—because there's enough pressure already. I've been meaning to begin one-on-one counseling with Eva like Ma has, but between training and deciphering Bautista and Sera's notes with Prudencia, I can't find the time. Too many people are counting on me. Myself included. Figuring out a cure is the only way I can piece my life back together.

I'm icing my shoulder while Prudencia and I flip through the dark blue leather journal with a gold fire-orb drawn onto the cover. Bautista writes in the sloppiest cursive, but dude could draw. Underneath sketches of extinguished flames, I make out his note about one of his attempts. He worked with a celestial who could neutralize other people's powers, but much like the gauntlets that enforcers use, the effect wasn't permanent. Between the handwriting, the art, and his fears, I wonder how much I'm me because of my own choices and how much has gotten passed down from Bautista like genetics. Maybe my attraction to phoenixes has always been because of my histories as Bautista and Keon.

Prudencia types more notes into her phone. "I've never heard of half of these ingredients Sera mentions. Bone tears? Water from the Shade Sea? Cumulus powder? Ghost husk? I can't tell if she's a brilliant alchemist or a know-nothing whose visions never helped her out."

"Bautista really believed in her," I say. "Why else would he keep being her test subject?" There was one potential cure where Bautista drank a potion mixed with the blood of water-casting celestials to try and put out the fire, but it was another bust. "What if those trials are why I never got Bautista's or Keon's memories? Maybe in trying to cancel out everything, all they did was extinguish that power."

"It's possible. Everything is just a theory, right?" Prudencia flips back to an entry about the Halo Knights that we dog-eared. It really hammers in how they're tremendous champions of the sky whose numbers have greatly diminished over the years, but they continue to devote their lives to the welfare of every phoenix breed. "If the Halos hadn't hated Bautista so much for hosting phoenix powers, they could've been helpful."

"True. But we need to figure out how to stop all specters."

"And make sure they can't just re-up on more blood."

"Totally a task for two people not trained in alchemy."

The door opens, and Iris enters. I've completely lost track of time for our session. Today we're working on arms and abs, but I can't imagine I'm ever going to be molded into having a six-pack like Atlas. "Hey, sorry I'm late, we've been going through the notes."

"Training is canceled today," Iris says. "You're coming on a mission with me and Maribelle to take down the specter you fought on the train."

So the enforcers didn't get their hands on Orton after all.

I dared to be happy for a second, thinking I could use that extra time to nap or chat it up with Eva, but in that breath of daydreaming, Iris had to hit me out of it like one of her brick-crushing punches. "Wait. Why me? What about Atlas and Wesley?"

"They're caught up with a job in New Jersey. We're training you to fight outside, not rescue dummies."

"I know, but I'm still so sore, and I'm only just getting the hang of things."

"Orton tried to kill you all last time, and we have to stop him now," Iris says. "I've been tracking several leads that can help us find the Blood Casters, and I found his new territory where he's been selling Brew. We have to figure out Luna's ultimate goal, and Orton is our best shot for intel."

Brighton closes his laptop and raises his camera. "I'm going too!"

Iris shakes her head. "Filming videos within Nova is one thing, but we're not risking your life out in the field." Brighton tries getting another word in, but Iris holds up her hand. "Emil, meet me in the locker room."

"She didn't even give me a chance to explain," Brighton says.

"It's Iris's job to protect us," Prudencia says.

"It's my job to build sympathy for gleamcrafters everywhere. Emil's been getting some positive traction online from celestials and sympathizers. He's giving them hope. But if we can't control the narrative, then the greater public will never come to their senses that the Spell Walkers and Emil aren't terrorists. Look at him, he doesn't even want to go out *now*—and people still like him!"

Prudencia lets out a deep breath. "I'll try to explain to her."

I drag my feet to the locker room. This is straight-up ridiculous. No matter how much training I've been through, I have no business out on the streets. No one would ask a doctor to do a firefighter's job, but everyone's cool with sending a museum gift shop employee after the person who tried killing him.

Brighton fixes his camera on me as Prudencia walks over to Iris, who's lacing up her boots while Maribelle is in the other corner stretching.

There's gear laid out for me. The gloves are deceptively

heavy, with fabric woven around brass knuckles for that extra damage. I haven't seen the others in elbow pads, but I throw them on because I want as much protection as possible; I'd put on a damn helmet right now if one was lying around. My long white undershirt is made from sun-dust, which feels like wool woven with feathers; it's the same fire-resistant fabric the Halo Knights wear into battle. I pull on the power-proof Spell Walker vest—midnight blue with the gold constellation spray-painted across the chest.

"You look badass," Brighton says.

The whole outfit is heavy, and even though I get to keep my jeans and sneakers, I don't feel like me.

"Get dressed," Iris says, with Prudencia by her side.

"What? I am."

Iris points at Brighton and Prudencia. "They're coming along for a trial run."

"For real?" Brighton asks.

"You and Prudencia have to stick close. You'll each be given daggers, and if this goes well, I'll be training you on how to use gem-grenades for future protection. We leave in three minutes. Suit up fast."

Brighton spins around, and I can tell he's expecting to find Spell Walker gear like mine. He puts on a black power-proof vest that has definitely seen some action; a tear from a blade, singed edges from fire, and three holes crossing the stomach from spellwork. I hope whoever wore this before my brother is okay. Once Brighton and Prudencia are dressed, we go down the hall. The whole time, Brighton is filming me as I march to my death.

Ma is shaking by the entrance, and Eva takes Iris into her arms.

"I don't want you to go," Ma says.

"Me either," I say. But I'm only going to get my freedom by serving as a Spell Walker.

"Take care of Emil," Ma says.

"We're his sidekicks. We will," Brighton says.

"As his brother and his best friend. All of you come home to me."

One group hug and we're out the door and back in the car that brought me here. We're on the road, and I can't believe I've gotten myself into this.

Maybe this is how every hero feels before they go into battle.

EIGHTEEN
BURNOUT

EMIL

On the morning of Dad's funeral, I refused to get off the train when we reached our stop. Brighton had to hold open the doors while Ma pleaded with me to take her hand, to be the strength she needed to get through the ceremony. Passengers saw that we were dressed in black and crying, but their sympathy and patience didn't last long before people started shouting at me. They didn't care that I wasn't ready to face my father in a casket.

I don't want to get out of this car and fight Orton.

"I'm not ready," I say to Brighton and Prudencia, who are in the backseat with me.

"We'll be there with you," Brighton says.

Maribelle turns around from the driver's seat. "You'll be keeping your distance."

"I don't have the power to stop Orton," I say. "I got lucky the first time."

"We've got the element of surprise again," Iris says. "And you have us too." Iris's powerhouse strength and Maribelle's levitation and agility are a boost, for sure. "The objective isn't to kill. We need to lay him out so we can question him on Luna's advancements in alchemy."

"But if you have to defend yourself, defend yourself," Maribelle says. "If it's kill or be killed, light him up."

"Do everything you can to avoid killing," Iris adds. But she doesn't disagree with Maribelle either. This is not the thing I wanted to see them bond over.

I get out of the car, and my legs are trembling as I follow them into an empty warehouse for Eternal Lerna Footwear, this company I hate since they produce shoes made of hydra leather. The lights must be busted, and the sun setting isn't helping us at all. I'm about to try and conjure a quick flick of fire when shards of glass from broken windows crunch under my boots. I freeze, terrified that Orton is about to pounce out of the shadows and strike me down before I can defend myself with a single lesson I've learned. I'd make history as a so-called chosen one who was taken down his first week on the job. But all is okay as Brighton turns on his camera's light, helping us guide the way. The smell of fresh kicks, rubber, and glue grows stronger as we pass waist-high tables where the factory workers handled business.

Maribelle hovers to a balcony while the rest of us creep up these steel steps, and we all freeze when we hear voices in the room ahead. I make out Orton's cruel laugh, and it sends shivers down my spine. I want to hit a one-eighty and hide in the car, but we're in too deep already. It sounds like a group of people in there, and I wish I could see through these walls so I would know how outnumbered we're about to be.

We press ourselves against the wall outside the door, and Iris gestures to Brighton and Prudencia to get some distance. Brighton is hesitant, but Prudencia drags him back by his vest.

"If she can't help me, then I'm done helping her!" Orton shouts from inside the room.

Iris counts down from three and punches the door off its hinges. I follow her and Maribelle in.

The office is cramped enough without the six people in dirty gray jumpsuits and crimson belts staring us down— acolytes who have sworn their lives to the Blood Casters. Orton hobbles around the table, and when he grins, I zero in on his red-stained teeth. Dark veins pop against his sickly white skin, like shadows coursing through snow. His eyes glow like burning coal as he shoots bright, screeching fire at us. I freeze, and Maribelle is quick to yank me out of the way; Iris would've ripped my arm out if Maribelle hadn't beat her to it. The fire explodes behind us, and I'm relieved that Brighton

ADAM SILVERA

and Prudencia aren't in here.

"Get them!" Orton shouts.

The acolytes charge. Three have switchblades, two have wands, and another has a battle-ax. One foolishly throws a punch at Iris, who catches his fist and swings him into another acolyte. Maribelle glides, careful not to bang into the low ceiling lights as she dodges spellwork. Two acolytes are closing in on me, and I back up, ready to run out that door, but I can't do Maribelle and Iris dirty. There's no shortage of fear to tap into as I hurl fire-darts into the acolytes. I hit shoulders and sides, doing my best not to kill anyone, even people who are trying to stab me. The woman with the battle-ax is screaming as she corners me, and as she raises it overhead, Maribelle pops up and snatches the weapon. Maribelle floats into a backflip kick, knocking the acolyte in her chin, and lands beside me.

"Show no mercy," Maribelle says as she hurls the battle-ax across the room, the blade digging into the leg of an acolyte who was sneaking up on Iris.

An acolyte aims his wand at Iris, and I catch him with a fire-dart from across the room.

"Nice, Emil!" Brighton shouts from the doorway with the biggest grin on his face.

Maribelle and Iris are so in sync as they knock out the remaining acolytes left and right.

The corner of the room glows with white fire as Orton casts an attack the size of a boulder. He hurls the blast and

160

catches Iris by surprise. She's thrown across the room and crashes through the desk.

She doesn't get up. I rush over to her as Maribelle pursues Orton. I'm relieved to feel Iris's pulse, no matter how faint. I call her name over and over and beg her to stay with us. Suddenly Prudencia is by my side.

"Help Maribelle," Prudencia says. I nod, but I don't get up. "Emil, go! I'll watch Iris."

I'm shaking as I rise. I'm nervous about everything—the stirring acolytes, my brother and best friend's safety, Iris's condition, how Maribelle and I will hold up against Orton.

We were idiots to come here without the full squad. Orton looks weak, but he's stronger than when we battled on the train. Maribelle is swinging nonstop, but Orton is legit untouchable. He surprises her with punch-kick combos, phasing again whenever she counters. I study his pattern, like when Wesley was running circles around me during training, and the next time Orton lunges, I catch him with a fire-dart to the back and blast him straight into Maribelle. I would've been in shock and tensed up, but Maribelle is quick, and she chokes Orton from behind. I can't tell by the look in her eyes if she's trying to knock him out or take him down for good. Orton is struggling, but he's not slipping away like air.

"Don't let go!" I shout. "I don't think he can use his power when you're holding him."

Orton's face is turning blue the harder Maribelle squeezes,

and then his eyes go dark. White fire ignites around his hands, and Maribelle screams as he burns her. Her grip is broken, and she's shaking on the floor. Orton's arms are glowing with flames, and he touches a desk, setting it ablaze. Black smoke begins to fill the room, and one acolyte picks himself up and runs away. The others probably won't be so lucky if they don't recover soon.

Brighton is continuing to film while checking on Iris with Prudencia.

"Get out of here!" I shout.

I have to try and take down Orton alone. Brighton and Prudencia don't have to die with me.

Orton stares me down, and I feel like we're about to have a shoot-out. We cast fire at the same time and our attacks explode against each other in dying screeches that chill my bones. I'm sweating as I unleash fire-dart after fire-dart, but the attacks phase through him. The sooner I handle him, the sooner we can focus on rescuing Iris and Maribelle. I'm catching my breath when Orton hits me with a fire-orb in the center of my chest. I'm thrown backward and slam face-first into the wall. The power-proof vest saved my life, no doubt, but my forehead is busted open and I can taste blood on my lips.

"You're okay," Brighton says as he appears beside me and studies my wound.

I cry out because the cut stings and stings, like whenever I would get sunburnt from the beach and Brighton would smack my back as a joke.

"Whoa," Brighton says. "It's closing. You're healing!"

Another phoenix power.

He reaches for his camera, and that's when we see Orton glowing in white flames against the growing smoke. The fire has traveled from Orton's arms to his back and is trailing down his legs. Someone might say he looks powerful, but there's nothing but anguish on his face.

"Move him!" Prudencia shouts at Brighton.

Brighton tries helping me up, but Orton is closing in on us. He grabs his dagger. My brother won't stab some dude—I know him. I'm about to raise my hand and try to blast Orton, but he stops. He continues taking slow steps, but he's not progressing, like he's stuck on some invisible treadmill. The white fire spreads throughout the rest of Orton's body, consuming him from head to toe. Brighton is quick to aim his camera as the flames work against Orton. His howling dies before his body can slam across the floor.

I don't know if this is rebirth or death. But we need to save our own lives.

I assist Maribelle as Brighton and Prudencia carry Iris. We step around the tomb of fire that's continuing to eat at whatever remains of Orton's corpse. Maribelle is in no condition to drive, and not having a license doesn't stop Prudencia from putting her weekend driving lessons to use. Hopefully we didn't survive this battle just so we can die in a car crash.

We pull out of the factory's alleyway as black smoke spills out of the shattered windows. I watch the glowing fire within until it's out of sight, and even then, I can't push the memory of the flames eating Orton out of my head.

"Is that going to happen to me?" I ask.

"What?" Brighton asks.

"Burnout," I say. "The powers turned on him. I'm not supposed to have mine either."

"Bro, you were reborn with these powers! It's different. You owned everyone in there like a hero."

I can't feel as hyped as Brighton. We didn't get the information we needed. Maribelle is biting down on her shirt to fight past the pain of her burnt hands. Iris has been hurt so badly that she's in need of healing—again. There were six acolytes, and I only saw one escape the factory. Orton is dead. I didn't kill Orton or the acolytes directly, but six people are goners now because of me.

I shouldn't get to be crowned as the hero when everyone's suffering is my fault. And maybe we're not the saviors this city needs.

NINETEEN
SPELL WALKERS
OF NEW YORK

BRIGHTON

Being Emil on social media is wild. He isn't doing great in real life since last night's fight, but he's tracking really well online—really, really, really well. His Instagram profile is now sporting the blue verified badge, and he's got over six hundred thousand followers showing him love and support. Some hate too, but he doesn't need to know about that. His Twitter mentions are so out of control that I can't keep up. Most notably, his Celestials of New York training montage has over three million views. BuzzFeed even cribbed my clips for their post! Between that and the twenty thousand new subscribers I've made overnight, I'm living the dream.

Last night, I handed over the full video of the battle against

Orton to the Spell Walkers so they could figure out why Orton burned out. When people's bodies react poorly to the amount of creature blood needed to turn someone into a specter, it usually happens at the beginning. Orton had his powers for at least two weeks. This was extreme. Lucky for them, I got most of it on camera. I stayed up editing the battle to fire it up on YouTube as soon as possible, but it sucks that I lost some moments, like when Orton's blast was flying straight at me and Prudencia so we had to take cover away from the doorway, or when Orton was walking in place as if he were shackled like some rabid dog.

The video is blowing up within the hour. I rush out of the library and back to our room to show Emil. I find him shaking, with a blanket wrapped around his shoulders, even though warm sunbeams are bathing him and Eva is sitting across from him with a mug of tea.

"Hey," Emil says weakly.

"What's going on?" I ask.

"Your brother and I are having a long-overdue talk," Eva says. "Would you mind giving us some more time?"

"We tell each other everything," I say.

The way Eva stares at me makes me question what I've said. "I'm happy to set up a time for us to do some group counseling, maybe even involve your mother, but this is a private session."

Someone thinks she's a real therapist.

"It's okay. He can stay," Emil says.

I'm tempted to throw an I-told-you-so smirk Eva's way, but I keep it together and sit beside Emil. Emil gets me up to speed, though it's nothing new—questioning his relation-ship with Ma, how he's terrified all the time, how he couldn't sleep last night because he feels so guilty over everything that happened with the factory. Talking it out with Eva is a solid idea because I refuse to grieve Orton and the acolytes, and Maribelle and Iris both received healing, so all's well that ends well. Figuring out how he feels about the big family secret and feeling bolder in battles is going to take time, but Emil will get there. He has to.

"What if using my powers overloads me too?" Emil asks.

"Bro, you're trying to talk yourself out of fighting. You see that, right?"

"Emil's fear is valid," Eva cuts in. "There's still so much we don't know about Orton's situation. Did he die because he was a celestial with phoenix essence? Maybe the creature's blood took longer to corrode his celestial blood."

"I want to do the right thing," Emil says. "But what if I screw up everything even worse than Keon did?"

Eva is about to tug a strand of hair and resists. "Back before there was so much disharmony between celestials and humans, our ancestors had a saying: 'The strongest power above all is a living heart.' Emil, your heart is powerful—you care, you ache, you feel. I don't know what Keon's intentions were, but his execution was disastrous. Your humanity is what makes you heroic, not your powers."

As Eva tells Emil more about how she swears by this mantra as a pacifist, my mind keeps turning the words over and over: The strongest power above all is a living heart. Humanity is what makes heroes, not powers. The strongest power above all is a living heart. Humanity is what makes heroes, not powers.

The strongest power is humanity.

"I got it!"

"Got what?" Emil asks.

"The key to winning."

I tell them to get everyone in the boardroom, and I run back to the library to get ready. I collect all the links and data I need to make my case. This is going to be a level up for the movement. My heart is pounding when I enter the boardroom to find the Spell Walkers and Prudencia gathered around. I haven't been this nervous about a presentation since my Advanced Placement Computer Science final—which I aced.

I go to the front of the room and thank everyone for coming.

"What's the big plan?" Maribelle asks.

"A six-part video series featuring all the Spell Walkers," I say. Maribelle glares at me like Dad used to when I would urgently wake him up to tell him about some new fun fact I learned, a fun fact that always could've waited until he was out of bed. "Eva told us about that old celestial adage, the one about the strongest power being a living heart. Why don't we post about why you all became heroes? Your origin stories. We can dispel all the rumors about how you're building an army to take down the government or getting stronger to attack the city again."

Maribelle stands up. "Dude, no one cares about us."

"I disagree." I share my report on the positive engagement I've seen across Emil's accounts and my own. People are rooting for all of us. They didn't know Emil two weeks ago, and now they're starving for more details. I remember what it was like waiting for the next time any Spell Walker would pop up on my feed, whether it was a clip of the latest brawl or even a casual sighting of them out in the world.

"We've tried the media route before *and* after the Blackout," Atlas says. "My own account included."

"You built your following by shouting out how many lives you've saved or lost. They only see you as a warrior. Let's take it to the next level and make it clear what you're fighting for."

"And you're the one to do it?" Maribelle asks.

"My platform has grown since Emil." I can't say it out loud, but it does sting that my personal fame isn't because of my own spotlight. The tables have now turned, and I've become Emil's cameraman. "I can get people to pay attention. We start with you all, and maybe we can expand to the innocents you've saved."

"Not every celestial wants to be exposed," Prudencia says.

"All the work they've done to blend into society gets thrown out the window."

"Everyone will have a choice to prove they're not walking weapons simply because they have powers. They can tell their stories through my Human Power campaign."

I give them the rundown. We lead with a special feature—Spell Walkers of New York—on my channel and every video will be tagged with #HumanPower. When it trends—and it will—we'll throw the question back at everyone: What's your Human Power? Celestials can share their stories. Humans can prove they're allies and energize others to step up their game.

Prudencia takes a deep breath and looks me dead in the eye. "I want to believe your campaign will work, Brighton. It's inspired. I'm not all that confident that someone who's a bigot learning that Spell Walkers have dreams and feelings will finally view them as equals. Then there's the fake activism, which is exhausting. People show up for a hashtag, spend an hour preparing a picture to post to prove they're good, and then they return to their regular lives where people don't swing at them."

It's a conversation we've had before, but my cheeks flush having it in front of the Spell Walkers.

"It's worth trying," I say.

"I agree," Iris says, and I hold back a smile. "Senator Iron is using the Blackout to silence Congresswoman Sunstar. It's unrealistic to expect Brighton's campaign to change everyone's worldviews forever, but maybe now is the time to try. This could be a big push to get Sunstar in office, where she can continue her work on a greater scale."

Everyone is talking over each other. Atlas is on the fence because not everyone's stories are going to be received well by the public. Eva is worried about what this could mean for Nova if enforcers and alchemists find out there's a healer on the team. Emil wants me to think about how this might backfire on *me*, but hateful comments are very different from what celestials face daily. Maribelle is resistant until she realizes the potential of this campaign catching fire—with a bigger platform, she can ask the world if they know the identity of the mystery girl who survived the Blackout. Wesley wants to talk it out with Ruth, but he's open to it if she is.

There are risks, of course, but the Spell Walkers decide to give me a chance.

Maybe this war can be removed from the streets and won online.

I set up my camera on the auditorium's stage, facing two chairs against the black curtains.

The Spell Walkers took the night to sleep on their involvement in my series, and now everyone is desperate enough for change that they're honoring their yeses. I prep them on how this is going to go down: I'll ask personal questions about their origin stories and lives, and the more honest they are, the better our chances will be at gaining sympathy for the campaign. We'll each film for fifteen to twenty minutes, and I'll stay up editing down to three to four minutes because of my viewers' attention spans. Emil is my cameraman like the good ol' days.

"Who wants to go first?" I ask.

Between his active Instagram and convention appearances, Wesley is the least camera-shy, but even he's tense as I ask him about being kicked out by his parents at fourteen and forced to use his powers for survival on the streets. He admits to abusing his swift-speed for personal gain, but he turned it all around when he met Atlas, who gave him purpose, and later Ruth, who grounded him with love. He needs this war to be over so she doesn't have to use her cloning power to raise their baby girl. Wesley will do whatever it takes to be the loving father he never had growing up.

Atlas hugs Wesley before sitting with me and opening up about his parents being locked up in the San Diego Bounds after using their powers to rob a bank, since no one wanted to hire them. At ten years old, Atlas was acting out as he bounced between foster homes, but after the high of saving someone at seventeen, he ditched Los Angeles to make a positive difference with the powers he inherited from his mother. He changed his name, dyed his hair, and set out to New York with the air of someone enlisting in the military. He prayed he would attract the attention of the Spell Walkers with his heroic deeds, all tracked on his @AtlasCounts account, and he's committed to creating a world where celestials won't have to abuse their powers to make ends meet.

Iris cuts in before Maribelle because she insists she has to get back to surveying specter activity to figure out what the Blood Casters are planning with the Crowned Dreamer. Iris tells the story of what it has meant to not only be a legacy Spell Walker, but to come from a line of women who are stronger with each generation. Leading the Spell Walkers after the Blackout has felt like impossible work, but her parents never shied away from the importance of the mission, even when the stars felt dimmest, so Iris will continue carrying the world on her shoulders instead of letting it roll away, hoping she can one day live as an ordinary twenty-year-old.

Maribelle joins me onstage with a photo in her lap. She defends her parents, saying that the media has got it all wrong about the Luceros and the Chambers. Instead of harping on how the Spell Walkers are responsible for the Blackout, she urges a deeper investigation on the girl everyone saw on the surveillance footage. She holds the missing pages of the story that the country is misreading. I'm about to ask her about what it's like to be in a relationship that was born from tragedy, but Maribelle storms off with red eyes, and Atlas chases after her.

Two more to go.

Eva's dark hair flows out from behind her rainbow cap,

gifted to her by Iris to beat any urges to yank more strands from her head. She doesn't make eye contact with me or the camera as she introduces herself as the hidden Spell Walker the world has never met because her healing power has made her too valuable. Three years ago, after losing her parents, who were working in a celestial shelter that was annihilated by a terrorist, Eva moved in with her lifelong best friend's family. Eva had exposed her power to heal a child who'd been hit by a car, only to be followed by men who tried to kidnap her and sell her off to some shady alchemists. Her friend's mother fought them off long enough for a celestial to come to the rescue, but she was shot in the conflict and died before Eva could heal her. Her friend watched, powerless, and soon after that, the friend sought out power to protect herself—she became a specter. Even scarier, she's now the Blood Caster with hydra blood.

I had no idea Eva was once friends with Dione Henri. I'll admit, I was curious how Eva's videos were going to track compared to the others in the series, but once this story gets circulating, I'm sure everyone is going to be holding their breath to see what happens between the Spell Walker and Blood Caster who have so much history together. I know I am.

Emil comes out from behind the camera, and Prudencia takes over.

"How honest should I be?" Emil asks.

"What do you mean?"

"Maybe if I own up to my past lives, we won't lose the spotlight."

"Solid."

Prudencia shakes her head. "It's not solid. Emil, there might be a bigger bounty on your head to make you pay for what Keon did. Violence against phoenixes will only increase. It's all too risky."

So we go with what's safe for the video. Emil talking about how he was excited for college and how things were picking up at work. It's fine, but it's all surface level. Everyone would lose their minds to hear about how he was adopted, how he was found on the streets. It was a plot twist that shook us greater than our favorite stories. It doesn't matter, I guess. If Emil is in it, people are going to treat it like a gigantic deal.

I pack up and immediately lock myself in the computer lab to work on edits. Ma makes sure I'm eating, and Prudencia urges me to rest, and Emil keeps me company while flipping through Bautista and Sera's journal. I pass out at the table while polishing Atlas's video, and when Emil wakes me up to go to bed, I get back to work. I clock out around five in the morning, only when I've done all my edits. I review everything when I wake up and present it to the team. Everyone is good, so there's one last thing left to do.

I hit upload.

The Spell Walkers of New York have broken the internet. The #HumanPower tag is trending globally, and people are taking it on like it's the latest Instagram challenge. It's only been fourteen hours, and Emil's video is leading with over two million views. The others have all crossed one million too.

My phone is absolutely blowing up with media requests and follower growth. I love the high of notifications, but I had to finally turn them off. Shooting past one hundred thousand YouTube subscribers was the big dream, and now that I've crossed that line, I want more—I need more.

I'm getting some heat from this conservative vlogger, which isn't that surprising—the so-called Silver Star Slayer is always spreading conspiracy theories about celestials. Anytime Senator Iron gets caught saying something that should work against his campaign, you can count on him to upload a video about how a shape-shifter probably posed as Senator Iron or some other celestial used their technological powers to manipulate the footage, as if that's even a thing.

The Silver Star Slayer has got his political neck of the woods believing the following: it's only a matter of time until Atlas follows in his parents' footsteps; Wesley's sob story about Ruth cloning herself to help out with their baby is a disservice to single mothers who are actually struggling; if Iris wanted to be a hero, she would disband the Spell Walkers; Maribelle is calling for an invasion of privacy of a young girl's life because she won't accept that her parents are murderers; Eva is selfish for not healing patients in need of urgent care; and Emil is being groomed to assassinate Senator Iron and any other anti-gleamcraft politicians.

"I'm sorry," I say to the group. "People are buying into it."

I never wanted to give anyone more ammo.

"But not everyone. Anyone willing to believe his lies isn't ever going to change their mind about us," Iris says. "This is a promising sign. You've proven that they're paying attention to us with their hashtag. Now we just have to figure out how to leverage this platform to cause some real change."

Prudencia walks over with bottles of cider and champagne. "You did it," she says with a true smile.

Everyone gets themselves a glass, and they toast me.

I may not be throwing fire, but I'm just as much a hero as anyone else.

TWENTY
NO ONE

NESS

Dione Henri is limping when she finally returns to Light Sky Tower with dark shadows under her venom-green eyes. Blood is caked in her curly red hair and splattered across her muscular, tattooed arms. I can't help myself, I'm always drawn to the white scars around her body—the thick line across the tulips on her forearm, another splitting the pink rose on her shoulder, a deep one at the base of her neck, to name a few—and the new one below her knee is still healing, like flesh stitching itself together. Why people continue to cut away at the girl with hydra blood as if that will stop her is beyond me.

A few months ago, I would've been thrilled to see her return in one piece. Starting over with no ties to my old life was lonely, and Stanton is too ruthless for true friendship. Dione's presence was more real, more human. I was sure we were in the same boat—indebted to the gang for saving our lives and heartbreakingly loyal because it was better than running from our pasts alone. Dione bad-mouthing the Senator when we watched the news together was a sign that she's good people, and she was the only one who checked in on me the night I killed that alchemist who put a wand to my head. But she's been on a power trip lately, throwing herself into more and more danger in the name of Luna's grand design, which she thinks will make her safe forever. That it will make all of us safe forever. The mission is what matters. No friends.

I've been wondering if she watched the video of the Spell Walker Eva Nafisi talking about how they were former best friends. Considering her current state, now doesn't seem like the time to ask.

"Where's the freak of nature?" Dione asks me and Stanton.

Always nice to hear that I'm not the only one still unnerved by June's existence.

"More blood tests with Luna," I say.

"Then we leave in two minutes without her," Dione says.

"You don't control me," Stanton says.

There are several Casters around the country, but we're the elite, we're in on the big plan. Stanton is the most senior of the New York gang by a year, but we only serve one leader and that's the person who gave us power. Our roles are constantly shifting, but for the most part, we're set. I spy on Luna's enemies and impersonate at her orders. Dione negotiates with dealers, traffickers, and politicians, and when that fails, she uses pure force so she doesn't return without good news. Stanton hits the streets to prey on potential Casters who first have to be initiated as acolytes to prove themselves—a step I'm grateful I got to skip, since Stanton's methods in testing their loyalty and fierceness are brutal. And June is nothing more than an assassin, far as I can tell. The killer who hasn't been seen by the world since the camera caught a glimpse of her in the wreckage of the Blackout. Luna has paid many favors to the media to keep June's face out of their circulation.

Dione ignores Stanton's bait and fills us in on the rare golden-strand hydra that's being transported from Greece for some trafficker's client who outbid Luna. The trafficker wasn't going to reveal the whereabouts and timing of the drop-off, not even after Luna offered to bless him with the powers of an ivory phoenix, so Dione assassinated his entire crew single-handedly, and he changed his tune. It's important that the hydra remains unharmed, which means preventing its delivery to the Apollo Arena, where it will be forced to fight another creature in a vicious cage match.

Everything is going down within the hour in Brooklyn, so Stanton rounds up some acolytes and we leave the tower. I pulled tonight's disguise from the security guard who looked at Luna with disdain when we first arrived at the end of August.

Wearing a dead man's face is good for my conscience; not like he'll get arrested for any crimes I commit tonight.

I'm hoping no serious action will be necessary, but as we all park and fan out across the marina, hiding in boats and behind bushes, I stay close to Stanton and Dione, because that's the key to staying alive. Luna tells us to look after each other like family, and even though that word has been meaningless for years, we know we better live up to her expectations. So many acolytes would love to take our places.

I tense up as the cargo ship pulls in to the pier. The door swings open, and while the hydra's growl is chilling, nothing freaks me out more than a dozen armed mercenaries exiting the boat with wands and daggers swinging from their belts. We don't have nearly as many acolytes as we need to survive this. To even attempt it.

"Let's call them off," I say. "Wait for them at the arena."

"Security at Apollo is tight," Dione says.

"We'll die if we move now," I say.

"We'll never truly live if we don't," Dione says.

Dione lunges into action. She reaches mercenaries with her bursts of swift-speed before their spells can be fired, and she snaps one's neck. The acolytes come out of hiding, distracting the mercenaries long enough for Stanton to strike.

Here we go.

My wand is charged to the max. I need to make these six blasts of lightning count. I enter the fray right as one acolyte takes a spell straight through his heart, falling over into the river. The mercenary responsible takes aim at me, and I shoulder roll out of the way, almost going over the edge and into the water myself. Before I can fight back, Stanton pops up behind the bearded man, sinks his teeth into his neck, and rips out a chunk of flesh. Blood gushes all over the dock, and the mercenary falls into it, writhing around.

Stanton grins and waves before spinning in time to catch the wrist of someone who was trying to stab him.

Objective: protect the hydra from harm.

Reaching the boat isn't simple. I only get two discharges out of my wand before a mercenary blasts it in half, burning my hand. An inch to the left would've been a head shot. I would've died as someone else. . . .

I hop onto the nearest boat and take cover in this ridiculous midlife crisis purchase. The little wobble of the boat is enough to trigger my seasickness. The couple times I rode the ferry with my mother were enough to keep me off water forever. I try to hold my dinner in, but when I look through the foggy window and onto the dock, I see a mercenary pin an acolyte under her boot and shoot a spell between his eyes. I throw up all over my boots.

Dione and Stanton and the remaining three acolytes are being overpowered.

"Ness!" Dione shouts.

There's fury all over her face as if I'm stronger than her, as if

I'm the one who said we should go and try to fight this battle.

New plan: Morph into one of the fallen mercenaries long enough to get past the survivors who are keeping my people at bay. Then we all run.

I'm in the process of modeling myself after the one Stanton thought was acceptable to bite like some vicious storybook vampire when someone tackles me from behind.

"I hate shifters," the man growls.

He flips me over. He swings his long red hair out of his face, revealing a thick scar that travels across his cheek. Who knows if the hydra that did that became a trophy in his home, but at least that creature managed to slash away half of this man's nose. The mercenary chokes me, and I'm hoping Stanton and Dione are going to appear out of the shadows and save me, but nothing. I lose concentration on my morph, and my entire glamour fades away.

"You . . ." His face goes white. "Aren't you—"

I rip the wand out of his holster and fire a spell through his heart.

"I'm no one," I say with my first breath.

The life vanishes from his eyes, and he collapses on me. His corpse is heavy, but I manage to roll him off. I tried to avoid this—so badly—but if it's my life or someone else's, there's no competition. Footsteps are coming my way. If I could swim, I'd throw myself overboard. But I can play dead better than anyone I know. I morph into an acolyte with blood staining my shirt and stay very still, even though my heart is alive and racing. Let everyone think we took each other out.

The Blood Casters failed tonight, but I can make this right.

I have to make this right.

May the stars have mercy on me if I can't.

TWENTY-ONE
HOPE

MARIBELLE

It's a couple days after Brighton's campaign before something worthy pierces the news cycle, but this late-night report of an attack on the Brooklyn marina catches my eye. There are images of dead acolytes being bagged up, and that's all I need to resist Atlas pulling me back into bed. This is a solid lead, and because Atlas is a gentleman, he gets up, and we rush out to his car with our gear.

"The couple that hunts together, stays together," I say as we take off.

Atlas yawns. "I vote for becoming the couple that stays in together and gets a full night's rest."

I had that once—didn't work for me. The only person I

dated before Atlas was Aquila, a powerful celestial who was rescued by Iris's parents. I was fourteen when I bumped into her outside the haven's bathroom, oblivious to who she was and why I was so attracted to her. I was able to talk through my feelings with Iris, who's always understood her heart. Aquila and I bonded over music and strong mothers, but unlike me, she wasn't committed to the fight and wanted to stay indoors instead. Going off on her because her power was more active and better primed for the fight than mine wasn't my finest hour. But praying to the stars that everything will sort itself out isn't me. I get out of bed to make a difference.

"Iris is going to be pissed we didn't wake her up," Atlas says.

"If she was really on her game, she wouldn't need us to."

"Mari, she can't be awake twenty-four seven."

"Why not, she's the all-powerful celestial who's going to save the world from itself, isn't she?"

I can't believe I didn't see all her arrogance when we were growing up.

"Sounds more like Emil," Atlas says. "What people are expecting, at least."

"I don't want to say it to Emil's face, but the wrong brother got powers. Emil's sensitivity and resistance to fighting is much more suited to doing all the behind-the-scenes activity. Brighton's take-charge attitude paired with those powers could've been truly revolutionary for us."

"I believe in Emil. He's doing his best."

"I hope his best gets better."

We park minutes away and almost bump into a couple holding hands as they exit a bodega, carrying groceries. I'm envious. No one is expecting them to save the world. They're not trying to avenge the deaths of their parents. They get to hold hands and breathe in peace. I'm tempted to reach for Atlas's, but we have to keep our hooded heads low under the moonlight and not draw attention to ourselves as we continue our late-night mission.

There's yellow tape stretched across the dock. All the body bags and police are gone. I step in puddles of blood that haven't dried yet, and I'm adding more crimson footprints to the grimy wooden panels. I investigate the insides of a metal cargo crate, using my phone's flashlight to expose the claw marks and scattered fur.

"Hydra," I call out, and my voice echoes within. I step out. "Luna must be creating another specter."

Atlas is standing still and staring at the blood.

"What's wrong?"

"So many deaths. Mari, if I die during battle—"

"We're not having this talk."

"—I want to be cremated. I don't want some open casket funeral where my body is stitched back together from whatever takes me out and people remember me wrong. I want my ashes scattered somewhere . . . maybe even tons of places."

We're too young to be thinking about this. But my parents

died without me ever knowing what they wanted. Not that they had bodies to bury, ashes to spread.

"Noted," I say. "Same for me, I guess."

Maybe we'll die together, sooner or later, and our ashes can be thrown into the same winds.

Someone's watching us, I can feel it thrumming through me like the sixth sense that aids me in battle. I look up and there's a girl in acolyte gear standing at the dock. When she sees me, she runs.

"Mari, wait!"

I get a running head start and jump into the air, gliding straight into her. I flip her over and see she's small with long blond hair. Her big eyes are frightened as I pin her down, my forearm against her throat. "When I let you breathe you need to tell me where Luna is. Understand?"

The girl sucks in a deep breath. "I don't know where she is. Luna is always moving around, and I go where I'm told. I snuck out of housing to see if my sister died in the attack."

"Your sister?" Atlas asks.

"I followed in her footsteps and devoted my life to Luna so we could one day be given powers. But she didn't return tonight, and . . ."

"Ease up, Mari," Atlas says. "She's a kid who doesn't know better."

I get off her and cross my arms. "What's your name?"

"Hope."

"Okay, Hope. I'm Atlas. Do you know anything about the mission? Why Luna wanted the hydra?"

"Not really, but she's working us all double time to intercept that hydra from the traffickers. Since we failed here, all of the Blood Casters will have to bust into the Apollo Arena's cage match tomorrow night to retrieve the hydra before it gets harmed."

"Does that include a celestial girl who is untouchable?" I ask.

She tenses. "Yes."

"Who is she?"

The acolyte looks around like someone might snipe her if she says another word. "I don't know much, except that she's an assassin named June who was contracted to kill the Spell Walkers. The ones before you."

The Blackout.

I grab and shake her. "How did she pull it off? Was she working alone?"

"I don't know! But Luna is very proud of her."

"Anything else?" I ask.

Hope shakes her head. "Please take me in, I can't go back," she begs.

"Luna doesn't even know who you are," I say.

"We appreciate your help," Atlas says, playing good celestial. "But we're caught in the cross fire of this war, and if you truly want to escape the Blood Casters, your best bet is leaving town. Do you have any other family?"

Hope looks like she might cry.

I'm not dealing with her.

I walk to the edge of the dock and try to breathe. I shut my eyes and June's face comes into the darkness.

She killed my parents.

I'll snuff out her light.

TWENTY-TWO
CAGE MATCH

EMIL

"Tell your mother how that makes you feel," Eva says during our morning therapy session.

Talking about the big family secret is difficult, but I don't want to keep shutting her out. "I can't trust you," I say to Ma with my eyes to the floor. "I mean, I trust you, but I feel stupid for doing so now. I know you love me and that you wanted the best for me, I get that. I always felt safe around you and Dad."

Ma nods. "Do you think you would've been okay with us telling you as a child?"

The thought has crossed my head a lot. I probably wouldn't have known better. The same way I didn't treat my sexuality like a big deal. But I can see myself spiraling growing up too, and questioning every little thing. Did Brighton get a bigger cookie? Why did Brighton get kissed first before bedtime? Would Ma and Dad have expected better grades if I shared their DNA?

"I don't know," I say.

Eva is about to ask another question when the door opens and Maribelle enters. "We're having a session. Why doesn't anyone respect therapy?"

"I figured out who killed my parents," Maribelle says. She looks like she hasn't slept all night. "Emil, I know you're wanting to sit some fights out, but the Blood Casters are going to be out in full force tonight, and we need you. Bonus perk: if you play your cards right, you'll be able to save a phoenix's life before it's ripped apart by a hydra."

So much for this session.

I'm pulled into a meeting with the rest of the group where Maribelle and Atlas give us the full rundown of their trip to the dock. Iris is hesitant to trust the acolyte who passed along this information, but Atlas really vouched for the fear in the girl's eyes. We're thrown straight into training, and my stomach is absolutely uneasy once we take off for Apollo Arena.

Cage matches between creatures are barbaric, and we've got the entire crew walking straight into one. I'm not trying to watch some phoenix and hydra battle it out, I don't have the heart for that, but I can't sit this out. I'm going to make good use of these powers I'm not supposed to have; the gray sun won't have died in vain.

We park our cars in front of this run-down boxing arena. People are being carded at the door and checked off a list. Maribelle is ready to bust in the front door to get her hands on the Blood Caster who played a role in her parents' death, but Atlas convinces her to practice some discretion for the greater mission. Wesley dashes out of sight and returns a minute later.

"Two armed guards at the back entrance," he says.

"Go disarm them," Maribelle says.

"I give the orders," Iris says. Wesley awaits instruction. "Go disarm them."

We make our way to the back, fanning out so we don't draw as much attention. I keep close to Brighton and Prudencia, wishing they'd remained at Nova. I stay away from Maribelle, whose fierceness is dark tonight. There's a dagger hidden in her boot and gem-grenades in her shoulder pouch, and I don't want to be around when she makes her move on June. We regroup behind the arena, where Wesley is lounging across the hood of a truck away from a group of unconscious guards.

Maribelle charges inside with Brighton closely following, his camera light exposing stains of blood and deep scratches along the floors and walls. It reeks of sweat and beer and wet fur. A thunderous roar echoes. I bet spellwork could explode back here and no one would notice.

We split up. Brighton and Prudencia head to the balcony

so they can film discreetly. I remain on the lower level, which can't be farther from my people, but Atlas assures me he'll stay up in the shadows above to keep an eye on them. Iris and Wesley blend into the crowd while Maribelle patrols.

It's a safe bet that tons of people here tonight have decorated their homes with creature heads. Maybe even hunted them personally as trophies to brag about. None of them give a damn that these creatures were ripped away from their families, carted over in darkness so they can be unleashed against their natural enemies. For entertainment.

Screw them all.

The ring is shaped like a diamond, with puddles of blood in the sand. There are sheds of serpent skin stretched across the ring, and man, I hope there isn't a basilisk slithering around tonight. An announcer in an oversized hoodie signals that the match is about to start. Four people appear from the low entrance, all wearing armor and helmets, and they're each carrying a chain and dragging the hydra. The golden-strand hydra is a ferocious beauty with flesh that's beige like the tropical beaches of its home. Its eyes are yellow and orange with cracks of red like the sun. The hydra struggles, dragging its clawed feet, scratching the path to the cage.

A low phoenix screech that sounds like a piercing firework taking flight pulls everyone's attention back to the entrance. The sun swallower's ankles are chained, and its bright orange feathers are shedding as it flaps its wings wildly. Its red beak is sealed shut with iron, preventing it from breathing fire before it's time. I want to lay into the two people as they pull the phoenix into its cage and unlock the muzzle and chains with the press of a button.

The hydra and phoenix are left alone in the cage and freeze as they lock eyes. The hydra roars, and the phoenix screeches, and I don't need to speak their language to know they're both frightened and prepared to fight for their lives. The hydra lunges, and the phoenix circles above, breathing fire. The crowd cheers as the hydra gallops around the cage, skidding across the sand and banging into the cell. The hydra bounces off the wall and smacks the phoenix out of the air with a tail that's as thick as a garden tree. Right before the hydra can stomp out its opponent, fire blasts into its under-belly; the phoenix missed the heart by inches. I'm shaking as the hydra howls in agony, rolling around in the sand even after the fire is put out.

"EMIL! EMIL!"

Iris points at someone in the front row—Stanton.

I want to back out. This is the first time I've seen him since the day everything changed. Stanton jumps over the barricade. Three security guards come for him, and Stanton bangs two of their heads together, kicking the third into the cage. If Stanton is here, the other Blood Casters might be too. There's no sign of June. I don't know if the shape-shifter is here. He could be the woman sitting next to me or the furious man behind me.

Anyone. Atlas comes down from the sky and binds Stanton to the outside of the cell with his winds. The cage rattles, and the hydra screeches, banging from within.

June appears and phases through the cage. She unlocks the door from within, and a muscular girl with curly red hair and bright sleeves of flowery tattoos follows her in. Dione, the Blood Caster with hydra blood—and Eva's former best friend.

I hop over the barricade and into the cage. I hurl fire-darts at Dione, but she ducks and weaves with bursts of swift-speed, and no matter how prepared I thought I was after hitting Wesley during training, I barely have enough time to brace myself before Dione uppercuts me. The hydra is running wild as my fire blooms around the cage, and right as it's about to tackle Dione, June grips her and they become untouchable. The hydra scratches at Dione and June, like an animal to its reflection, and then gives up.

The cage door rattles as Iris fights Stanton. She bangs him into the bars over and over, and then she swings at him, which he narrowly dodges. If he hadn't moved, there would've been a hole in his face, no doubt. Iris's punch snaps the bars out of place, and the roaring hydra leaps at the broken barrier and squeezes itself out.

Pandemonium strikes.

Everyone who's been cheering on the creatures' deaths is now running for their lives. The hydra barrels through people in the stands with no sense of direction. I don't want to save any of them, but I can't let the hydra hurt anyone. This is how I'll help prove the Spell Walkers are innocent. I chase the hydra, not sure how to stop it without hurting it, when a jet of light shocks the hydra.

A white boy with brown hair is at the top of the steps with a wand. I don't recognize him, but he clearly knows who I am when he fires off three more shots my way before the wand loses charge. I catch up to him, and the boy kicks me into a chair before dashing the other way. The hydra is breathing, so I pop up and hurl fire-dart after fire-dart at the boy, doing my best not to knock out innocent people. I strike him in the shoulder, and he tumbles down the steps, taking others down with him. There's a muted gray light within the pile of bodies—it's the shape-shifter. I rush down, but I can't figure out who he became. I grab an older man's wrist and he's straight terrified, but this might be some act. I spot a woman running off, and she's massaging her shoulder . . . that's him. I bullet for him but stop in my tracks when someone screams.

Dione is pinned underneath Maribelle's foot, and her hand is no longer attached to her wrist. Blood pools out from her stub. Maribelle holds an explosive gem-grenade over Dione.

"Make yourself solid," Maribelle says to June. "Or she won't have a body to regrow."

"Don't kill her," I say.

"They're all going to have to die one day," Maribelle says.

The fierceness in her eyes is burning as June approaches.

The soft glow around June fades away, and Maribelle lunges. June swings a killer kick into Maribelle and snatches the gem-grenade. Before June can drop it, I blast her with fire-darts and she flies into the cage. The gem-grenade rolls out of her hand.

"Grab her!" Maribelle shouts.

I'm quick, and I grab June's arms, holding them behind her back. This doesn't feel right. Dione is bleeding out, and I've got June bound, but winning shouldn't feel this sickening. It's hard to believe we're going to come off as the good guys in Brighton's video.

Maribelle picks up her dagger and saunters toward June. "Start talking about the Blackout." June isn't reacting. Not even fighting to break free. "Nothing? Fine."

I look away as Maribelle unleashes punch after punch.

"You . . . killed . . . my . . . parents!"

Maribelle swings back her dagger, and I let go of June. June fades, and Maribelle catches herself just before she drives the blade through my heart.

"What the hell did you do?"

"I can't kill, I'm sorry!"

"You just had to hold on to her!"

"I'm sorry, I just . . ."

"She's a Blood Caster, Emil! She's not innocent! If June kills anyone from here on out, that's on your conscience!" Maribelle throws the dagger, crouches, and runs her hands through her hair.

I'm shaking and catching my breath, and my face is warm like I'm sitting in front of a fireplace.

Iris drags Dione out of the cage, but not with her usual ease. The fight against Stanton must've worn her out. I'm guessing we'll bring Dione back to Nova for some questioning.

Then Iris rubs her shoulder.

Son of a . . .

Up in the seats, acolytes are wheeling away the chained hydra.

I'm going to get the shape-shifter before he can keep tricking us. The real Iris and Atlas are recovering. I hurl fire-darts at the shape-shifter and accidentally light up some seats. In no time, the fire is spreading. I brave through the gray and gold flames. Iris is running behind me, and Atlas flies above. I shout for Atlas to get Brighton and Prudencia out of here. I can't believe I'm out here giving instructions, but time is wasting. The higher I get up the steps, the more my rib cage aches. I throw a fire-dart and catch the shape-shifter in the leg. He falls down, taking Dione with him, but Stanton catches her. I grab the shape-shifter as June fades in.

"Leave him," Stanton says.

The shape-shifter looks up at me with Iris's eyes, and he's too weak to fight. The real Iris hoists him over her shoulder.

"Looks like we got a win of our own," Iris says.

The arena is fully catching fire now. The smoke is suffocating, but we all manage to break free with my light guiding the way. Out in the parking lot, I turn around, and the destruction is blinding—a mountain of gray and orange fire, the flames licking away at the dark sky. The sun swallower emerges and flies into the night. Its freedom reminds me how happy I am to watch this building turn into ashes.

Iris drops the shape-shifter to the ground and kneels beside him. "Tell us why Luna needed that hydra."

"And where I can find June," Maribelle adds.

A laugh sneaks past the shape-shifter's groaning. "You're insane if you think I would sell out Luna." He props himself against a car door. "You can kick me around all you want, but that's nothing compared to what Luna will do."

"I'm happy to step outside my comfort zone," Maribelle says. "Pick your poison."

She was ready to kill one Blood Caster. The odds aren't looking great for him.

"You're bluffing."

"You're underestimating how much I want to punch that face you're wearing." Maribelle clocks the shape-shifter in the jaw, and he falls over. She turns to Iris.

Iris rolls her eyes. "Was that necessary?"

"Better him than you," Maribelle says.

The dull gray light spreads across the shape-shifter and washes away Iris's features. His Spell Walker gear fades, and he's left in nothing but sweatpants, sneakers, and a tank top that reveals the kind of toned arms the world has always told me I should have too. He's about my age with light brown skin, dark eyebrows, and even darker hair that's curly on top and shaved down on the sides.

I know his face. The entire country knows his face.

It's Senator Iron's son, Eduardo.

The one who died in the Blackout.

TWENTY-THREE
INTERROGATION

EMIL

We're discreet when we return to Nova. It's wild that Eduardo is somehow alive, but that's got to stay a secret until we know what's what. Iris carries him into an old supplies closet, and Maribelle locks him up. I try telling Maribelle that chaining his ankle to a busted radiator isn't necessary, but she's not having it. Everyone is grouped together out in the hallway, in desperate need of showers and sleep, but they keep peeking into the closet like Eduardo is the wildest celebrity sighting ever.

Iris crosses her arms. "We can't fit the entire team in there."

Maribelle already has one foot back in the closet. "Don't even try to stop me."

"It'll only be the two of us," Iris says.

"I should record," Brighton says.

"We're not documenting this," Iris says.

Brighton squints. "Why not? Iron has built his campaign on public fear and the death of his son—who isn't dead! This could be the final push to get Sunstar in office."

I wonder how much Brighton is dreaming about the Pulitzer he could get from uncovering this story.

Iris doesn't offer another word as she and Maribelle step in, closing the door behind them.

My brother is fuming. I rest my hand on his shoulder, knowing I got to be gentle about this. "It's one thing to film me, Bright, but we can't put Eduardo on blast like that. You should go edit the video or something."

Brighton shrugs off my hand. "Don't 'or something' me like editing the video is equivalent to literally anything else. Not after I've personally started turning the tides to restore this team's reputation."

Atlas and Wesley exchange a that's-our-cue glance and take off together, leaving me alone with Brighton and Prudencia.

Brighton stares at the door. "You do realize they're about to interrogate Eduardo, right? There's no way Maribelle is going to go easy on him."

"Even more reason why you shouldn't be in there filming," Prudencia says.

"Whatever."

He walks off.

"Nothing is ever enough for him," Prudencia says.

Truth. We've given him access to the missions, even though I hate risking his and Prudencia's lives. We let Brighton film the Spell Walkers exposing their stories to launch his campaign. His hunger can't be satisfied, like when his power brawl video did astronomically better than anything he's uploaded before, but he was down on himself because it wasn't viral enough. I really miss those simpler days when we were brainstorming names for his channel. Dad was his first subscriber. Ma pawned off family jewelry to buy Brighton his first camera. Maybe Brighton's ego is our fault.

I'm about to chase after him when I hear commotion inside the closet. I stare at the door with a pounding heart. There's no way Eduardo has gotten the jump on Iris and Maribelle.

"Want me to stay with you?" Prudencia asks, watching Brighton turn the corner.

"Yeah, but no. Go ahead."

She nods at the supplies room. "Good luck with that."

"Back at you."

I let myself in. Maribelle is hovering over Eduardo, who is massaging his new bloody lip.

"What are you doing?" I ask.

Maribelle ignores me. "Tell me how I can find June."

"Also how Luna infused a celestial with creature essence," Iris adds.

"And maybe how you survived the Blackout?" I ask, my voice cracking.

Eduardo shakes his head. "It may not seem like it as you turn me into your punching bag, but this is not some negotiation. Besides, I've already won."

"Oh yeah? What did you win?" Maribelle asks.

Eduardo looks from wall to wall. "I mean, I could go for a bed and some rosewood candles to get rid of the dirty mop smell. But I'll take whatever security I can get from the Casters."

"Are you serious?" Iris asks.

"I'll settle for vanilla candles if that's all you have."

Iris folds her arms. "You can turn into anyone. Move across the country. They would never find you."

"The last time a shifter specter fled, he didn't make it very far before the gang tracked him." Eduardo goes still as a statue. "He was tortured for so long that he died between morphs—absolutely unrecognizable. Stanton very kindly showed me pictures the night of my initiation. Friendly warning." He looks up at us. "The only way I can truly be safe from Luna and the Casters is in this hideout. Wherever we are."

Maribelle crouches and gets in his face. "Tell us everything we want to know or we'll release you."

"That would be more threatening if I wasn't holding the keys to the car you want to drive. There's no way you're letting me out of your sight." Eduardo's cocky grin reminds me of his father's confidence during speeches. "You won't find anyone alive more calculating than Luna. She's taught me how to play the long game."

"I promise you're not as smart as you think you are," Maribelle says.

"Maybe not, but I was clever enough to get you to the arena," Eduardo says.

She doesn't say anything.

Gray light washes over Eduardo, and he shrinks into a shorter white girl dressed in acolyte gear. He plays with the long blond hair and stares at Maribelle with bright blue eyes. "Have hope," he says in a high voice.

"I don't get it," I say.

Maribelle glares. "She—he—was Hope, the acolyte at the dock who tipped me off about where we could find June and the other Blood Casters."

"I knew you were gunning for her because of that YouTube interview. Figured I would give you what you want." Eduardo morphs back into himself. "If you're pissed that I manipulated you, then go ahead and release me. It's win-win for me as long as I don't sell out Luna."

I can't believe the boy we have chained up is the one who has us cornered. He's definitely the son of a corrupt politician.

"You're right that we won't let you go," Maribelle says. "If you're not going to tell us how you're alive or who June is or what Luna is up to, then you leave me with no other choice but to beat it out of you."

She arches her fist. I speed forward and catch her punch with both hands. I can't know what she's going through in trying to avenge her parents. The only mystery revolving around Dad's death is whether or not he would've lived longer if he hadn't gone for the clinical trial. Maribelle's heart may be in the right place, but she can't come undone to get answers. I have to believe the person who helped train me is better than this.

Maribelle rips her fist out of my grip. "You have no idea what the hell you're doing. You've been here for what, two weeks? All of a sudden you think you know what we're about."

"I know what you're supposed to be about," I say. "We can't go attacking people for answers. That doesn't make us better than their side."

"I want justice, and treating our prisoners with comfort is not how we're going to get it."

"Couldn't hurt to try," Eduardo says.

Maribelle looks like she might throw me across the room so she can stomp out Eduardo, and I can't blame her if he keeps running his mouth. "Emil, I would love for this to be black-and-white, but war makes us do things we didn't know we were capable of. We've shown compassion, but we've also had to become violent to stay alive. To try and win."

"That's not me," I say. "I'll be a soldier, but I'm not a murderer."

Eduardo's posture straightens as he eyes me.

"Take a walk, Maribelle," Iris says.

"You don't boss me around!" Maribelle gets all up in Iris's space and looks down at her. "We're going to lose. We don't stand a chance under your leadership or with Emil playing nice with the other side." She spins, and she's so close to me that our noses almost touch. "What do you think soldiers in the military do? Do you think they gear up for battle and then lay down their wands? No. They take their shot, and they do their best to not miss."

"I get that, but our endgame is peace with the rest of the world. So many deaths will be in vain if we can't get everyone to trust us, right?"

"Don't talk to me about deaths that will be in vain. Not while you get in the way of me figuring out who assassinated and framed my parents." Maribelle closes her eyes and shakes her head. "I was wrong to put my faith in you. We all were."

She storms out, and the door slams behind her.

I've never pretended I was going to be some incredible savior, but I still ache from that guilt laying into me like a boxer.

"Will you talk to us now?" Iris asks.

Eduardo points at me. "I'll talk to him and him only."

"Not happening," Iris says.

"Good luck cracking Luna's big plans before the Crowned Dreamer goes away," he says.

Iris releases a deep sigh. "Be careful with him."

She leaves me alone with the shape-shifter. I'm trusting it'll all be good since he's tied up, but if he gets funny with me I got to be quick with a fire-dart.

"Why'd you only want to talk with me?" I ask.

"You're fascinating," Eduardo says. He's eyeing me with pure wonder. "I'm in the business of never being seen more than once, but we've crossed paths serendipitously multiple times already."

"I wouldn't call you trying to trick me in my home or leading us to the arena as serendipity."

"Before that."

Eduardo's eyes burn like a gray eclipse as he glows and transforms. It takes me a minute, but he's the same guy I saw on the first night of the Crowned Dreamer, the one who was filming the brawl. Then he transforms again into James, the guy who was selling Brew with Orton—the one who had the same phone case. Then again as the only acolyte who fled the fight at the factory. And one last glow and he becomes himself again.

"Pardon me if I got some of the details wrong—keeping track of eye colors or hair length or height doesn't matter in this moment. But you get what I mean now? New York is huge, Emil. You will see someone once while you're out and about and never again for the rest of your life. But you keep popping up like a firefly at night."

"You're one to talk, Eduardo. You're supposed to be dead."

"That's not my name anymore. Eduardo Iron died during

the Blackout," he says. All his intrigue has been swallowed by darkness. "You're not the only who gets another shot at life."

He knows about my origin. More than ever, I hope the Spell Walkers keep him here.

"So what's your name?"

"Ness Arroyo," he says.

If I remember right, Arroyo was his mother's last name. He's erased every connection to Iron.

"Does your father know you're alive?"

"No."

"Maribelle can use that against you if you don't speak up about June."

Ness nods, like he's considered this already. "I imagine the enforcers have a unit devoted to locating this haven, but if the Senator gets word that I'm alive, then that's when every officer will be dragged out of bed to track me down. He can't risk the country discovering that his entire campaign is a lie, not this close to the election."

He calls his father the Senator. It reminds me of when Brighton and I were kids and he got pissed at Dad, so he called him Leonardo for a week. It was so impersonal, and Dad refused to let Brighton win by showing how much it bothered him.

"Is teaming with the Blood Casters really better than living under Iron's roof?" I ask.

Ness rises. He's maybe an inch or two shorter than me, but my heart races because of how powerful he feels with his leveled shoulders and intense stare. "The gang has turned me inside out. They carved me into someone dangerous and brilliant." He shakes his leg, and the chain clinks against the floor. "This can't hold me. I can morph into a child and escape and snap your neck." He steps toward me, and my fist is on fire. The gray and gold flames light up Ness's face—the shadows under his eyes, the exhausting defeat I see in the mirror as well. "The Senator used me as a pawn and mouthpiece of my generation time and time again. He made sure everyone saw a child grieving a mother he lost to celestial violence. The Blood Casters aren't innocent by a long shot, but I won't ever allow the Senator to use my face again." He turns his back on me and lounges across the floor, using a paper towel roll as a pillow. "Good night, firefly."

TWENTY-FOUR
POWERLESS

BRIGHTON

I'm on the roof, cooling down with the Crowned Dreamer glowing above me. Emil only has authority because of his power, but I'm still a contender for some power of my own because of my bloodline. Ma hasn't shown any sign of taking after her mother, but the Crowned Dreamer can hook me up with visions. I could become the powerful clairvoyant my abuelita never was and I can foresee Luna's next move and protect our team from surprise attacks.

I would prove once again why I shouldn't be shrugged off.

The door opens, and Prudencia steps out. The chilly wind greets her immediately, and she rubs her bare arms. "I've been looking for you."

"You found me."

"How are you feeling?"

She sits beside me, and her presence calms down the rage that's been heating me up. I'm still running hot, but I feel more like I'm sitting by a cozy fireplace instead of standing in a burning building. I'm tempted to wrap my arm around her and keep her warm.

"Undervalued," I say. "Do they not realize what I've done for them? And what was with Emil's garbage about running off to go edit my little video?"

"He didn't call your videos little."

"He may as well have. I'm saving the world too."

"You are, Brighton, but this is a team effort. We all have different roles to play. There are some meetings we shouldn't sit in and some battles where we should hang back."

"If Emil is there, I'm there. That's that."

Prudencia turns away from the Crowned Dreamer, and I can't look her in the eye. "Are you there to protect him or prove yourself?"

"I've already proven myself, Pru. Sorry if my accomplishments don't stack up like Emil's."

"There is no reason to be jealous of him. He is not enjoying this, but he's doing his best. You're both brilliant in your own ways, and you can't forget that."

"Oh, come on. There's nothing brilliant about lucking into powers and having your hand held every step of the way. I'm incredible at what I do because I have worked hard for years."

Prudencia gets up. "You're being a lot right now, so I'm going to give you some more time to yourself. Maybe you'll remember that we're all in this together."

She leaves, and I'm not calling her back or chasing her down.

I stay out with the Crowned Dreamer until it becomes uncomfortably cold, and I go inside and get to work on my "little video" in the computer lab. It's hard rooting for Emil the same way, I can't lie. He's running around and throwing fire-darts, and if it wasn't for me, he wouldn't have all this glory. I could easily cut some of these clips of his finer moments; fewer Emil-related GIFs to cross my timeline. But the only thing I'm getting rid of is when Maribelle lunged for June to kill her. Even though June is rolling with the Blood Casters during a cage match, the last thing viewers need is a reason to paint Maribelle as a killer. We have to control the narrative, and this is what's best.

I'm too exhausted to get up now and find a second eye on this, so I upload the video and squeeze onto the couch. My subscribers are all over it. I picture their notifications waking them up all night; posting late is a new tactic to build my following. If someone wants to brag about how they saw the video early, they have to subscribe to get my notifications. When the content is epic like this, you don't want to be late to the show. I spend twenty minutes reading through the comments as they roll in. Lots of people are impressed with how Emil's aim has improved. Others are blown away by the hydra and the phoenix. A few praise me on how brave I was to go in there with no powers. They're calling me a hero, and I drift off into a well-deserved sleep.

I don't know how long I've been knocked out when I'm pulled out of a dream where I was flying. Emil is calling my name and shaking me awake. "I'm not going to our room," I groan, shutting my eyes to try and rest some more.

"Get up!" Maribelle shouts.

I pop up to find Prudencia, Iris, and Atlas behind Emil and Maribelle. "What's going on? Did Eduardo speak?"

"His name is Ness," Emil says. "He hasn't said anything."

"So he's not Iron's son?"

Emil keeps his eyes low as he runs his hand through his curls. "I'll catch you up later. Your video took a turn."

"As in, everyone has turned on us," Maribelle says.

"It's your fault too," Iris says to Maribelle.

While they argue, ignoring everyone asking them to calm down, I open my laptop. I feel sick reading the comments. People are calling us liars and asking me to explain myself and telling me I should delete my entire channel. Subscriber count has dropped by nearly ten thousand, which is a sign of what's to come. This has always been one of my fears as a creator. Trusting that something I put my heart into will turn on me.

This is all going to hell because of Silver Star Slayer.

Turns out there was a straggler back at the arena who recorded Maribelle attempting to kill June. The user shared the clip online, and Silver Star Slayer uploaded it to his channel to disprove all my messaging, saying that no one should trust me or the "violent and destructive Spell Walkers." My face is hot, and I might throw up. I wouldn't even wish this moment as a nightmare—the heroes I've been hyping up are going at it with each other because I've screwed them over. Looks like there's still some support online for Emil since he let June go, but other commenters are calling him complicit.

Maribelle snaps back to me. "Your channel was supposed to help us."

"I'm sorry. I edited it to protect our image."

"It backfired," Maribelle says. "Everyone thinks I'm as evil as the Blood Casters."

"This backfired because of your actions," Iris says. "Whether Brighton posted the video or not, this was going to leak. He just got the jump on this guy, and now the optics aren't great. End of the day, Maribelle, you were about to kill someone, and it doesn't look like self-defense."

"She killed our parents!" Maribelle looks so confused, like maybe she's wondering if she's speaking a whole other language because Iris doesn't seem to understand her pain. "I'm not some bloodthirsty killer. I want vengeance."

"We're seeking justice, not revenge. Celestials are depending on us to get this right."

"Specters too," Emil says.

"I know you're not defending that shape-shifter," Maribelle says. "His crew is getting away with actual murder while we're being persecuted because I attempted to kill the celestial who screwed us over." Emil tries to speak, but she talks over him. "If it wasn't for Atlas showing up that first night when he did, then Ness would've kidnapped you and probably had your brother killed. Ness made his bed, and he has to lie in it."

"You tried to kill June, and you now have to live with that," Iris says.

"No," Maribelle says. "I'm going to live with the fact that I will be the one to kill her."

She storms from the room.

Atlas sighs. "I'll talk to her."

"If you can't get her to cooperate, you know what's going to happen, right?" Iris asks.

"I will do my best, but Mari is Mari. She's just as heartbroken as you are."

"It's different!"

"How?"

Iris shakes her head. "I'm older. More time with my parents and fighting alongside them. More weight on my shoulders. Just . . . do your best to get her to cool it. We need to be united."

Atlas nods and leaves.

Everyone is quiet.

"I can make this right," I say. "I'll film an apology and own it."

"We should hold off on videos," Iris says. "We can't react impulsively."

"But . . . I'm still going on missions, right?"

"We'll talk."

Those two words tell me everything. I take a deep breath and run past everyone. Emil and Prudencia chase after me. I snap around. "I'm fine," I lie. "I just need some space."

"Let me get some space with you," Emil says.

"Just me," I say.

"Brighton," Prudencia calls, but I run back onto the roof and stare out into the bright city.

I screwed up. I did so much good and had more to accomplish, but I screwed up. This isn't like the couple times I didn't study properly for an exam. This is colossal. I made the heroes look like heartless terrorists. I have to figure out how to bounce back from this. If not, who am I? What's my role?

It's one thing to be powerless and another to be completely useless.

TWENTY-FIVE

INFINITY CYCLE

EMIL

Everyone is falling apart.

Maribelle and Atlas have been hitting the streets the past couple nights, trying to track down any acolyte or alchemist or dealer who has a direct connection to Luna. When Iris isn't locking herself away she's been negotiating with Ness for some intel, but he's not budging on what the Blood Casters are up to. Eva is bone-tired as she bounces between therapy sessions with celestials who are feeling more hopeless by the day. Wesley is clearly itching for a trip to Philadelphia to visit Ruth and Esther, but remains close to shop for supplies and coordinate moves to other shelters for the celestials who no longer feel safe under our care.

I wish I could send Brighton, Prudencia, and Ma elsewhere. Brighton has been damn near manic since he pulled his video offline. He's locked himself in the computer lab, and from what I can see, he's monitoring our social media accounts but not posting anything as Iris instructed. I think he's looking for an impossible solution. Sort of like Prudencia, who is spending all her time in the library to unearth more information about the mysterious ingredients Sera listed in the journal. I try to help, but she's been rejecting my company. I can't help but feel like she blames me for everything that's going wrong in her life, like having to turn her back on her aunt and Brighton turning his back on her. Ma was running dangerously low on heart and anxiety meds, so Wesley braved returning to our apartment to get more for her, but since we can't exactly risk Ma personally going to get her prescription refilled, it's only a matter of time before we'll have to break into a pharmacy to steal everything she needs; more ammo for Senator Iron's campaign if we get caught.

There's a shift whenever I walk these halls. The people in our care used to admire me, and now they walk past me like there's nothing I can do for them. Honestly, I'm with them. It's becoming clearer and clearer that we're fighting a losing war. Iron will be elected president. The future for all celestials will grow grimmer by the year. They'll lose their rights and will be forced into camps—or worse—for their powers. History repeats itself, and in my past lives, I die young for the cause.

This one won't be any different.

Instead of hiding under the covers and dreading whatever mission we'll have to go on next, I take care of Ness. The others haven't been particularly sympathetic considering that Ness has been rallying hate against celestials since his early teens, but I can't forget that he's a human who was raised by a monster. Iron won't ever change his ways, but I have hope that Ness can bounce back. So I get him time in the bathroom to wash up and handle his business. I give him an air mattress so he doesn't sleep on the floor. I make sure we're feeding him as much as anyone else, sometimes even hooking him up with extra portions from my plates that I can't eat since they're not plant-based.

I've been doing more research on shifters too, ever since Ness's threat that he could kill me if he wanted to. I was getting nervous that he could morph into some six-foot-six bodybuilder and crush my skull with one hand, but his power only allows him to take on the physical glamour, not to gain strength or speed or mimic abilities that aren't there. Still doubt that I would win if we threw down fists, so I got to be quick with fire if he comes for me. I don't think he will. He's been harmless—he doesn't thank me for the food or books I bring him, but it's all good as long as he doesn't swing at me.

I've got dinner for him tonight, so I go to his room and knock gently. He doesn't invite me in, but that's usually how it goes down. I enter, and where Ness usually rests, there's an older white man murmuring in his sleep. The first three times I walked in on Ness sleeping as someone else—a woman who was balding, a young boy with burnt fingertips, a man with greasy hair and a mousy face—I assumed he was playing some weird game with me. But this is the first time I've seen him so distressed. The man's long red hair is plastered to his sweaty forehead, and a deep scar runs across his face. On closer inspection, he's missing a chunk of his nose.

"Please don't, please don't," the man mutters.

I set down the plate of food and rub the man's shoulder. "Ness?"

The man snaps awake, and his hand finds its way around my throat quick as a blink. His nails are digging into my flesh and have trapped my next breath from reaching me when I need it most. He's missing an eye, but the bright blue one that remains burns with more than enough hate to make up for it. I pound at his wrist, his arm, his chest, but every punch is weaker than the last. I'm fading, and a gray light and loosened grip and new breath keeps me awake. Ness is himself again, and he's shaking. He removes his hand from my throat.

"That wasn't me," Ness says. "I didn't do it."

Of course that was him, of course he did it. What is he running his mouth about?

I fall on my back, breathing in and out, in and out. He hovers over me. He's been threatened by Maribelle left and right, but this is the first time I've seen pure concern on his face. I massage my neck while my heart runs wild.

"I'm sorry. That happens sometimes," Ness says as he helps me up, resting me against the wall closest to the door. "Turning into other people when I sleep."

I'm so thrown by all of this—the strangling and the apology and the opening up.

It takes me a minute, but I get the words out: "Who is he?"

Ness sits against the opposite wall. There couldn't be more space between us. "He was a trafficker who tried killing me that night on the dock. So I killed him first."

I figured Ness had taken a life before, but the confirmation still pins me. I'm afraid to ask, but I have to know. "So those other people I've seen you turn into . . ."

"I don't know who you've seen or haven't seen, but I'm haunted by people who I haven't killed too. I get so deep into some of these nightmares that my power mistakes it as concentration to morph into them. Dione was the only Caster who showed any sympathy. June doesn't care, and Stanton thought it made me weak."

"You're not weak," I say. "The strongest power above all is a living heart, right?"

"You pushing your brother's campaign on me?"

"No. I'm heartbroken because we're eighteen and we've been turned into weapons. You have to lie about being dead so your father won't find you. You had to manipulate your way to safety. You had to kill for a gang you don't want to be in.

It's only a matter of time until I find blood on my hands too."

My eyes drift from Ness to the floor as I go off about all the pressure I've been under. I unload about all my guilt that's tied up in Keon's alchemy. But I talk the most about how I'm being so hard on Ma when she raised me right and gave me a home. It still feels impossible to forgive her since learning I'm not a biological Rey came right after another devastating surprise that has truly upended my life. Everything that's happened the past three weeks is so wild. I crack and cry so hard that I wish anyone, even a stranger like Ness, would take me in their arms and lie to me about how it's all going to be okay.

"Why are you telling me all of this?" Ness asks.

"I don't know. Maybe because I'm freaking out about how to be a good brother and a good son and a good best friend and a good hero, and you're the only person not expecting anything from me."

There's something about his silence that pulls more words out of me. It reminds me of whenever I was upset as a kid and Dad would ask me what was wrong, and I would swear that I didn't want to talk about it, but he kept me company until I eventually burst and got everything off my chest.

"I wonder what my dad would think about me today," I say.

Before Ness can ask me about him or tell me to go away so he can eat his microwaved pancakes in peace, I tell him all about how accepting Dad was. He never questioned my sexuality and was quick to encourage me to shoot my shot with

Nicholas because maybe I would marry my high school crush like he did. He made sure I never felt inferior whenever Brighton's report cards were glowing and mine were disappointing.

"I really miss him, but maybe it's a good thing he's dead. He won't have to watch me turn into someone I don't want to be."

"I think the same with my mother," Ness says. "I grew up wanting to be an actor. We used to go to musicals and movies, and I felt this . . . this pull to be on stages and sets. Broadway, blockbusters, indies. All of it. We ran lines for school plays while our driver took me to acting classes an hour away. If she knew how much I was using all those lessons as a Caster, she would've told me to forget my dreams like the Senator did."

Losing Dad at seventeen was hard enough, but I can't imagine losing either of my parents at thirteen like Ness did.

"What was it like when she died?"

"Confusing," Ness says after a beat. "It was so sudden, and the Senator told me how to feel—anger, hate, disgust. He forced me to grieve in front of cameras. I was a poster boy for children who lost loved ones because of celestial violence, and I leaned into that role because it's the only way I got support from the Senator. Don't get it twisted, I'm not talking about hugs. Handshakes on some days and pride on others. But it was something to fill that emptiness my mother left behind."

I tell him I'm sorry for his loss, even though it's too many years too late.

"You too," Ness says. "You're lucky that your last living

225

parent loves you so much that she protected you at all costs. Mine threw me into the fire."

He gets up and sits in the center of the room. It feels like an invitation, and I do the same. This time I'm able to breathe in the smell of the cheap lavender soap we've stocked in the bathrooms, and it settles my nerves like a well-lit candle.

"What was it like losing your father?" Ness asks.

I tell him how it was confusing too, even though we had months to prepare. Sometimes Dad pretended he was healthy, but we couldn't play along when he was coughing up blood and had fevers burning so hot we would rush him to the hospital. Going to school was brutal because we didn't know if he would still be alive when we got home. When it was looking beyond hopeless—wills were signed, goodbyes were had—the doctors suggested it couldn't hurt to explore clinical trials. Except it did hurt, and the blood poisoning blindsided us all—especially Brighton, who will never be fully right after finding Dad dead.

"You're lucky you've got your whole immortality thing going on, firefly."

"You think it's luck? This infinity cycle is a curse. It hasn't even been a month, and I can't look in the mirror because I don't see this savior, this chosen one, this hero that the Spell Walkers are counting on me to be. I'm not trying to fight for the rest of my life—the rest of my lives."

"But my mother would be alive if we could all be immortal,"

Ness says. "Your father too."

"You think immortality is a solution to the world's problems?"

"I don't believe in the world anymore. This country is about to elect my father—the Senator—as their president, and no one with powers will be safe. It's only a matter of time until he discovers I'm alive, and he would have me executed to protect his image. That lifelong security of yours would be welcomed. I could run forever from the Senator and Luna and live my life."

"Running and fighting forever isn't life," I say.

"It's better than death," he says.

I don't get where all this is coming from, but this sounds like a nightmare. "I don't want to lose loved ones, Ness, but I also don't trust a world where we can't die. To be hunted or tortured forever."

Ness's amber eyes are fixed on me. "You're lying if you say you would give up resurrecting if you could."

"I'm already trying to figure out a cure. I don't want to die, but I refuse to live forever."

"You don't get it, firefly. It's too late. Luna is a chess master who has been setting up the board before any of us were born. She is patient and calculating. She could've given herself power years ago, but what use would that have been to her? She's like the Senator that way—powerless herself, but one of the most powerful people out there. But now she's dying, and the Crowned Dreamer has arrived in time for her to make her final move."

Prime example of someone I wouldn't ever want to live forever. "What's wrong with her?"

"Blood illness," he says, and my chest squeezes. "Once a host has taken in blood from one creature, it can't take another."

That's great news for whatever cure we come up with to bind powers.

"Luna's attempts to merge multiple essences have only gotten people deathly ill and weakened the power from the original creature significantly. It was pointless to her end goal."

"Which is what?"

"Immortality," Ness says.

"True immortality is impossible," I say. "Even phoenixes die."

Ness nods. "Yeah, but when Keon first died and he wasn't reborn, Luna realized she wouldn't have what was necessary to create immortality for herself on phoenix essence alone. She didn't quit like many alchemists before her—she went darker."

"Is there something about me that she thinks is the key?"

"No. She can't drain you for your blood. It has to come pure from a creature. And Luna isn't looking for the key. She already found it. Your old friend Orton is proof."

"What is it? Celestial blood mixed with creature blood?"

"Orton wasn't a celestial. He was full specter."

"But he could phase through solid objects. No creature has that power."

"Correct," Ness says. He lets me sit with it, but I got nothing. "It's the most superior blood of all, and Luna partnered with alchemists who specialize in necromancy to get it—she's been killing ghosts."

Oh, come on. I feel played, like he's been telling me some campfire story all along. "But you can't touch a ghost."

"Tell that to June, the first ever specter with ghost blood, who not only possessed Maribelle's mother and framed her for the Blackout, but saved my life when that explosion went off," Ness says. "This is what I'm talking about, firefly. Luna is next level. She will unite the blood of three entities—a hydra, a ghost, a phoenix. If you decapitate her, she'll regrow a new head. If you try to harm her body, she'll fade away. If you somehow manage to obliterate her completely, she'll be reborn."

"But it doesn't work. Not for long, anyway. Her test subjects are dying."

"Luna hasn't been using pure blood on her test subjects. But for her true elixir, she needs the head of a hydra that's never been decapitated before, a phoenix who has never been reborn, and ghosts with ties to her bloodline. Unite them all underneath the Crowned Dreamer's zenith at the Alpha Church of New Life, and she'll have her so-called Reaper's Blood. She will be the closest thing to Death to walk the streets, and she will make history by never becoming history."

I wish this was some story, but it's all truth. Luna has lived a life engineering essences to make herself invincible. There's no winning.

"But if she dies, she'll have to start over like me, right?"

Ness shakes his head. "If her calculations are correct—and let's count on them being right—she'll be away from the world for a single moment and reborn as herself."

"So she's got the hydra now. What's her next move?"

"What's today?"

"Tuesday."

He takes a deep breath. "Luna moves for Older Cemetery to capture the ghosts of her parents—tonight."

"What? We're screwed."

"Probably. But the summoning is tricky enough that she's hired Anklin Prince, this top alchemist, for the assist. The longer someone has been dead, the harder it is to catch their ghost. Unless they died violent deaths and didn't have a chance to make peace with their lives. Luna murdered her parents when she was seventeen. The only time I believe she's ever gotten her own hands dirty."

"If it was that long ago, they'll never find their ghosts."

"They died very, very violent deaths. Luna was just as creative back then as she is cruel today."

So Luna's parents have been lost and wandering for decades,

and she was going to bring them back to obliterate them forever. I don't want to go up against someone so twisted.

"What about the phoenix?" Then I figure it out, the light
bulb moments I always envy Brighton for having, but this one
scares me. "The century phoenix."

Ness nods. "If you want to put an end to her madness, you
have to end her, firefly. Period. Problem is, you don't have a
killer's bone in you. You wouldn't even let Maribelle murder a
remorseless assassin. Face it. Luna has you beat."

I hug my knees, tight, and hold back a scream.

"Why are you telling me this?" I ask after a stretch of
silence.

Ness holds my gaze. "You're the only person not expecting
anything from me either."

TWENTY-SIX
RISE

EMIL

The Spell Walkers are hitting me with questions left and right. How do we know Ness isn't sending us straight into a trap? Why did he reveal everything to me? Is June stoppable? Do we have any chance in hell at actually beating the Blood Casters? There are no sure answers, but we're thrown into a frenzy as we suit up and head for the cars. Iris tries convincing Ness to come along, but he simply tells her that the only way he's going to the cemetery to face Luna is if he's a dead body they can bury.

I can't find Brighton for a see-you-later when we head out, and it turns out it's because he's been sitting in the far backseat all along.

"Get out," Iris says as she takes the driver's seat.

"No. If Luna is actually going to be there then I can film her, and we can finally pin her to her crimes."

"It's too dangerous," I say. "Please, Bright, sit this one out."

"You guys are going to have to drag me out, and that's time better spent getting to the cemetery," Brighton says.

"I hope the stars are with us," Iris says.

Maribelle, Atlas, and Wesley get in, and we take off. Prudencia isn't here to watch his back either.

The Spell Walkers are hoping to use the Crowned Dreamer for that much-needed power boost to get us through this night. They'll have an advantage over the Blood Casters too, since their gleam is natural, which makes me lucky to be on the right side. But as we pull in and park, my chest is so tight. There's no preparing for these impossibilities.

Older Cemetery is so damn winter-cold that everyone's breath is clouding the air around us as we continue searching for the Blood Casters. This darkness is too much for a city boy; I need streetlights the deeper I go across the field, past unmarked graves, but all we have to guide us are the brightening stars of the Crowned Dreamer, whose shape is becoming clearer every night. If we don't stop the gang, Luna will be closer to remaking the world. And if there's any possibility for a power-binding potion, who knows if it'll be enough to work on Luna once she drinks the Reaper's Blood.

"We should invest in coats," Wesley says.

I cast a fire-orb for warmth and light. What I swore were branches snapping underneath my feet have actually been a trail of thin blackened bones that lead into a tree. Brighton follows the trail with his camera.

"Bright, look alive."

"Documenting," Brighton says.

"You really shouldn't be here."

"Neither should you."

"I don't want to be," I say. "But it's different and you know it."

"I messed up, and I'm going to make this right. Showing more initiative than your favorite shape-shifter, who's lounging at Nova and probably sweet-talking his way to get some Netflix going."

I'm not going to get pissed at someone who doesn't want to fight because they want to live. I get it.

"If he didn't want powers, he shouldn't have signed up for them," Brighton presses.

I'm about to beg him to cut the hero act and turn around and leave when Iris signals to us to shut up. She crouches behind the statue of a headless hydra. Even though wintry winds are doubling down, I clasp my hands and crush the fire-orb, my fingers instantly cold again, so it won't give us away.

Down a hill, the three Blood Casters are spread out like a pyramid with dark ropes connecting them, and they're surrounded by a dozen acolytes in ceremonial robes. They're all protecting a short man with deathly white skin and hair as gray as storm clouds. The alchemist, Anklin Prince, is standing between two graves while holding a metallic urn with a stone rim. I can't make out the golden glyphs emblazoned on the base, but they're burning bright as Anklin chants.

Across from Anklin is none other than Luna Marnette. She's never out in the open. If Ness wasn't detained at Nova, I would've sworn he was posing as her. But this must be legit. Her face is gaunt, and she's staring intently at the urn. Her tangled silver hair reaches down to her waist, and there are three sheathed daggers hanging from her belt. She's wearing laced gloves that twinkle under the moonlight. I don't know the sound of her voice or her eye color, but I already feel so haunted by her. Ness said that she doesn't need power to be powerful, and I get it.

I shiver as the cold strikes again. I guess messing with the dead must be responsible for these chills.

"Keep your distance, okay?" I whisper.

Brighton shakes his head. "You do your job and I'll do mine."

He's going to get us killed, I know it.

We're all huddled together, doing our best not to be seen by Luna's people.

"We got to get that urn," Atlas says. "Wesley, that's all you."

"We have no idea what those ropes do," Iris says.

"It's probably ceremonial," Maribelle says. "Wesley can be

in and out and we should take advantage while we still have the element of surprise—"

A bone snaps behind us and someone shouts, "SPELL WALKERS!"

An acolyte.

Atlas blasts him off his feet.

Spellwork explodes around us, blowing apart the statue's body. Everything we planned in the car has already gone to hell, but we'll do whatever it takes to stop Luna from capturing her parents' ghosts. Two acolytes chase me, and the cold air is filling my lungs like the times I would run from the train station to my building during winter just so I could get inside somewhere warm. Bolts of electric blue light sail past my shoulder and blow up around my feet. I jump behind a tree that shakes after a spell shoots through it. I pop out and nail an acolyte in the ankle with a fire-dart, and the other trips over him.

I keep it moving, relieved to find Brighton crouched behind some bushes that must belong to someone who was rich as hell in life. The Blood Casters have got me straight scared with how still they are. Why aren't Stanton or Dione or June dropping the rope to fight? It's got to be more than ceremony. In a blur, Wesley charges toward the triad of specters and leaps into the air, but once he crosses the rope, a radiant gold force field rebounds him. Wesley flips through the air, and his back bangs against a massive headstone.

Wesley falls face-first into the dirt, the stillest I've ever seen him.

"Wesley!" Leaves swirl around Atlas, and he punches the air, his winds carrying six acolytes off their feet and collapsing all around.

We run to Wesley and flip him over. Atlas shakes him, but his eyes remain closed.

"Is he breathing?" I ask.

Atlas nods when he feels a pulse. "We got to get him to Eva."

I look back and forth between the Blood Casters and Wesley. "Let's get him out of here."

Spellwork continues unloading around us. I don't think I'll ever get used to the sound or the idea that someone is trying to shoot me. Can't imagine Luna wants me as a weapon. You don't go around snapping swords in half that you intend to stab someone with later.

"Iris!"

She fights her way back to us, hurling acolytes left and right. Every time a spell hits her, she stumbles, but none are strong enough to pierce her skin. Her eyes widen when she sees Wesley. "Tell me he's not dead."

"Not yet. We got to get him to Eva."

"I should've let her come along, I'm so stupid—"

"No time for a guilt trip," Atlas interrupts. "I'm going to knock out everyone, and you get Wesley to the car."

I forever wish I had the power to teleport instead of creating fire, especially now, when it means I could get Wesley to safety. But his health is counting on me to be on the offense, so I follow Atlas back into battle. He's doing his best to hurl funnels of wind while dodging spellwork. Maribelle is floating around, kicking wands out of the hands from acolytes. She throws a gem-grenade at June, but the force field sends it back, exploding in midair.

I take a deep breath and go off on all these acolytes. Fire-dart straight into the acolyte aiming a wand at me and another into the one shooting at Atlas. An acolyte jumps out of a tree with a net to try and capture Maribelle and I cast a fire-orb, timing it perfectly to explode against his chest.

The path is as clear as it's going to be, and I have to break past this force field. I charge a fire-orb and release, hoping phoenix power will drive through, but it slings back at me at a speed I can't dodge. The orb hits me like a hammer to the gut and knocks the wind out of me. I'm not immune to my own power. Good to know, bad time to find out.

I'm staring up at the sky from the ground when Atlas is shot out of the air. He falls twenty feet and crashes into the dirt beside me.

"Atlas!" Maribelle appears beside us.

"Mari, Mari, I'm okay," Atlas weakly says.

There's fury in her eyes. "Watch him," she says to me.

Maribelle picks up a wand and takes off into the air, showing no mercy against the acolytes.

The cemetery gets even colder, like I'm lying naked in streets of snow. There's a howl that's so piercing I'm convinced I'll never sleep again, and it digs deep into my heart, making me feel incredibly lonely, like no one will care if I die this very second.

Anklin is no longer chanting.

Two shadows of black light appear out of nowhere, above the graves of Luna's parents, and turn into ghosts so lifelike they could be living people. The ghosts stare at Luna with confusion, then horror. The person before them is much older than the young woman who violently murdered them. The Marnettes try holding hands, but they slip through each other.

Luna's laced gloves begin to glow. The ghosts step back as she stalks toward them like a predator. The Marnettes move their mouths, but no words come out, just that awful howling that makes me feel painfully empty, like I'm starving for crumbs of happiness. Unlike June, Stanton and Dione look to be suffering from this agony too, but they hold on to the ropes, locking the Marnettes in as they try escaping. They pound on the force field like it's a door someone will open for them, and Mr. Marnette even goes so far as to bang into it with his shoulder. Mrs. Marnette howls in Dione's face. Dione closes her eyes, but there's no shutting out that ghost song.

Heroes aren't supposed to feel so easily defeated, but I'm damn near down for the count. I don't have the heart for this life. I can throw fire but it'll get deflected. I may as well be powerless.

Luna corners her father while Anklin follows her with the urn. She doesn't even say anything to him as she grabs him by the throat, her gloves sparking as she presses his face into the urn. He isn't sucked in easily, so Luna keeps pressing down on him as if her father is simply a pair of shoes she's trying to fit into a full suitcase. Within a minute, her father's ghost is gone, trapped in the urn, to be vanquished later. Mrs. Marnette's ghost howls even louder as she falls to her knees. Luna circles her like a vulture and shoves her into the urn too. Anklin seals the urn and hands it over to Luna.

Her grin sends chills down my spine. "Kill them," she says in the silence.

The force field vanishes when Stanton, June, and Dione drop the rope.

Me and Maribelle are the only active Spell Walkers, with Iris tending to Wesley and Atlas a couple feet away. This is it; this is not only how we fail everyone, but where we're going to die. Where we're going to be killed.

Stanton charges me, and I'm quick with a fire-dart, but it only stalls him for a second. He races forward, grabs my neck, and flings me through the air. My world spins as I soar across the cemetery until I slam into the ground and bang into another headstone. I'm fading in and out, fighting to keep my eyes open. Maribelle is locked in hand-to-hand combat with

Stanton. They're anticipating each other's punches, but Stanton speeds up, surprising her with a kick to her chin. Dione runs at me, screaming as two extra arms punch out of her sides, and she leaps. I'm not quick enough to attack back, but Iris jumps over me and catches Dione in midair, slamming her to the ground.

"Get the urn," Iris commands as one of Dione's new fists clocks her in the chin.

I get up, fighting past all limping and dizziness. Luna is watching the chaos and doesn't flinch when I approach her.

"You don't have the fire I thought you would," Luna says.

"I've come this far," I say.

"This is where you'll end, my little wonder." She slides a dagger out of a sheath. The handle is made of bone and charred black, and the serrated blade is yellow. "You're familiar with the infinity-ender, yes?" Anklin joins her side, and she hands him the blade. "I made the grave error of not stabbing Bautista in the heart when I killed him, my dear Anklin, so be sure to pierce Emil properly so we can end this bloodline once and for all."

Luna walks off with the urn, and Anklin barrels into me before I can make a move. He pins his knee deep into my stomach and drives the blade down on me. I catch his wrist and try wrestling the weapon out of his hand. The phoenix cries within me, guiding my reflexes like never before, like its essence is aware that our fire might be snuffed out for good.

Anklin gains control, and the tip of the blade kisses my heart, and I pray Brighton isn't watching and has the common sense to get the hell out of here. I don't want to kill this man, but I have to fight for my life. I'm sweating and shouting as I ignite fire, burning Anklin's hands. Gold and gray flames crawl up his sleeves. He drops the blade beside me as he tries to extinguish the fire.

I don't bother with him. I charge after Luna. I'm beat, but I'm still fast enough to catch up with her. I jump into the air and tackle her to the ground. The urn rolls out of her grip. I cast a fire-dart, aim, and the second before I throw it, Luna redirects my wrist and it shoots into a plaque. Luna punches me, her ring cutting into my cheek, and man, if I survive this, Ma is going to give me hell for fighting an elderly woman, no matter how corrupt she is. I clock Luna in the chin, but it's not enough to lay her out, and I wonder how many times she's been hit during her journey that she knows how to take a punch so well.

I shoulder roll and grab the urn, running back in the direction of the car. I dodge recovering acolytes, holding on to the urn for dear life, and damn, I could've been a boss at football. Stanton steps in my path with a bloody nose. Maribelle is aiming a wand at June. It's a distraction, and she's falling for it. Dione and Anklin pop up behind me as Luna approaches too.

"You come closer and I'll pour everything out," I say, trying to twist open the urn's cap. They grin and laugh at me like they knew this would go down. "Fine, fine. Stay the hell back or I'll burn it."

They all calm down.

"Hand it over," Luna says.

Phoenix song screeches higher and higher within me, and my arms are set ablaze, bigger than ever before—true wings of gray and gold flames. I shoot into the air right as Stanton lunges at me. My legs are dangling and what-the-what, I'm actually flying. Flying isn't as weightless as I thought it would be, it's more like the worst pull-ups of my life, but I can't sink with this urn in my possession, so I work harder and harder to rise high as a tree.

"Get him down!" Luna shouts.

I shift my body, holding one fist ahead of me, and I soar through the air with the wind and fire roaring in my eyes. The urn is tight in my grasp, and I fly out of the cemetery, happiness overpowering fear for once.

TWENTY-SEVEN
FALL

BRIGHTON

Emil is blazing like a comet, gray and gold flames streaking against the night.

I lose focus on filming as my brother flies away with my favorite power. How long has Emil known he could do this? Was he keeping it a secret so he could bust it out in some blazing moment of glory? Unlike him, I'm not running away from battle. He can go back to Nova and play it safe with Ness; I don't care. But this fight doesn't end just because he got the urn.

Maribelle and Iris are struggling to hold their own against Stanton, Dione, and Anklin.

There's a wand on the ground, and I drop the camera.

Stanton spots me and is confused long enough for Iris to punch him so hard he hurtles into a trio of beat-down acolytes. I scoop up the wand, which feels as heavy as a steel bat even though it's only as long as a cutting knife. My fingers are tight around this weapon, and I'm as powerful as I've always felt.

This isn't some video game. This is the real deal.

I hold the wand like I've seen so many heroes and enforcers do on YouTube.

I may only get one shot, so I choose the most important target.

I squint at Luna and flick the wand.

The ember-orange bolt misses Luna by inches and sets a tree ablaze. The force of the spell knocks me on my back, and my arm is shaking so hard, like an earthquake in my wrist, and I drop the wand. Luna stares at me with a cocked head, grins, and points at me. Acolytes are on top of me in moments, and I reach for the wand, but they're dragging me away. I dig my nails into the ground, shouting for the Spell Walkers to help me, but I'm flipped around by Stanton, who hovers over me with his bruised face. He pins me down with his viselike grip and punches me between the eyes.

TWENTY-EIGHT
HEARTS

EMIL

Minutes after taking flight I'm not strong enough to stay up, so I ground myself on a street far away from the cemetery. I don't know if I'm having an easier time with powers than other specters would since my body was never fully human, but it's still so much work, like how Wesley runs out of breath after minutes of speeding around or how Maribelle also feels weighed down when levitating.

Someone films me as I'm descending with my gold and gray wings of fire, and I jet around the corner when she asks for a picture. I go into an alley, dig through a dumpster, and fish out a Trader Joe's paper bag to hide the urn. I don't think I'm above the law as I melt a chain to steal a bike, but I can't exactly get on the subway with trapped ghosts that our city's greatest enemy needs to make herself indestructible.

I take off on the bike, the well-bagged urn hanging from the handlebars. No one is following me, and I stick to less traveled paths, turning a twenty-minute ride into an hour. I'm so banged up and drained, but when I pull in at Nova I'm ready to see everyone and hope that Wesley and Atlas are getting the healing attention they need. Eva, Prudencia, and Ma are waiting by the door.

"Password," Eva says.

"Break Luna before we can't," I say, and we're good.

I hug Ma and Prudencia, so surprised and grateful to be back in their arms.

"Why aren't you with the others?" Eva asks.

"Turns out I can fly. They're not back yet?"

"Should be any minute now."

I show them the urn, which is depressing all over again. Luna was ready to bleed the ghosts of her parents so she could live forever. We have to find a way to free the Marnettes.

The front door bangs open. Iris is shouting the password with Wesley over one shoulder while also carrying Atlas's legs as Maribelle holds him up under his arms. Why isn't Brighton helping out Maribelle? Eva immediately gets to work on Wesley, howling as she absorbs his pain. Maribelle is rushing her. My chest tightens. There's nothing I can do in here so I go outside to see what's what with Brighton. Maybe he was banged up too and limping in. He's not outside or in the car either and I run back inside.

"Where's Brighton?"

Iris takes a deep breath and shakes her head.

"Where is my brother?"

"The Blood Casters grabbed him," Iris says.

Ma sucks in a breath and she presses her hand against her heart. Prudencia is holding her up and I remain motionless.

"It all happened so quickly," Iris says. "You flew away and we were losing the fight. Brighton got his hands on a wand and when he missed Luna they got him. We wanted to pursue them, but . . ." She looks at Wesley, who's recovering.

"You left him!" Prudencia shouts.

"We had to act fast," Iris says.

My brother is hostage to the city's worst gang and death no longer seems like the worst thing that could happen to Brighton. This urn no longer feels like a victory.

I want out of this war so badly it hurts. I want to rip out my hair and my teeth and my nails and bones. I want to scream so loud that I lose my voice. I want to stay beneath the ocean until this phoenix fire is washed out forever.

I cross the hall to take Ma's hands in mine. "I'm going to get him back, I promise."

She's inconsolable. "They're going to kill him, Emil, they're going to kill him."

"No they won't, they must need him," I say. Brighton is the

biggest idiot for not listening to me to hang back, but I'm the biggest traitor out of all my lifetimes. I promised Ma I would keep Brighton safe, her only son by blood, and I abandoned him when I flew away. "I'm going to bring him home and then we're all done."

Her arm is shaking and her breaths are sharp, and she grips me with one hand and slams her chest with the other.

She's having a heart attack.

TWENTY-NINE
EXTRAORDINARY

BRIGHTON

Stanton got me good with that punch.

The room is dark with no windows. I'm stretched across concrete ground. I could be underground. Probably not a sewer since it doesn't smell like waste, and it's too quiet to be subway tunnels. Wherever I am, the Blood Casters didn't tie me up. Maybe they didn't think I'd recover so soon. I stand, wobbling. I peek out the door and the hallway is cold with shafts of light coming from a flickering light bulb. This reminds me of every horror video game I refused to play at night, and I go right back inside because there's being brave and there's being stupid. The Spell Walkers are probably questioning how I ever became salutatorian since attacking Luna wasn't exactly brilliant, but I had a weapon then, and I'm certainly not exploring this building without one. I open a locker, thinking this might be some one-star gym until I find a toolbox. I tuck the screwdriver inside my belt and carry the wrench and hammer out into the hallway.

I obviously have a bad feeling about this, no need for my blood-and-bones instinct. The Blood Casters must want me to walk into some trap, but my options are limited, and I'm certainly not going to hang around in that room hoping to hammer someone to death. I turn the corner, and an acolyte crosses from one door to another with a crate of potions. I count to three and sneak along the walls until I'm inside the room he left.

It's a lab that's smaller and messier than my bedroom. The lighting is bright enough to worsen my headache. There are old-school cauldrons that reek of gas. Trays of feathers and scales and fur. Jars of yellowed fangs and human teeth. There are unmarked ingredients that look like tree bark and crushed rubies among others. I set down the hammer and wrench on the counter, inspecting these vials of glistening celestial blood and potions of all colors that are labeled with powers. There's an open logbook with data in tight cursive, tracking where they received each power. So many have come from outside of New York. There are side effects listed, such as nausea, fever, and blood poisoning, that the drinker might experience.

Will drinking one give me power?

I don't know how tested these potions are, but a fraction of power is more promising than using these tools to protect me. I probably shouldn't try more than one, but I could escape with shape-shifting by posing as an acolyte or break through the walls with powerhouse strength. I hold a gray potion, dreaming about flying out of here.

The door opens, and Luna enters with Dione behind her.

"Ah, it's the boy who tried to assassinate me," Luna says.

My aim sucked with the wand, but maybe Luna is close enough for me to throw this hammer at her head. Do everyone a favor before Dione can tear me apart. My wrist is shaking as I keep close to the screwdriver in my belt. If they come near me, I'll drive it into their necks, I don't care.

"You're dying anyway," I say, lower than I hoped. "We won't let you become immortal."

"I truly hope you had to torture my dear Ness for information about the cemetery."

"He's on our side. He doesn't want to see you rise to power either."

"Fascinating. I didn't see him fighting alongside you." Luna coughs, wiping blood from the corner of her chapped lips with a handkerchief that's stained red and brown. There are dark shadows underneath her eyes. Some of us stay up all night editing YouTube videos and others work on formulas for immortality. "You believe I don't deserve to live," Luna says.

"You brought your poisoning on yourself," I say.

"Would you say the same about your father?" Luna's mocking grin twists my insides and tightens my fist. "Of course I know all about Leonardo Rey's illness. I've studied up on Keon's scion, your adopted brother. It's tragic what happened to your father." She walks around the center table and tidies her station, rolling up a blueprint I didn't get a chance to examine. "You like stories, yes? Do you know the one about how my younger sister, Raine, was sick, and every alchemist and practitioner I trusted to save her failed us? You're so willing to dismiss me as power-hungry, when everything I do has been for life."

I can't believe that this queenpin watched my videos on YouTube.

"You've got a lot of blood on your hands for someone who cares so much about life."

Luna is absolutely fearless as she walks past me, smelling like woodsmoke. Her back is to me as she trails a finger through some black powder, pressing it to her tongue and sighing deeply. "Unfortunately, life must be lost to figure out how to preserve it, restore it." She turns around, and her thinning eyebrows narrow. "You aren't worth killing in my grand design. You weren't even worth locking up, unlike Emil, whose true power would require us to use the heaviest of chains. You are nothing but a pawn in my possession to collect the urn your brother stole from me."

I grab the screwdriver and thrust like it's a dagger, but Luna smacks it out of my hand. I shove her against the table and grab the lightning potion as Dione leaps across the room.

I uncork the vial. If I'm struck with blood poisoning, it won't go away with rest and water like some common fever, but desperate times call for desperate measures—Luna knows it, my father knew it, I know it. I drink the potion, and it tastes like cough syrup, rotten berries, and iron. I gag, but I don't spit it out, even when I get instantly dizzy, like whenever I was a kid and Dad would spin me around in his desk chair at work. I fight back a cough as Dione grabs me by the throat and slams me against the wall.

"I have no problem snapping his neck," Dione says with her menacing eyes.

Luna balances herself against the table. "He remains not worth it."

Blood rushes to my head the tighter Dione squeezes, and there's a charge running through me, crackling throughout my arms. I think back to Atlas coaching Emil on how to call his power. I've heard it all a thousand times from editing those clips. I focus on bringing the lightning to the surface, can feel it right beneath my skin, needing just a little more of a push. . . . I press my hands against Dione as if to shove her and bolts of white lightning blast through her. Dione's eyes widen and her grip loosens and she falls at my feet, smoke rising around the hole in her stomach. I expect flesh to regrow and piece her back together, but she's still.

It was self-defense. I killed her in self-defense like the Spell Walkers have. I'm more in shock over how quickly it happened than I am having had the power to protect myself in the first place. Dione has done a lot of harm, so I'm not going to twist myself up over this, especially when I can slay the monster who underestimated me.

I step over Dione's body, and Luna backs into a corner.

She thought I was harmless. The acolyte I saw before with the crate returns, and I hurl a bolt directly through his heart. He crumples with his mouth open.

I'm a first-timer calling my power with more ease than Emil ever has; this is what I've been saying all along. He may have been reborn, but my blood comes from a long line of power that's beginning again with me. Luna tries escaping, and I strike her down with bolts of lightning.

"I was wrong," Luna whispers while pressing down on her bloody arm.

"About what?"

"You're extraordinary."

I nod. "Unfortunately, Luna, life has got to be lost to preserve it."

I stand over her and cage her in lightning until she's dead.

I've done what no one else could do. I killed the one Blood Caster who Eva feared confronting on the battlefield, and I executed the queenpin before she could become unstoppable. I can't wait to bust out of here and get back to Nova to celebrate with my family and Prudencia. I'll ask the crew what we can do about getting me some proper Spell Walker gear and then we'll take down the next threat.

The room spins and everything reverses in rapid flashes—what little color there was returns to Luna's face as lightning retreats back inside my hands, she's running backward, the acolyte's corpse rises and exits, I'm pressed against the wall again and Dione's hand is back around my throat.

"You're supposed to be dead," I say in choked breaths.

"Never," Luna says. "Especially not at the hands of some fool who cannot tell an illusion apart from reality."

"Illusion?"

Luna eyes one of the vials. "These are potions of mine that failed to convert humans into celestials and were revealed to have hallucinatory side effects. I couldn't keep risking the health of my acolytes, so we've been selling them on the streets and filming the drinkers in the event one proves to exhibit actual powers so we can study the subjects. We've been marketing it as Brew—Ness's idea, but surely he told you this given that he's on your side, correct?"

I'm powerless and speechless. Of course I was drinking Brew like those clowns in the park. It was so lifelike, but the reality of Ness being a traitor is just as crushing. My brother thinks Ness is trying to turn over some new leaf and make an honest guy out of himself.

Dione drags me through the hall with ease, even though

I'm resisting and dragging my feet. She throws me into a room where I skid across the concrete, scratching my arms and face, and rolling into Stanton's feet. June continues reading through a dusty book, not glancing up at me once. Luna is the last one in and locks the door behind her, as if I stand any chance at getting that close to escape with three Blood Casters here.

"Your fantasy of what makes someone a hero is your downfall," Luna says. "Not a long fall, of course, since you've never known great heights. To save and rebuild the world demands a soul that will do what is necessary. You don't possess the nature or the heart that I do. But that's okay. Everyone has their role."

Stanton lifts me by the back of the neck and forces me into a chair against the wall.

My camera that I dropped at the cemetery for the wand is here and facing me.

"You crave the spotlight so badly," Luna says. "Go ahead and give us a smile."

THIRTY

THE BRIGHTEST FIRE

EMIL

I'll never forgive myself for putting the world before my family. Turns out Eva can't heal hearts, but Wesley was quick to grab Ma's nitroglycerin, and we've got her stabilized down the hall while the rest of us are working away in the boardroom. I'm about to check in on her again when I get a notification alert on my phone.

Celestials of New York just uploaded a new video:
Return the Urn.

"Brighton!"
Everyone turns to me. Prudencia snatches my phone. He's

got to be alive. No one else knows his super complicated password for any of his accounts. Unless they tortured it out of him. I've imagined so many nightmares for what they're doing to Brighton the past four hours I've been without him. If Luna was so cruel with her parents and their ghosts, she would be merciless with my brother. Not going to lie, if things are as horrific as my gut thinks, death might be better.

"Play the video," Prudencia says.

Atlas projects it onto the wall, and all the Spell Walkers are still.

The thumbnail shows Brighton with a scratched cheek and swollen eye. I thank the constellations that Ma took the sleeping pill so her heart could have a break. If she almost died imagining what was happening to Brighton, this video would finish the job. Prudencia is shaking, and when she grabs my hand, I don't have the strength to clutch hers.

In the video, Brighton is in a chair with a grimy wall behind him. I'm immediately hit with all those memories of when Brighton watched wild spectacles, and how I never thought he would be the subject of one. My heart is slamming when I hear Stanton's voice from the other side of the camera.

"Tell your brother what has to happen," Stanton demands.

Brighton sits up. "Go to hell."

"Do what they say!" Prudencia shouts as if this is a video chat.

Stanton comes around the camera, growling, and chokes

Brighton. Brighton's face is a deep red in moments and his eyes are bulging. I almost look away, but I'm never turning my back on my brother again.

Stanton releases him and he gasps for air. "Do it," he says through clenched teeth.

Brighton is near tears, all stoic broken. "Emil . . ."

I have no idea what he's going to say. Maybe that this is all my fault or how he's about to die because of me.

"The only way to get me back is to return the urn and prisoner by seven a.m." Brighton is shaking. "If you don't, I'll be executed on a live feed. Meet us at the place where we spent the last few minutes of our birthday." Stanton brings the camera closer to Brighton, and he flinches. "If you don't bring the real urn, they will kill me. If you show up without the prisoner, they will kill me. Do not play games. His life isn't worth mine."

Stanton clocks Brighton so hard that the chair rocks back and Brighton hits the floor, laid out.

The video ends.

This was never fun and games, especially not since I joined the Spell Walkers, but it's never felt realer. I've never wanted to set another living person ablaze the way I do now. I'm not a killer, but I'm already so outside of myself that I could become one to save my brother's life.

Prudencia sinks to the floor, crying. Maribelle slams her fist against the table. Wesley stares out the window.

Stealing powers from creatures didn't mean the Blood Casters had to be monsters. Threatening Brighton's life wasn't enough; no, they had to go ahead and humiliate him on his own channel. No doubt waking him up from Stanton's lights-out punch to upload the video himself. The views are coming in fast, and I wonder how many of these people have reported it or called the authorities. I bet people are sharing links left and right like our lives are some drama series they can't believe is unfolding in real time.

"Brighton's talking about the rooftop of our building," I say. No one says anything. Too stunned, I guess. I'll get the phoenix singing. "I don't know if I can fly again, but I'll show up with the urn, and once we trade for Brighton, then we can ambush them. Come back with Brighton and the urn."

Iris holds the urn with a grip so tight I'm surprised she's not crushing it. "We can't risk losing the urn. We may not be able to stop Luna if she has the ghosts again."

"She'll definitely kill my brother if we don't!"

"Luna will do far worse if she becomes indestructible."

"We rescue innocents," Atlas says. "This is what we do."

Iris takes a deep breath and doesn't look me in the eye. "The one for the many. I want to claw out my own heart for saying it, but the mission has always been to stop Luna and the Blood Casters. The mission my parents died for."

"My parents died too!" Maribelle says.

"It's not the same!" Iris shouts.

"Because your parents were leaders? Get over yourself. Seniority is the only reason you and your parents were ever trusted to lead. You must be living in some fantasy land where blood isn't on your hands just because you're not doing the killing, but wake up. Brighton was brave enough to take a shot that you never would in a million years, to do the very thing our parents fought for, and now he has to pay the ultimate price?"

"We all risk paying the ultimate price," Iris says.

Maribelle shakes her head. "Unbelievable. You don't deserve to lead this group. No one else agrees with her, right?"

Eva folds her hands on the table and stares at the ceiling. "I'm sorry, but I do. We're already trying to protect a country of celestials, and if Luna can take command, she will go global and have us all killed for opposing her."

Wesley stands by Eva and Iris. "I think Brighton is the man, and he's done a world of good for us. But we almost died in the cemetery. This won't be a fair trade. There's too much to lose."

"I would die to protect you," Atlas says.

"Bro, you know what I'm saying," Wesley says.

"No, I don't. If you were captured by the Blood Casters, I would be out this door already. But if we're too careful with our lives all of a sudden, then we should go out and live our truths while we still can, because everything we've set out to do will come to a full stop once Luna rises to power."

"We have to make sure we're around to fight," Wesley says.

"I have a family, man, and I owe it to them and everyone else to make sure Luna doesn't become unstoppable."

I can't believe people are debating whether my brother's life is worth saving.

"If you want me on your side, I have to have my brother," I say. "This is how we started our alliance, and this is how we'll end it. You're really going to tell me to my face that you'll let my brother die when he was risking his own neck to shine a light on your lives?"

Everyone is quiet.

"I'm getting Brighton back, even if that means showing up alone and without that urn. I'll die fighting so he knows I didn't abandon him when he needed me most. Good luck fighting your war without us."

I storm out knowing damn well I won't survive this alone. I didn't grow up with powers, but I've been a brother for eighteen years.

No fire burns brighter than that.

It's almost six when I call Kirk, and I'm relieved when he answers.

"Emil?"

"Hey, Kirk. I—"

"How are you doing? I've tried reaching you. I want to

understand why you made the decision to become a specter and—"

"I know, I know. I'm sorry I haven't been in touch, but everything has taken a turn and only gotten worse and worse."

"Is this about your brother? I saw the video."

Of course he's seen it. My life is some show for people to consume.

"Brighton's in trouble, and I might not be able to save him. But the Blood Casters won't win if you keep Gravesend far away from the museum. Cancel the gala, get her out of the country."

I tell him everything I know about Luna's plan to use Gravesend's pure blood to make herself immortal.

"Immortal? Emil, that's not possible."

"I would've told you the same before I came back to life," I say. He's quiet. This is the first time I've trusted anyone outside Nova with the big secret. "In essence, at least. Turns out Keon could resurrect. He became Bautista, and . . ."

"Now there's you." Then Kirk is quiet. "Emil, this is astonishing news, truly. I would love to help you work through this, but in the meantime, we can't cancel the gala. The museum needs this funding to keep its doors open. The Halo Knights will already be present to protect Gravesend, but I'll alert them to the threat."

"Luna is planning to create her potion at the height of the Crowned Dreamer. Delay the gala."

"Gravesend will have hatched by then. The Halo Knights are capable, I promise you. I'd like to ask you more about this resurrection business—"

I hang up. Between the Spell Walkers turning their backs on me and Kirk not taking my warning seriously, I've lost the little hope I had that we might defeat Luna.

I go to Ness's room. He's lying on his air mattress and puts down the book he was reading. "Finally, firefly."

I sit in the center of the room, relieved when he joins me. I tell him everything—Luna pulling off the ritual, me flying away with the urn, Brighton being taken hostage.

He watches the video and hands me back my phone. "She wants me back."

"It's not fair, I know. I'm sorry. But Brighton is innocent."

"What's the plan? You offer me up, and once we secure Brighton, we all get away?"

If only it were that easy. "Iris would rather sacrifice Brighton."

"She may have a point," he says.

"I don't care about some greater good. I didn't ask for these powers and I'm not my past lives. I don't know when Keon was born, and I can't tell you what Bautista's favorite meal was, and I'm already carrying around enough guilt for a war I didn't cause. But Brighton getting jumped by the Blood Casters? That's on me. No one matters to me more than my brother, and I won't be able to live with myself if he dies."

The door opens, and Maribelle and Atlas walk in.

"The good guys are here," Ness says dryly while feigning a clap.

"They backed me up in there," I say.

Atlas pats my shoulder. "We're here to help you now too. You and Brighton have done more than we should've asked of you."

Maribelle flips a dagger between her fingers while holding eye contact with Ness. "You coming willingly?"

"He has to make this decision himself," I say.

"You're truly not cut out for this life," she says. It feels more like an apology than an insult.

Good on all the Spell Walkers who have stayed in this fight, even when they've wanted to bust out too, but the soldier life is too suffocating for me. Someone shouldn't have to be a walk-ing weapon simply because they possess powers. I'm not about it, and I'm done once I save my brother.

Ness stands. "I got myself into this, and I'll get myself out of it."

I don't know how to thank someone who is willingly marching back into the life he doesn't want for himself. "I'll protect you too," I promise.

"Sure."

This would be easier if Ness were as awful as Stanton, but as far as I can tell, he's a Blood Caster who was torn between two conflicts and chose the option that scared him the least.

"Eva has the urn," Atlas says. "She's not going to hand it over to anyone but Iris. This is where you come in, Ness."

Ness looks puzzled. "You trust me to shift into your leader?"

Maribelle scoffs. "Not my leader."

"I trust you," I say.

Ness takes a deep breath and begins morphing before our eyes. There's that muted glow as he shrinks, and his skin darkens while his hair shortens and turns green. There's pain on his face the entire time, and within a minute, the transformation is complete. He looks like Iris, but still in his clothes. "I don't know what she's wearing," he says in a voice that sounds like his own before it transitions into Iris's halfway. He makes the necessary changes as we describe her resistance shirt, white jeans, and combat boots.

We walk down the hall. I sense Atlas is uneasy with all of this, but he's going to do the right thing. Like Ness. If he had some master plan, this wasn't going to be the time to make a move. Once we get the urn, I have to figure out how to save us all. I'll honor my promise to Ness.

Maribelle barges into the professors' lounge, which I haven't been in before. Eva is stretched across a fold-out couch and comes out from under her pillow. "We need the urn before your girl has a change of heart," she says, gesturing at Ness, who is standing tall as Iris.

Eva rubs her eyes. "It's never going to work."

"We have to try," Ness says. It's nice to hear what Iris

would've sounded like had she said these words herself.

"I'm not going to let the Blood Casters get away with the urn, but I have to get my brother," I say.

Eva gets out of bed, goes into a closet, and opens a safe, and when she hands Ness the urn, she turns to me and holds her stare. "You get one shot." She knows what's up, and she's allowing it anyway. But there's no mistaking the look on her face—this pure anguish and hope that she won't regret handing the world over to someone who will risk it all to save his brother.

We grab our gear but don't bother changing. We rush inside the car before Iris or Wesley find out what Eva has done. Prudencia comes banging out the doors, and she looks dressed for battle too. She pulls at the backseat door, but I keep it locked.

"Let me in," she says.

"No. Brighton is in this mess because he couldn't defend himself. I'm not risking you too."

"I can handle myself," Prudencia says.

"Please hang tight and explain everything to Ma in case . . ."

I'm not as hopeless as I was when I thought I was going into this fight alone. I will survive, and I will save Brighton, and Ma will never have to panic over the death threat.

I tell Atlas to drive, and we move a couple feet before the car stops. My face and Ness's slam against the backs of the front seats. The wheels continue spinning like we're stuck in a ditch. I think Iris must've caught up to us and grabbed the rear, but when I turn around, Prudencia is the only one there, and she's walking toward the car with her arms outstretched as if she's inviting me in for a hug. When she's outside my window, she snaps her fingers, and the lock switches. She lets herself in, pushing me against Ness.

"I told you I can handle myself," Prudencia says. Her eyes are fiercely glowing like ping-ponging stars. "I'm going."

THIRTY-ONE
THE TRADE

EMIL

My best friend has been a celestial all along.

"I wanted to tell you," Prudencia says to me as we speed away from Nova.

"Why didn't you?"

No matter how often Brighton, Prudencia, and Ma have been there for me, these have been the loneliest weeks of my life. When Dad passed, we were all united by grief. But no one could fully be there for me when I came into these powers because they didn't understand firsthand. That's what I legit thought.

"Enforcers only mistook my mom as a celestial, Emil, but my dad was. My aunt made me promise to never use my powers again if I lived with her. That was fine. I didn't want them after seeing my dad killed for his." She shifts to me with this energy of someone who's finally able to share her secret with the world, but I still hate that I'm making her relive this decades-old horror. "I was so torn because I could've been training to fight back like the Spell Walkers, but I also didn't want to be defined by my power, so I fought back in other ways. The podcasts, protests, any activism I could manage."

"Does Brighton know?" I ask.

Prudencia shakes her head. "Only Iris."

Maribelle flips around. "She what?"

"My power was the only way Brighton and I could go on the missions."

"She's not supposed to have secrets," Maribelle says. "I cannot believe her."

Ness lets out a long whistle. "Drama galore, but we'll use this to our advantage, right? No one knows you're a celestial."

"I wish Brighton hadn't taken off to the cemetery without me," Prudencia says. "I could've protected him like I did when we fought Orton."

Everything is clicking into place. When Orton was blazing up and charging at us, it wasn't the fire holding him back, it was Prudencia. I remember the moment on the train when it seemed like she was about to chop Orton in the neck, but she was actually about to swing with her power. All this time I've been going off about how difficult my life had become while she privately suffered, so determined to lead a normal life that she didn't even open up to us.

"I'm sorry," I say. "We're going to set all this right."

"I hope so," she says.

Thirty minutes later, we're a couple blocks from home with a plan in place. I never thought I would find my way back here. In my heart, this place will always be home, even if I'll never be able to live here again, no matter if I manage to expel these powers or not. We park on the opposite corner, and I instruct Ness to go out and see if the Blood Casters are here yet.

"Wait," Maribelle says. "He'll morph and run away."

Ness looks out the window and studies a man who's carry-ing grocery bags. He closes his eyes and shifts into him. "Can't wait to surprise you," he says in his own voice.

"Do you really trust him that much?" Maribelle asks.

"I trust him enough."

I'm counting on our interests being the same—stop Luna and get out of this life.

A few minutes later, a woman enters the car.

"Sorry, this isn't a Lyft," I say.

"The Blood Casters are here," the woman says as she morphs into Ness. "Stanton's cycle is parked around the corner, and I spotted Dione on the rooftop. No sign of June, but there are acolytes in the lobby turning residents away."

"So we stick to the plan," Prudencia says.

We get out of the car and enter the neighboring building

from the back entrance. As we go up the stairs, I'm reminded of the times Brighton and I would hide from our friends during rounds of manhunt, when we were so hard to find that they would text us when they gave up. This isn't a game. We reach the roof and there they are. Brighton is on the ground with his hands tied behind his back and Stanton is holding a wand to his head while staring straight at us. Luna is nowhere in sight, but Anklin Prince is here.

I summon my blazing wings and shakily glide across one rooftop to the next. My landing isn't graceful either, but I stand tall. Atlas and Maribelle carry Ness and Prudencia across the gap and join me.

"Give me my brother," I say. Brighton has never looked so scared.

Stanton smirks. "Luna is looking forward to seeing you again, Ness."

Maribelle draws a dagger. "Not enough to show up herself."

Stanton digs the tip of the wand against Brighton's temple harder. "Luna learned her lesson after this one took a shot at her."

We coordinate how this will go down. I'll accompany Ness in the middle, and Anklin will release Brighton after he's verified the authenticity of the urn. Once I have Brighton back, I will clock Anklin, and Prudencia can call for the urn before the Blood Casters can reach it. I don't want to hang around and

ADAM SILVERA

fight, but if it comes down to it, we've got them outnumbered for once.

We meet in the middle. Anklin takes the urn from Ness and it shakes, as if the ghosts are trying to fight their way out. Brighton's eye is swollen shut, and there's dried blood across his face and arms. Brighton keeps shifting between me and Ness with his good eye and subtly shaking his head. I don't get what he's trying to say, but spellwork explodes across the roof and we all duck.

Acolytes come running up from the fire escape, and Dione tackles me out of nowhere. I cast fire and slam down on her back with my burning fist so I can escape her hold. I pop up and chase Anklin, only stopping when Stanton fires off a blast at Brighton. Prudencia telekinetically sweeps the white bolt away, sending it sailing off the roof to meet some other fate. Brighton halts in shock, just like when my powers first surfaced on the train. Then Stanton throws down the wand and leaps at Brighton while he isn't paying attention. Prudencia's power isn't strong enough to hold him back, and Stanton bangs straight into Brighton's back. Brighton rolls across the concrete and stops at Prudencia's feet.

"Brighton!"

Atlas and Maribelle are locked in combat with Dione and her four arms. Prudencia looks like she's running on fumes as she suspends two acolytes from reaching her.

She will protect Brighton, and I have to focus on the urn. I call for Ness, and we run at Anklin from both ends, cornering him at the ledge.

"Hand it over," I say.

Anklin tries hurling himself off the roof, but Ness catches him from behind. My heart steadies as Ness snatches the urn and holds it up like a trophy. Ness's smile vanishes when he sees that Stanton is closing in on us.

Then Ness swings the urn into my face, lights out.

THIRTY-TWO
THE DARKEST FIRE

BRIGHTON

My eyes are closed as greens and pinks and blues and oranges pierce the darkness. I'm hot, like I'm directly under a spotlight, but it becomes relaxing in no time—until the screams start. I squint past the lights to find Eva and her healing hands. It's too bright to keep staring, but I chill back while Eva does her thing since I'm safe at the nurse's office at Nova. When I'm all good, Eva wipes the sweat off her face with the hem of her shirt and sinks into her seat.

"Thanks, Eva. Sorry you had to go through that."

"Not the worst," Eva says.

That's alarming considering that's the greatest pain I've ever been in.

The last things I remember are Emil shouting my name and Prudencia's eyes glowing as she saved my life. I'm suddenly hot again.

"Where is everyone?"

"Scattered. Mostly everyone is in the boardroom, and Prudencia is keeping your mother company as she rests. While you were . . . when you weren't here, she had a heart attack."

"What?!" I shoot out of bed. "Did you heal her?"

"I can handle most wounds and some internal bleeding, but healing hearts is not within my range."

"Then why isn't she in the hospital?"

"Enforcers are on the lookout for your entire family, Brighton. I promise we are doing our very best around here."

"It's not good enough."

"I'm sorry that my power isn't more miraculous," Eva snaps.

I'm not going to apologize again. I get to be upset that my mother's life is in the hands of people who can't do anything about it. Then again, people can surprise you. "Where's Emil?" I stand and move for the door. I'm going to see how long he's known about Prudencia's power. Eva stares at the wall like she tuned me out. "Okay, I'm sorry, Eva."

"I wasn't waiting for a fake apology. I just didn't want to be the one to tell you that Emil was taken hostage by the Blood Casters."

It feels like I'm captive again, trying to survive Stanton's heavy fists. Luna said that she would chain Emil if he was there, and his powers aren't going to be enough to protect him. "How did they let that happen? Where the hell was everyone? Did Wes and Iris have something better to do?"

"You should talk it out with them," Eva says.

"Happily."

Even if I weren't fully healed, I have no doubt adrenaline would drive me forward. I pass a celestial who rolls his eyes at me, and I almost want to shove him into a locker. At least I'm out there fighting while he hides. I barge into the boardroom and find Maribelle, Atlas, Wesley, and Iris all seated at the table.

"You're better," Atlas says.

I ignore him and go straight for Wesley and Iris. "Where were you? Tell me to my face right now that I wasn't worth saving. Was it because I messed up with the video? Was it because I wasn't reborn into this life with powers worth your time? After everything I've done for you, not showing up to rescue me is the worst way to say thank you."

Iris pulls her face out of her hands. "It wasn't personal. But we have to do what's right for the entire community of celestials within our care and in the country. If it was my own brother on the line, I would've done the same."

"But you don't have a brother. Would you risk Eva?"

Iris is teary and shakes it off. She points at Maribelle and Atlas. "Go be pissed at them too. They're the ones who ran out of here half-cocked and not only lost your brother but returned Ness and the urn to the Blood Casters."

Maribelle glares at Iris. "Stop turning this on us when we're the ones who tried. Emil was going to go whether we backed him up or not, so I'm not going to apologize for trying to save Brighton's life. Maybe we could've kept the urn if you showed up to fight."

Wesley stands before Maribelle and Iris can get another word in. "Brighton, man, we have a lot of respect for you, but our hands were tied. We can't justify a single life over the world's fate. That's not how wars are won."

I can't believe one of my heroes is telling me that I wasn't worth saving. "Let's not pretend you're not about to make an exception for Emil. The one everyone is rooting for."

"We have to be more strategic," Atlas says. "We all should've been more united before, but the stakes are higher now. We don't know what purpose Emil could even serve to them. So we can't plan a rescue mission unless we know . . . you know."

"That there's someone to rescue."

"Our best hope now is cutting the Blood Casters off before they can get their hands on the phoenix Luna needs to complete her elixir."

I've never felt more hopeless about the people I've been cheering on for years. They couldn't be bothered to save me or even back up Emil. "Whenever you head out, I'll be there too." I turn to Wesley and Iris. "I'll prove to you why no one messes with my brother."

I storm out. They better not try to leave without me.

I go to Ma's room, where she's eating with Prudencia. They both look like they haven't slept the past several nights. I don't know the last time anyone has had a full night's sleep. Prudencia tries to hug me, but I take a step back and look at Ma.

"My shining star," Ma says. Her bottom lip trembles. "You're okay."

"But now Emil isn't. I'm going to get him back."

"No, please, you have to stay here. Let the Spell Walkers handle this," Ma says.

"They didn't even back him up the first time!"

"You can't risk yourself the way Emil could," Prudencia says. "I know that's the last thing you want to hear, and I know you want to be the one with powers, but you aren't, and you have no business being out on the battlefield again. Look what you and Emil are putting your mother through!"

I look her dead in the eye. "I'm sorry, have we met?"

Prudencia comes around the bed and gets in my face. "You don't get to be upset because I didn't tell you I'm a celestial."

"Yes I do! What, all those times you were looking over the journal with Emil, were those actually meetings to talk about how amazing it is to have powers? What a shame that I'm not in on the fun? Laughing behind my back, I bet."

I will never tell anyone about my Brew experience. How powerful and victorious I felt when I believed I killed Luna and Dione and that acolyte. I'm a big enough fool without anyone knowing all that.

"Brighton, I had no intention of ever using my powers again. I would've loved to have trusted you with that secret, but I didn't want you to pressure me into doing some piece for your series or shame me for not nurturing my telekinesis. I care enough about you and Emil that I broke my own promise to myself to look after you both on missions."

"Some good that did."

Prudencia's eyes fill with tears, and then they fill with rapidly moving stars. The deep breaths she takes are probably the only reason I'm not flying through that window.

"You're not being fair, Brighton," Ma says.

"What do you both know? You're both liars."

Ma inhales deeply, and I regret what I've said, but I'm too pissed to take it back, and if I stay here any longer I might make it worse.

"I've got work to do," I say, and leave.

I'm exhausted and starving and want to shower, but I can't stop thinking about if Emil is still alive.

I get back to my room, pop open my laptop, and go straight to YouTube, that reflex of mine that's as strong as breathing. There aren't any trending videos of Emil's captivity. I search his name online, and nothing new pops up beyond the standard praise and hate. I check out the stats on the video where Stanton beat me around. Over two million views since Stanton forced me to upload it early this morning. The comments range: Lore keeping me in their prayers; Silver Star Slayer and his followers claiming this is staged; I apparently shouldn't have stuck my nose in any of this and left everything to the authorities, as if the enforcers were rushing to save my life; people speculating on where the meet-up was, like it was going to be some opportunity to get photos with Emil; and the last one I read is someone trying to get a bet going on how long it takes for Emil to save my life. How little they know.

The door opens, and Maribelle comes in.

"We messed up trusting that shape-shifter," she says. "We followed his lead, but we should've known better."

"Emil would trust Luna if she promised to turn over a new leaf. His heart is too good."

"You've got fire in you." She crosses her arms. "Taking that shot at Luna took a lot of guts. Come train with me so we make sure you don't miss next time."

I put down the laptop and rise.

I'm going to be my brother's hero. No matter what.

THIRTY-THREE
INFINITY-ENDER

EMIL

I wake up to find four acolytes aiming wands at me like a firing squad. My wrists are chained above my head, and my arms are sore. This migraine eclipses the one I had after my first casting. I cannot believe I trusted Ness—that two-faced bastard who played to my fears of escaping war. Dude straight seduced me.

I have no idea where I am, but in the silence, I hear the golden-strand hydra's howls. Another life that's going to be lost.

Maybe I screwed up this war even more. If I'd never agreed to fight and just hung around Nova minding my own damn business, then Brighton would've never found himself doing

283

fieldwork, and I wouldn't have bothered connecting with someone who has committed crimes for the city's greatest queenpin. I don't know what went down after Ness laid me out with that urn, but I hope Brighton and Prudencia and the Spell Walkers are all good. I'm shaking hard thinking about what comes next, but better me than my brother. I suck at saving lives, but sacrifice is heroic too.

The door creaks open, and Luna and Ness enter.

"How far you've fallen, my little wonder," Luna says while twirling the infinity-ender she thinks will extinguish me and my phoenix fire for good. "Keon was a mastermind, the first of many specters. Despite Bautista betraying me because he was enthralled by an even greater traitor, he still managed to establish a movement that has impeded me plenty. But what have you done? All this power and no fire in your heart."

"Maybe my next life will impress you," I say.

"You weren't supposed to be reborn, but it was a valuable lesson for my purposes. When I struck Bautista down with the infinity-ender, it wasn't somewhere fatal. I didn't believe it would matter, since all phoenixes die once struck with the blade, even a nick in the belly. Since a specter's body is still human, he bled out, but I didn't end his line. Ness has informed me you possess no memories of Keon's or Bautista's lives, and I'm positive I at least fractured that ability."

So it wasn't because Bautista experimented with all those power-binding and power-expelling potions. Which means that I can die for good if struck by the infinity-ender.

"You serve a purpose," Luna says. "You've shown me the reaches of power that a specter can experience. How lovely it will be to fly with those glorious wings and live on forever." She holds out the infinity-ender, and Ness clasps the bone handle. "Luckily for you, you're more valuable to a client of mine alive than you are to me dead, as tempting as it is to snuff out your line once and for all. Still, the weaker you are, the better for everyone."

Ness approaches me.

The fire bursts across my arms, but I can't hurl any fire-darts at him. If Luna wants to see impressive, I'll show her someone who won't go down without a fight. I fly as high as I can, my neck craned against the ceiling. The chains prevent me from escaping, but I can relax my arms enough to let fire-darts rain down on the room. The acolytes scatter, and I nearly catch Luna, but Ness hops up and slices the exposed skin above my ankle. Scorching pain surges up to my waist, a metallic silver light flashing so brightly through my dark jeans. My wings vanish. I crash onto the foot where my ankle's been cut and the chain pops my left arm from my shoulder.

"Get up," Ness says.

"Please kill me," I say. If he has any mercy, he'll end me quickly and claim it was an accident. If someone reborn after me manages to carry Keon's memories, they could be tempted to continue his work, and I want this entire conflict to die with Luna when the Spell Walkers take her down.

"Get up," Ness repeats.

"I can't." My leg is in agony, like it's being stabbed over and over.

Luna instructs an acolyte to help me, but Ness waves them off. He drops the dagger and roughly picks me up, slamming me against the wall. His eyes are red, and I like to think there's an apology in his stare, but trusting him is what got me here. He bites his lip, and I brace myself. He cuts across my rib cage, and I scream in his face, crying and spitting as my insides run so hot they feel like they're melting. He cuts the other side too; twin wounds that burn so fiercely I should black out from the pain, but the pain igniting within every few seconds keeps me awake.

"Marvelous, my pure miracle," Luna says, taking the bloody dagger out of Ness's hand. "You've made me very proud, as always."

She instructs the acolytes to bind my feet in chains, even though she doesn't expect my powers to recover soon.

Within minutes, I'm left alone.

Every time I get the sensation that I'm healing, my pain doubles, then triples, and I bite down on my lip so hard I taste blood. I'm drenched in sweat as these flames eat me alive, and I'm praying to the night skies that I die right here, right now. Blood soaks up my sleeves and the bottom of my shirt, dripping down my legs and to the floor. I cry for help, knowing damn well no one here cares. I remind myself that Brighton is okay because I was brave enough to stand up for him, how I will always suffer for his safety.

Times passes, and the agony doesn't go away.

The faintest phoenix song begs me to survive, but I'm tired of the music and wish someone would put out my fire for good.

THIRTY-FOUR
MANY FACES

NESS

I'm shaking hard in front of the mirror and I grip the sink with bloody hands.

Gray light bathes me, and I'm Peter McCall when he was thirteen. Brown eyes that feared me whenever we crossed paths, thin lips that quivered whenever I cornered him. He was so small that only half of his face reflects back at me now. He was the first celestial I bullied after my mother was killed, and he transferred schools after his parents caught him trying to take his own life. Gray light. Fourteen-year-old Harry Gardner. Black eye and missing teeth courtesy of my fists. He was the first celestial I attacked. I went home pissed because he hadn't used his power on me, which would've gotten him locked up. Gray light. Fifteen-year-old Rhys Stone. Blue eyes, immaculate smile, bright future ahead of him. We never met personally, but there's no forgetting the face of the celestial who was killed because of my convention speech, because of words the Senator wrote for me. Words I once believed.

Gray light after gray light, the many faces of people I've hurt go on and on. Some personally, others indirectly. Some alive, others dead. A few murdered by my own hand.

But there's one that strikes hardest.

Gray light. Taller than me, hazel eyes, curlier hair, a face that I've never seen smile but hope I will. Emil Rey. Firefly. But I got him all wrong. He's too clean, too perfect. He's been ruined tonight—I ruined him.

I don't want to, but I add the scars to my glamour and stare.

I will forever be haunted by the tears that filled his hazel eyes, the spit building over his lips, his cheeks flushing as he screamed for death, and his blood on my hands.

Gray light.

I'm me again. I wish I wasn't.

THIRTY-FIVE
GALA

EMIL

I've lost all track of time without windows. Sleeping while strung up by chains has been near impossible, but my body continues to shut down until acolytes wake me up for meals of crackers and dirty faucet water. I begged an acolyte for a chair at one point, and he laughed at me. Could've been Ness in disguise again, getting off on his winning mind games. The only mercy I was shown was an acolyte bandaging me, but I'm sure Luna didn't want me to bleed out.

I'm fading when Stanton enters the room and pulls the chain from the ceiling, making me drop. Stanton drags me across the concrete halls, my bandages coming undone. He carries me up a flight of stairs to a loading dock where he hurls me into the back of a van. Everything is blurry as I fade in and out, but I can clearly see Ness looking unaffected among acolytes. Wands are aimed at me even though I haven't been able to cast any fire. Ness is holding the infinity-ender, and the blade hasn't been cleaned. No point wiping it down when I've got more blood to spill.

The ride is bumpy, but at least my legs, which have been so numb, finally get a chance to rest. I want to sleep too. I always prided myself on being able to nap in noisy auditoriums at school and drift away on the train, but now fear keeps me awake. Not because of all the weapons that'll kill me if I make a wrong move, but because of where I'm being taken to and why I'm more useful to Luna alive than dead.

The van stops, and I breathe in the fresh air, feeling pulses of strength under the Crowned Dreamer, so close to its final form in the night sky. I recognize the parking lot of the Museum of Natural Creatures immediately. I wish Kirk weren't so stubborn and would cancel the entire thing, but maybe the Halo Knights will be enough to combat the Blood Casters and protect Gravesend. June phases through the back door and opens it from the inside, welcoming everyone in. I've never been through this hallway, but June leads the way with confidence. Smart money is on June having spent time in the museum, unseen and unheard, studying the ins and outs to become a walking map. I can't believe I'm back, and I don't know why, but I'm curious how long Kirk will wait until he updates the

Sunroom to reflect my history as the gray sun specter who accomplished nothing but misery for his family.

There's a flicker of hope. The Spell Walkers know the Blood Casters will be making a move on Gravesend's egg, and I'm counting on them being here. Every corner we turn, I fantasize about Atlas popping out and pinning everyone down with his winds long enough for Wesley to zoom in and carry me to safety. Eva will have to go through hell if she wants to heal me, which pains me on a whole other level.

We lose some acolytes before we enter the staircase, where a lovely phoenix melody can be heard coming from the gala. Right as I think we're heading up to the Sunroom, praying to every damn star in the sky that the Spell Walkers are fully united and in place to protect Gravesend and rescue me, we all go downstairs. The lights in the Hydra House are off for the night, and we approach a see-through vault that's heavily guarded by five people.

Halo Knights.

The fiercest warriors are here to protect Gravesend. They'll consider me a traitor for possessing phoenix powers, but it's all good as long as they can stop the Blood Casters. They're dressed in their clay masks with golden beaks, and sun-dust armor with feathered sleeves that are midnight blue and scarlet. Two are wielding iron crossbows while others are carrying axes and swords.

"Strike, my children," Luna says.

June sinks through the floor while Stanton and Dione charge, using their advanced reflexes to dodge arrows with flips and slides. Ness squeezes my arm, like I have any chance of making a run for it. Dione snatches the ax and spins it into the gut of a man. Right as she swings at another, a short Halo with long dark hair jumps through the air with such epic distance that she could be flying and slices her bronze blade across Dione's neck. Ness's grip tightens, and I fight back every impulse to throw up, but my throat stings as Dione's head rolls off her shoulders and her body crumples like an abandoned marionette.

The four Haloes pile on Stanton, and I relive my own pain as they cut him with their blades. Then June reappears and steps inside the body of a muscular knight with dark hair, using his sword to stab two of them in the back before the last catches on. It's one thing to hear about possession, but a much greater horror to see it in action.

The dark-haired Halo who decapitated Dione holds her shoulders high. "Nimuel, what are you doing?"

"He's possessed!" I shout, and Luna personally backslaps me.

"Get out of my husband or I'll end you too," she warns. June approaches her, and the Halo Knight grips the obsidian hilt of her bronze blade. "In another life," she vows, running her sword through her husband's heart, but not before June can step out of his body. The Halo Knight is too distracted by the horror she's committed, and Stanton rises and snaps her neck.

Hope was short-lived.

Ness guides me through the hall, and I gag as we avoid the blood and Dione's head. Luna doesn't seem particularly worried about Dione, and I wonder if she's ever actually seen her regrow her head or doesn't care that she's dead.

"Stay away," Kirk says from inside the vault. A generator whirs, and a dome of yellow energy surrounds him and the egg. June reaches a hand in, and she's thrown off her feet. "No one is getting through."

"We don't want to go inside," Luna says. "We'd like you to come out."

"This phoenix isn't yours to mutilate," Kirk says. I'm proud of him for standing his ground. "Enforcers will be here any minute."

Luna laughs. "We're standing in the blood of Halo Knights. Enforcers won't hold us for long."

"I only have to hold you back long enough for the Crowned Dreamer to go away."

"It's tempting to burn this entire museum and its rare collections to the ground," Luna says. "But the aftermath doesn't interest me. I have a proposal for you. I understand you're familiar with Emil. He's a promising specter, one who recently flew, a power neither Keon nor Bautista exhibited. I'll give you this scion to study for your own sciences, to write about in your own journals, in exchange for the phoenix."

Yeah, only Luna can mock me for being a nobody and still make me sound promising.

"Don't do it! You know she wants to kill the phoenix to become immortal!"

"Ridiculous theory," Luna says. "The purity of the phoenix is what's necessary for my health and will prove to be a marvel to the rest of the world should I succeed."

"But . . . the gala is ongoing, and the tickets . . ."

"Tell everyone the phoenix died. Refund everyone. There is more money to be made in the journals of a phoenix specter than a viewing party. This is a sign from the universe—the boy phoenix was under your nose all along. Unlock the answers you've always wanted. Creatures are going extinct, and you know specters are the next step of evolution."

Kirk looks curious. "And you don't want Gravesend for immortality?"

"Immortality is impossible. The greatest hope anyone can have is to live as Keon has relived. To exact the science of rebirthing and to maintain the memories through each cycle of life. I require the phoenix to attempt this." Luna pulls me by the chains around my wrists. "We've lessened his powers with an infinity-ender for the time being, and I trust you'll have your own methods to keep him grounded, to tame him like the phoenixes of your past."

Tears are forming in my eyes. I can't believe this is how I'm going to go down. "Kirk, this is insane! I'm a person, a human person!"

Kirk never looks me in the eye, and I know my fate.

"I always honor my word," Luna says.

"You said he was flying? Fascinating. I wonder if he can slip into previous lives or—"

Luna holds up a hand. "You can perform all the experiments you want. Do we have a deal?"

"Deal," Kirk says.

The shield comes down, and Kirk exits the vault with Gravesend's egg. Every step he takes, I'm surprised there isn't some head shot. He doesn't appear as disturbed by the dead bodies as I would expect, and who knows what other shadiness he's been up to in order to get where he is today.

Up close, the egg is truly beautiful and unlike any I've ever seen before. The shells we showcase are aged and spotted. This feathered egg has life inside of it and glows as if it's resting above a fireplace. I can hear Gravesend's song, a melody that's both beautiful and chaotic, like a bunch of keys in a piano that are all being played at once. I can sense that Gravesend isn't simply battle-hungry, but war-hungry. If Gravesend is given the chance to live, she could grow into a killing machine. The last thing the world needs is Luna walking around with this blood inside of her, escalating her violent instincts to dangerous new heights.

Ness pulls me back by the arm. "Where would you like him, Kirk?"

"The storage room down the hall, for the time being. I'll sedate him there."

"I'm a human, Kirk, come on!"

I know he isn't falling for any of Luna's lies. He's just doing what's best for himself.

Ness drags me. "Stay close, firefly. I'm going to get you out of here," he whispers.

There's an uneasiness in my stomach. I don't want to trust him, but hope ignites again when he relaxes his grip around my arm and his thumb brushes circles against my skin.

"Please, please get me out of here."

I don't care if begging makes me look stupid if he plays me again; I'll do whatever it takes to not be locked up in some cell or killed.

Stanton calls after Ness. "You passed the office."

Ness turns to me. "You said it was past this room. You lying, Emil?" Then quietly, he adds, "Make Stanton pay for everything he did to you and your brother."

I wait and listen to the song thrumming within me, fight past the pain that flares when I reach for the fire, and when Stanton is close enough, I hold up my hands and shoot fire-darts into his chest.

"Run!"

My wrists are still tied, but Ness carries the chains, and this is it, we're running up the steps. I guide us through the museum, leading us all the way to the Sunroom, where enforcers will be better equipped to protect us. My chest aches from using my power, my heart is speeding and my legs aren't strong enough, but adrenaline drives me through into the gala where countless guests are dressed up in outfits that are so fancy I'd probably punch a wall if I found out how much they cost. Spellwork explodes behind us, charge after charge. Winds lift us into the air, and Atlas is standing by the balcony, struggling to carry us over until he succeeds.

"He's good," I say, nodding at Ness. "I think."

"You look like hell," Atlas says.

"I'll be better now. Luna is downstairs and has the egg. Are you alone? Maribelle here?"

"She's here, and we're not alone."

Wesley is dashing into acolytes while Iris guides patrons to a safe escape. Maribelle is locked in combat, and Prudencia telekinetically snaps the suspended phoenixes down from the ceiling so they rain down on the people pursuing her.

And there's Brighton. He isn't holding a camera. He's armed with a wand.

THIRTY-SIX
WINDS

MARIBELLE

Where is she?

The gala guests are taking forever to clear the room, too busy tripping over each other's dress hems, and making it hard for me to track down June. There's no way she's sitting this one out. Luna's life's work is dependent on this phoenix.

Once I get my hands on her, I won't let her go.

I'm not messing around as I lay out acolytes left and right. I flip out of the way so an oncoming spell slams into an acolyte trying to sneak up on me with a dagger. One acolyte boldly swings at me, so I duck and rise with a scissor kick, breaking her nose. I carry another into the air and drop him through a display of different phoenix eggs. I'm sure someone is filming this, and it's all going to be used against me, but the world needs to know that someone as deadly and deathly as June exists. A barrage of spells presses me into a corner, hiding behind the stage with the massive screen intended to air the phoenix's birth. I peek, and the acolytes are rounding the stage any moment, and I can't float high enough to get above the screen to escape back to the other side. I'm about to call for Atlas or Wesley when I hear grunts and screams. I check for the damage with a pounding heart and see Brighton standing proudly with his wand outstretched.

"There she is," Brighton says, pointing his wand across the museum.

June.

I don't take my eyes off her as I call for Wesley. He appears by my side in moments. "June is at two o'clock. Grab her and don't let go."

He dashes away up the wall, and I take off into a hard run so she sees me coming, long enough to distract her. Atlas calls for me to watch my back, but that's what he and the others are here for. Glass shatters behind me, and I don't care, the target is June. Wesley's blur shoots down from the wall behind June, and he collides into her, his arms tightly wrapped around her as they roll across the floor. June's eyes glow as she tries escaping his grip, but it's no use.

"You're finished," I say as I grab her by the throat.

"Maribelle," Wesley says with concern.

"Go!"

She's all mine.

This girl possessed my mother and took my family away from me. There's no sign of fear in her eyes. There's still time.

I carry her into the air and slam her face-first onto the floor. I flip her over and lay into her. Punch for Mama. Punch for Papa. Punch for Finola. Punch for Konrad. Punch after punch for every celestial who's been blamed and hurt and locked up and killed because of the Blackout. The flesh on my knuckles is splitting open, and my glistening blood is mixing with hers. I don't even feel the pain. Having this assassin pinned under me and at my mercy is a surge of adrenaline like never before.

"Mari! Mari!" Atlas calls.

I keep my hand around June's throat as I turn, feeling her struggling underneath me. The Spell Walkers are being over-powered by spellwork. Emil is up on the balcony with Ness at his side and he's throwing fire-darts, but not at his usual speed or strength. Wesley is running around Stanton, doing his best to avoid that poisonous mist while also trying to get some hits in. Iris is fighting a six-armed Dione, whose neck is caked in blood. I finally find Atlas in the chaos, and he's bleeding from his left shoulder and right forearm, making it harder for him to use his power against the onslaught of acolytes.

I have to end June now, otherwise Atlas and I will never truly be safe. She will eventually find our haven and slice our throats in the middle of the night.

I get a chill, a warning, and then shake and scream as something sharp digs into my side—a piece of glass June grabbed off the floor from a shattered display. She twists the shard in me, and I lose my grip long enough for her to shove me off her. I lunge, but she's untouchable and staring up at me with her face masked in our blood.

June saunters toward me. She's not threatening. She can't hurt me unless she's corporeal, and I can't imagine this silent assassin is feeling good about round two. But she doesn't stop, and her eyes that glow like flickering eclipses come closer to mine until she vanishes from sight, and I become so cold it's like I'm naked in a freezing ocean.

My body doesn't feel like my own anymore. I stand without meaning to and take steps like I'm on autopilot. June has possessed me. I don't know if she can hear my screams. I'm panicking and suffocating inside my own body. I can feel the movement of every muscle, the floor underneath every step, but none of the decisions are mine. This is how helpless Mama must've felt, and out of all the experiences we dreamed about sharing together as mother and daughter, being occupied by a ghostly assassin wasn't on the list.

There is so much chaos. Luna is watching by the door with the phoenix egg, and I want to call for Wesley to snatch it and run far, far away, but he's dizzying Stanton. Atlas is hovering above the acolytes, dodging spellwork. He calls my name again, but this isn't me walking toward him, not really. June picks up a wand with my hand, and I can feel a faint hum against my palm—there's still enough charge in here for one spell. When June raises the wand, I expect to find it against my head—but to kill me, she'll have to kill us both.

I aim—no, June aims—the wand at Atlas and the winds carrying him vanish as the spell hits his heart.

THIRTY-SEVEN
DARK YELLOW

MARIBELLE

Atlas crashes through glass right as June falls out of my body. I don't bother with her as I run straight for Atlas. Iris is suddenly beside me, hurling acolytes far across the room. I push past the destroyed relics to reach Atlas. He has never been this still. I scoop up his neck.

"Atlas, Atlas. No, come on, my love." His eyes are half open, and blood is soaking up his shirt. "Please see me, please see me." I slip my hand underneath the vest that was too damaged to protect him and his heart isn't speaking to me. But this doesn't make sense, because this is Atlas and he has to be around because I wouldn't be alive without him and we're supposed to one day have kids who will fly through the air with us and we will live, live, live until we grow old.

I press my forehead against his and beg him to keep his promise. When that doesn't work, I scream in his face, and that doesn't wake him up either.

I shot him.

June made me.

My teeth clench, and I fight back this urge to vomit and my arms are shaking and a cold shiver runs down from my head to my heart. Then I'm warm like when I was sick in bed, always waiting on Mama's tea with honey, lemon, and garlic. The fights around me continue, and June staring me down sets me off. I rise and scream, and my body feels so hot I swear I'm inside the sun. There's pressure on my eyes, especially the left, and I hear a roar that comes out of nowhere. A ring of dark yellow fire explodes around me and collides into everyone twenty feet from me. I'm the last one standing.

Flames run up to my elbows.

How?

Everyone is looking up at me. Luna is watching me in awe by the exit when an acolyte takes her by surprise and punches her in the face. The acolyte snatches the egg and runs. He glows gray the closer he gets—Ness.

I don't care about the phoenix or the elixir. I look back at Atlas, lifeless, and I want to put this fire to use before it goes away. A flow of dark yellow flames blasts from my palm, but June sinks through the floor before it can reach her. Dione has already charged away and I'm lucky enough to strike Stanton down, even briefly, before they all reach Luna and flee.

The flames vanish, and I feel faint, the emptiest I've ever felt. I stumble back to Atlas and fall on top of him, cuddling against his chest, and even though he doesn't wrap his arm around me, I fall asleep.

THIRTY-EIGHT
ASHES

MARIBELLE

I met Atlas on the Brooklyn Bridge.

I was there with Iris to take down a trio of celestials who were threatening to kill everyone if enforcers didn't release their boss from the Bounds. It was a poetic moment for us since our parents were the reason their boss got locked up. But we were ambushed when people we believed to be potential victims in cars stepped out and began attacking us. We considered leaping into the East River, but we had to prove ourselves. One celestial was telekinetically pinning me to a wall and preparing to launch a dagger into my heart. He would have succeeded if Atlas hadn't dropped from the sky and blasted him off the bridge. I recognized him from his attention-thirsty Instagram account, but in person, Atlas was dedicated to the mission. Same for Wesley, who was carrying people away from the action at an exhausting speed. Then a celestial was about to strike Atlas out of the air, and I drop-kicked him into a car's windshield. He thanked me for saving his life, and I called it even.

Then tonight when he needed me to back him up, I killed him.

I've stayed in our room for an extra hour by myself, punching holes in the wall and screaming and crying into the pillow that smells of him. I want him in bed with me, to feel the world roll off my shoulders as he embraces me for the night, like we're the only people in the world.

Mama and Papa were bold with how they wore their hearts on their sleeves when out saving the world that hated them. It inspired me growing up. Even after the Blackout, I was still determined to fall in love and fight for it. But I shouldn't have said anything. June could've killed anyone, but she targeted Atlas to destroy me. At least my parents died together.

I wander the halls and find everyone in the boardroom. Wesley is balled up against the wall and sobbing; he even kicks at the floor. Emil, Brighton, and Prudencia are sitting around the egg, and they freeze when they see me. Eva is massaging circles into Iris's back. Iris is in her own daze.

"Where is Atlas?" I ask.

"Maribelle, I'm so sorry," Eva says. "There's nothing I—"

"I know you can't heal him. Where is he?"

"Downstairs in Wesley's room."

I'm running hot again, and if I can't control myself, that mysterious ring of fire might kill everyone in this room. Seems appropriate since I'm truly a killer now. The boy I love more than anyone else is gone because of me.

"What's wrong with me?" Atlas isn't here to calm me down. "I'm heating up."

"Power advancement?" Eva says.

"I can levitate. Flying higher and further would be a development."

"You sure your parents didn't have fire-casting in their bloodlines?" Brighton asks.

Everyone keeps speculating except Iris.

"You know something," I say as I approach her.

She refuses to make eye contact. "No one knew . . . no one thought this would happen. My parents believed your power had advanced as far as it could. It just came so late, and your blood glistens, and you've shown no other signs of being . . ."

"Being what?"

"A specter," Iris says. "This is phoenix fire, Maribelle. It just surfaced differently than Emil's. Flight before fire."

I'm going to blow this building to the ground. "How do you know all of this?"

"I was told everything in confidence. The fact that you're experiencing both sets of powers is exceptional, especially since . . . especially since Bautista didn't. He only possessed phoenix fire."

"What the hell does Bautista have to do with me?"

"No way!" Brighton's hands fly to his mouth.

"Lestor and Aurora raised you," Iris says. "They're your parents, but—"

"Save it, Iris, I don't care about your secret intel. I'm a Lucero. End of story."

"You're Bautista and Sera's daughter, Maribelle. To our knowledge, you're the first child born from a specter and celestial."

No one says anything. Even Wesley stops sobbing and stares in confusion. Emil is the only other person in this room who has a sense of what I'm going through, and even then, our experiences are different. His past life is my biological father. I have no idea when Mama and Papa decided to raise me as their own or how that even unfolded. Was that Bautista and Sera's idea? Finola and Konrad's? Why didn't anyone tell me? Why was this a secret?

The question that pains me: "Who else knows?"

"No one," Iris says.

Even Eva is shaking her head. "Iris, how could you not tell her? This wasn't some intel like before. This is her family."

"I was sworn to secrecy! Maribelle, I didn't want to disturb your history. That wasn't my place."

"The hell it wasn't! You were the only person who knew!

Atlas died without ever knowing the real me. I could've died never knowing the real me!"

"My job was to protect you. It's what Lestor and Aurora wanted."

"Don't you dare use their memory against me!" Everything suddenly makes sense about why Iris would keep up this lie. "Oh my stars, no wonder you kept it all a secret. You thought that if I knew that I came from Bautista and Sera, then I would take over as leader of the group."

Iris pops up from her seat and slams her fist on the table so hard that it caves in. "You have never once tried to make this impossible job any easier! You were my best friend, you were like a sister to me, yet all you do is come down on me when something goes wrong, and you never credit me when I get us a win. I have sacrificed my life to lead this group." I can't remember the last time I saw Iris crying. "You don't care about my pain because you think I'm unbreakable, that I'm strong enough to carry everyone on my shoulders. News flash, Maribelle, I've been heartbroken since the Blackout too. Thanks for asking."

I turn my back on her. I'll never forgive her. I sit beside Wesley and try to understand my life. I'm a celestial and a specter—it's possible after all. The levitation isn't an extension of Mama and Papa's flight. Are their powers the reason they were chosen to raise me? To trick me? If my powers are coming from Bautista, then what do I get from Sera? She had powerful visions, and I have . . . I have good instincts. Intuition when the going gets tough in battle. The dream and sickening gut feeling I had before Mama and Papa left me for the last time—I knew they weren't going to come back. It wasn't paranoia, it was a warning.

I could've prevented the Blackout if I'd understood and nurtured my power.

"What do we do now?" Brighton asks with some take-charge spirit. "We have a building full of celestials who need to be more involved. I can—"

"You're not doing anything, Bright," Emil says.

"You don't speak for me," Brighton says with a fire that's missing around here.

"We've got Gravesend's egg. We won. Luna is screwed."

"This isn't what victory looks like."

"We have been tortured. We're lucky to be alive. Time to call it quits."

"Then you can stay out of it. We'll stop Luna without you."

"You cannot come on any more missions," Iris says. "We just lost one of our best celestials—one of our best friends. Atlas was powerful and good, and now he's dead. If we couldn't bring him home alive, we can't guarantee your protection. It's too big a risk, and if you hop in one of our cars again, I will throw you out myself."

Brighton's face is red. "First I'm not worth a rescue mission. Now I can't enlist in this war because I might die? You're not safe just because spellwork can bounce off your skin. Wesley isn't so quick that he hasn't been hit. I've seen more action than Eva."

"Brighton, enough," Prudencia says. "Be with your family. Be with me. No more blood should be lost."

"I'm not turning my back on everyone," Brighton says. "But good on you all for being able to do so."

He leaves.

Iris approaches Wesley. "We need to relocate everyone. It's too dangerous."

I'm energized by Brighton's fire, and I stand. "Don't worry about the Blood Casters. I'm going to get to them first. Take care of June and the others for good."

"Spell Walkers don't kill," Iris says. "Can we at least see eye to eye on that?"

"You all don't kill. But I will." I get up and head for the door. "I quit."

My first thought when I see Atlas underneath the blanket is that he must not be able to breathe. I pull back the blanket, and I'm frozen for seconds before the sobs burst out of me. Too many memories rush through me, like the date I planned for him on Nova's rooftop and whenever we showered together and when I kissed him for the first time and whenever he made me laugh so hard that I forgot all my pain. He became my home, and now I don't know where to go.

Before I leave Nova, I have to take care of him.

I step out to grab rags and water and find Emil sitting in the hallway. I keep walking, but he follows me.

"I get what you're going through—the family thing. If you want to talk—"

"That has no effect on me," I interrupt. "You're not my father."

"I know I'm not. Definitely not trying to pull that card. It's so . . . bizarre. But I know what it's like to go through something life changing and discover your parents didn't give birth to you. It's not the same thing at all, I know, but it doesn't have to be so lonely."

I spin around and get in his face. He backs up with teary eyes. "I'm not interested in some support group, especially not with you. If you had held on to June like I asked you to, she would be dead instead of Atlas."

"I'm sorry—"

"Will Ness know where June is?"

"He said the gang routinely moves around. They won't be in any of their usual spots now that he's betrayed them."

Just my luck.

"Maribelle, I'm seriously sorry, and I—"

"It's great that you're done with this fight. You don't belong here. But before you go, tell Wesley to come see me. No one else."

The Spell Walkers have fallen apart, and I don't care. I'm a one-woman army.

I go to the bathroom and return to Atlas with a bucket, water, and rags. I wash the blood and debris from his face, apologizing over and over. Wesley arrives and offers to help, and I don't fight him.

"He wanted to be cremated," I say. "Say your goodbyes while I pack my bag."

"Mari, don't—"

"He's the only one who could call me that."

I don't take my time in our room. Atlas was my home—wherever he was, that's where I felt happiest and safest. I throw everything that matters into the duffel bag—the star-touched wine Atlas gifted me, Papa's binoculars, Mama's reading glasses, and the daggers I will drive into June. When I return downstairs, Wesley and I carry Atlas out to the playground and lay his body on top of a stretch of glass.

"What if he didn't see June possess me?" This question will haunt me until we're reunited. "What if all Atlas saw was me pointing a wand at him and firing a spell? He wouldn't even have had time to think about it. It was all so fast, Wes. I hate that it was so quick that he didn't have time to register that it wasn't me, and I hate that I'm upset that his death was swift."

"He knew you loved him," Wesley says.

"He would be alive if I didn't."

Wesley stays quiet. It's true.

"I'm technically the one who killed him, so I should be able to bring back his ghost. But only after I've killed June. Then I can send him to rest in true peace."

"I want to be there if you'll let me."

I nod.

"I'll see you soon, Atlas."

I call for my power, focusing on getting vengeance on June, and I close my eyes once the dark yellow flames enshroud Atlas's body. I won't leave him, but I can't watch. For an hour, I sit with my back to Atlas's body, crying against Wesley as we breathe in charcoal and other odors. Then, when Atlas's body is gone, I empty the bottle of star-touched wine in a dying plant. I scoop up Atlas's ashes with a gardening shovel and pour as much as can fit of him into the bottle and I pray to the mightiest of constellations it will be enough to summon him back for a proper goodbye.

"When will I see you again?"

"I'm sure our paths will cross. Take care of your family, Wes."

"Be safe, Maribelle."

I head for the parking lot with the bottle of ashes close to my chest. Being a Spell Walker, I didn't always want to save everyone. Too many people hated me so fiercely, but now, I'm sure of my calling. Pure vengeance.

Out by Atlas's car, Brighton is waiting by the driver's seat with his laptop under his arm and backpack over his shoulder. "Do you need some company?" he asks. "I'll do whatever it takes. I'm not like Emil. I won't hold you back."

I nod.

"Let's go. We have a ghost to kill."

THIRTY-NINE
FIREFLY

EMIL

Tonight has been beyond miserable. I'm carrying Gravesend's egg, feeling torn between who needs me the most—do I sit with the group, make things right with Brighton, help Ma and Prudencia pack? I need a break from it all, so I go to the person who isn't expecting anything from me. Ness didn't think it was appropriate to be with everyone in the boardroom while we were grieving and strategizing, so I set him up in an old art supplies room. Not a huge upgrade from the closet he was camping out in before, but at least this one has better lighting and smells of paints and paper. He's staring out the open window, breathing in that fresh air.

I'm still not sure what's what between us, but for now, he

saved me and got the egg from Luna. That's enough of a spark for trust.

"Everything okay?" Ness asks. "That's a stupid question, isn't it?"

I sit in the center of the room, admiring Gravesend's feathered blue egg as I catch up Ness on everything that's gone down since we split two hours ago. Eva failed to heal the wounds inflicted by the infinity-ender blade—inflicted by him. I tensely sat between Brighton and Prudencia as Maribelle discovered the true source of her power. Brighton flipped on all of us, and I haven't seen him around since. Then Maribelle rightfully blamed me for Atlas's death. I don't know how I would live with myself if I helped her murder someone, but it would feel a lot easier knowing an assassin was dead instead of a hero.

"Will painting you a picture help?" Ness asks.

"Can you paint?"

"Technically, yeah. It won't be good, though."

It's a lovely gesture, something I would treasure no matter the quality, but it doesn't feel right to have a painting party when people are panicking as they wrap up their lives so we can evacuate as soon as possible.

"Maybe another time," I say.

"Can I explain myself instead?"

He keeps his distance, which should make me feel safer, but I'm thrown over how lonely I feel, like we're both stars in the sky that aren't close enough to shine brightly together.

"I didn't want to leave Nova, but you were so ready to risk everything for Brighton. You were ridiculously kind to me, and I had to repay that. But when we were on that roof and Stanton had us cornered, I had to grab the reins."

"So you laid me out with the urn," I say. "Then Luna made you cut into me."

"No, she didn't make me," Ness says. "She was furious because I exposed her cemetery plans. I had to convince her I was double-crossing you, and since she wanted to punish you, I volunteered to prove my loyalty to her. It pained me, but it was the only way I could make the best of a horrific situation. Dione wouldn't have been careful. June would've shown no mercy. Stanton would've gone too far and possibly killed you." He can't look me in the eye. "She believed me."

"I believed you too," I say. He would've made a great actor in another life.

"Did Eva clean your wounds?"

"No. Between Atlas and how worn out she was from trying to heal me, I didn't ask for more help. I should be good."

Ness opens a drawer and pulls out an apron, cutting it up and running the sink. "Take off your shirt. I'll help you."

"It's okay."

"You have to wash it. Come on." He squints. "What's the problem?"

I fidget with the sleeve of my baggy shirt. "I'm not used to someone who looks like you asking me to remove my shirt."

"Someone who looks like me?"

"Your face is solid and you're no doubt on top of the rest of your body too."

"You trying to call me cute and fit?" Ness asks with the hint of a smile.

"In my own words."

"Look, you're sweet, but I don't live in the gym." Before I can stop him, he removes his shirt and presents himself like I shouldn't be impressed with his toned chest and build. "It's not that serious. Believe me, when I first got my powers, I saw dozens of different versions of myself, but I like who I am."

"Of course you do. I would morph into you if I could."

"That's sweeter." Ness pulls his shirt back on. "Your face is solid too, firefly. I'm sure the same goes for the rest of your body."

I'm running hot. I know he's not into me—no one has time for that anyway—but it's hard to believe him when no one else has ever been able to convince me of this. Smart money is on Ness lying so he can help me and ease his guilt over these scars that I'll have for the rest of my life.

I tell him why I always wear baggy shirts. My body is either too skinny or not skinny enough. Never enough muscle. But it's always easier to hide inside shirts where no one can figure out what my body looks like. I used to wear tank tops at the beach, even to go in the water, which always led to chafing, but seeing everyone with their six-packs stopped me from going altogether. I was always promising myself that every summer was going to be the summer I could finally walk shirtless and feel desired and accepted. Then there are all the guys on Instagram whose bodies I zoom in on, and when they post their exercise routines I try them out and deprive myself of any sweets because my joy isn't worth being ignored.

"Even the Spell Walker gig makes this impossible," I add with tears in my eyes as Ness sits across from me on the floor. "Everyone has their idea of what heroes should look like, and that's not me."

"You're really not kidding, are you?" Ness asks.

"I don't need you to tell me how skinny or strong I am, I get it, but it's this voice in my head that—"

"That needs to shut up," Ness interrupts.

"I don't think I'll ever feel good about myself. I could have the six-pack and the V-cut and people saying they want me, but I will never feel beautiful enough for everyone in the world."

"You should only feel beautiful to yourself," Ness says. "And only be with someone who gets that you're beautiful because of who you are. Look, firefly, the first night I saw you I almost broke concentration and morphed back into myself. Make of that what you will." He blushes, which is wild, but if anyone can fake that, it's a shape-shifter. "I shouldn't have pushed. But you really should clean your wounds. Get your brother or mother to help you. It doesn't have to be me."

I stand. "Do you promise not to comment on my body?"

"Of course. If it makes you feel more comfortable, I can close my eyes?"

"Let's try that."

We go by the sink, where he wets the rag and closes his eyes. I lift my shirt, immediately puffing out my chest, an instinct that's been burned into me from locker rooms and the rare instances when I changed in front of friends. I guide Ness's finger to the cut on my forearm, and he's gentle, but presses down more when he's worried it's not properly cleaning the area. Then I watch his face when I direct him to my ribs, wondering if he's going to cringe in any way over how bony I feel, but he remains as focused as anyone can be with their eyes closed. He asks if he can put his hand on my lower back to better anchor himself, and I say yes, and the sensations burning through me still take me by surprise. I bite down on my lip when he applies too much pressure on my rib cage and he apologizes. The tip of my hair rests on his curls as he washes the last cut on my left arm.

"Should I keep going?" Ness asks.

"All good," I say, even though I'm not ready for him to back up.

"Let me know when I can open my eyes."

I'm tempted to tell him now, but if his face betrays his words, this memory will be stained, and I'll never believe anyone again when they call me beautiful. I put my shirt back on.

"Thanks, Ness."

He still doesn't look at me. "I'll never forgive myself for putting you through that. I'm sorry."

"You got me out of there and got us Gravesend. We're good."

"Speaking of," he says, finally opening his eyes and pointing at Gravesend's egg. "You got to handle that."

"Don't tell me to kill her. We just have to wait out this constellation."

"Your best bet right now is that the Casters won't feel good about storming into a place where you'll have home field advantage. But one mistake costs us everything, so you have to get that egg far away from here."

"We're working on it. You should come with us," I say. It's going to take Brighton, Prudencia, and Ma a minute before they trust Ness, but they'll have to get over it because we all need fresh starts, second chances. "We're going to be hiding too."

"But everyone is going to be looking for you. Fire-Wing," Ness says. It's another reason to hate how famous I've become. "If it wasn't so risky, it would be really hard to turn down that invite. But it's for the best. I should figure out my own path. If there was ever a time to run and start over, it's when Luna is focused on tracking down that egg before the Crowned Dreamer goes away. I have to discover who I am outside of the Senator's watch, outside of my debt to the Casters."

He's never been able to make his own choices. I respect this one especially. "You've got to protect yourself. I hope you don't have to hide the rest of your life."

"Pray to the stars that Luna and the Senator die sooner rather than later."

I wonder who has to die before I can come out and live my life in peace.

"I should get going before it gets too dark," Ness says.

I don't know what else to say to him. When he closes the space between us, good nerves explode within me. I almost even get my lips ready. But when he pulls me into a hug, I'm not disappointed. A kiss would've made me feel wanted, but that's not what this is. Right now, I feel comforted for the dark times ahead. Figuring out a new home, making peace with quitting this war, raising Gravesend with no experience. I rest my chin on Ness's shoulder. Our ears brush, and I strangely wish I could somehow listen in on his thoughts to see if I'll be on his mind too when he leaves.

When the hug breaks, my gaze doesn't leave the floor.

"I hope you find yourself," I say.

"I hope you pop up again, firefly," Ness says, and the door clicks behind him.

FORTY
TRUE COLORS

NESS

Before I leave the illusion's perimeter, I morph into a white man so no one will bother me. Every step away from Nova is terrifying, but I don't let that show. I maintain this guise that I'm someone with a great life who's simply out for a late-night stroll. No one will suspect this man is thinking about fleeing to the Dominican Republic where his mother was born, so he can connect with roots that the Senator didn't encourage growing up. To get far away from everyone who ruined his life in this city.

Maybe when I'm older and the world has completely forgotten me, I can exist in the world again without a morph. Some people I pass on the street may question why I look so familiar, but no one is going to make the connection that I'm that kid they believed died in the Blackout.

I'm about to ask someone for directions when sirens approach. Cars clear a path, and enforcer tanks speed past me. They park, and a young man steps out. He pokes at the air with a glowing hand before yanking his entire arm back, like someone pulling a tablecloth out from underneath a dinner setting. There's a massive flash that funnels away, and I can see everything—the empty gas station, and ahead, Nova.

The celestial broke the illusion.

The tanks speed toward the school, and I don't understand how celestials can turn their back on their own kind. But who am I if I turn my back on Emil and the Spell Walkers when they may need me the most?

FORTY-ONE
GRAVESEND

EMIL

On the way to pack, I wish I had more than scars and memories to remember Ness by. I should've taken him up on that amateur art. Maybe he would've painted two boys sitting closely together on the floor. But after seeing how Atlas was used against Maribelle, maybe it's best if we don't let anyone get to know our hearts.

I enter the room and almost bump into Prudencia.

"I was about to come find you," she says. "You okay?"

"Yeah, I was . . . I was seeing Ness out."

Ma is on my air mattress beside a stuffed duffel bag, and she stops folding a shirt. "He left?"

I nod. "How are you two?"

"We're done," Prudencia says. "But Brighton's stuff isn't here. No clothes, no bag, no laptop."

He's probably camping out in someone else's room. "I'll go find him."

I put down the egg, and it glows brighter than before and begins hatching.

"It's happening!"

The room gets warm. I can't believe I'm about to witness the birth of a phoenix—especially a century phoenix. Brighton should be here for this once-in-a-lifetime experience, getting it on camera like I always wanted for him, but there's no time to find him. The shell cracks on one side and within seconds, a bronze beak is hammering away, yawning a song of chaos. Then Gravesend breaks free from her egg with her crown of midnight-blue feathers and eyes as big and shiny as marbles.

"What a beauty," I say as I scoop her up in one of my shirts. She's as light and soft as a bouquet of flowers. Her war-hungry cries grow louder and louder as she squirms around my arms with one wing shielding her eyes from the light.

"She needs to be fed," Ma says.

"Good luck making Gravesend vegan," Prudencia says.

"Challenge accepted," I joke, even though I know it's not in her breed's nature to eat anything but other animals. "I'll see if there's anything left in the kitchen and—"

Gravesend squirms more viciously, and her song chills my bones like when I'm walking through a bad neighborhood and can see shady characters watching me.

Then spellwork and screams echo in the hallway.

The Blood Casters are here for Gravesend.

"Turn off the lights and lock the door," Ma says.

Was Gravesend warning us?

"We can't stay here. Gravesend is too loud. Pru, get Ma somewhere safe."

"You're coming with us," Prudencia says.

"I have to find Brighton."

I can't believe I'm doing this to Ma again, I can feel her heart breaking every time, but I'm not leaving without my brother. I peek out into the hallway, and a familiar blur is moving door to door, banging on each one.

Wesley appears before us, sweating and panting. "Enforcers. Enforcers are here. Get to the back and go past the fence. Cars will be waiting on the other side."

"How did they—"

Wesley dashes off. How they found us doesn't matter right now.

I hug Ma and Prudencia and tell them I'll see them soon, then I run with Gravesend in my arms before they can stop me. I go for the roof first, shuddering whenever spellwork explodes, shaking the floors. I shout for Brighton, but he's not up here. Over the ledge, I see six enforcer tanks parked by the front entrance. I rest Gravesend in the corner of the roof, praying to the stars this will be the safest spot to leave her while I hunt down Brighton. I kiss her forehead and rush back down. Her cries follow me the whole way.

The halls are crowded. In the chaos, I see an enforcer kick down one door. Then there's a whistle, and the enforcer falls asleep on the spot, allowing that celestial Zachary and an elderly woman to escape. I burst into rooms, calling Brighton's name and ushering stragglers out. I round the stairs when an enforcer hurls a citrine gem-grenade at me, and I'm quick and precise with a fire-dart. The grenade explodes midair, and the shock wave blasts the enforcer down the stairs. My wounds burn when I use my power, but I have to fight through it. I run to the lower level to find Eva healing that girl Grace, the one whose loud voice Maribelle hoped to use for security—like tonight. Once the colorful lights close the hole in Grace's stomach, I guide them into an empty classroom.

"Eva, what's going on?" I ask.

"They broke in. They must've gotten through our defenses, and our evacuation plans have all gone to hell without Atlas and Maribelle. I haven't seen Iris. . . ."

"Wesley said there are cars in back, beyond the fence. Go there. I'll send Iris your way if I find her."

I can't imagine Brighton would be in the music room right by the entrance, but if enforcers or anyone got their hands on him, maybe there will be some evidence that he was there in the first place, like his laptop or clothes. I cross paths with a duo of enforcers, dodging their spells that explode against the lockers behind me. Fire-darts take them out and I make it to the room. Everything is wrecked—sheet stands have fallen on their sides, holes have been blown through drums, and the piano has folded in on itself. But no sign of Brighton.

Where the hell is he?

I move for the back door that leads to the auditorium's stage when someone shouts for me to freeze. I don't know if it's one enforcer or half a dozen, but I don't move.

This is it for me. I hope Brighton is okay, that Prudencia and Ma escaped, that Ness got far away, that the Spell Walkers win, that I won't be reborn into a world where Luna and the Blood Casters are living forever.

I brace myself when I hear a spell discharge. An enforcer blasts past me and slams into the wall, unconscious. I turn around to see my savior, expecting Iris, but it's another enforcer who's very muscular and taking deep breaths as gray light transforms him.

Ness.

"You're back," I breathe, and I feel so energized and strong, like I could fight every day for the rest of my life.

"I saw the tanks. I wasn't fast enough to warn you, but I had to help."

I crash into him with a hug and squeeze hard because everything is going wrong and he came back for me. "Brighton's missing, and Gravesend is alive and crying on the roof, and I can't do this alone."

"I'm here. Let's find your brother, grab Gravesend, and get the hell out of here."

We run through the auditorium, where two celestials are dead onstage. Ness drags me away, reminding me to focus as if forgetting dead bodies is easy to put out of my mind. The celestials here are trying to live, even if that means holing themselves up in an abandoned school so they won't be treated as threats to society. At the entrance to the cafeteria, Iris is deflecting spells with her fists as Eva guides a dozen familiar faces out the back. She's alive and they found each other. Between Ness popping back up like he's the firefly, I have hope for Brighton.

"Maybe he left already," Ness says.

If Brighton and I were living that ultimate Reys of Light dream where we were unstoppable and had unlimited powers, we could reach out to each other telepathically to let each other know we're good, that we're alive, that we're sorry for letting this war get in the way of our brotherhood. But since we can't, I have to do this the painfully slow way and search room by room, even as this building is being blown apart by spells and gem-grenades.

Everything on the first floor is a bust and we're doing one last sweep through the second when three enforcers pop out of Ness's old supplies closet.

"There he is!"

I blast the ceiling lamps to slow them down and while we're

cloaked in darkness, we sneak into a classroom.

"I have an idea." Ness takes a deep breath and begins morphing—his brown skin goes pale, he inches a little taller, his hair becomes curlier, and his face becomes mine.

"No."

"They want you, right?" he asks, his voice unchanging. "I'll lead them away from you while you check the last couple of rooms. But if Brighton isn't here, you have to grab Gravesend and leave. Promise me."

"No, this won't work, I—"

"Promise me, firefly!"

I put my face in my hands as terror squeezes me and I nod a promise.

Doors are being kicked down nearby, and watching Ness boldly run while wearing my face feels a lot like watching myself being so unlike myself in Brighton's videos. Spells light up the hallway as they pursue Ness and when the coast is clear, I check the remaining classrooms and closets, but Brighton isn't here. Gravesend's song has only gotten louder in these emptied halls and a figure steps out of the darkness—June.

Her face is bruised and covered in dried blood. She looks to the roof.

No.

I run, but she's faster, fading in and out several feet at a time. She's inches from me on the way up the steps, but when I lunge, she's gone, and I fall hard on my chest. I force myself back up, and when I reach the roof, Gravesend is inside June's arms. I run so fast I almost trip over myself, I have to get ahold of her, but June sinks through the floor, and Gravesend's cries vanish.

"NO!"

I hold myself up by the ledge, and that's when I see enforcers carrying Ness—unconscious and with no glamour. They load him into the back of an armored truck, and once it takes off, all the enforcers return to their tanks and follow, even though they never got me.

Except maybe they were never here for me. Maybe it's Ness they wanted all along.

I don't know how they knew he's alive, but between losing him and Gravesend and not knowing where the hell Brighton is, I feel so lost.

My fiery gray and gold wings burst into life, painfully, and I leap over the edge, praying to the Crowned Dreamer above that my brother will be home waiting for me.

FORTY-TWO
EDUARDO IRON

NESS

I don't feel right when I wake up.

This room is unfamiliar, but it's not tough to figure out I'm on a boat—a life jacket sits in a corner, framed pictures of an anchor line the cabin's wall, the floor is wobbling, and the smell of salt water fills the small space. I just don't know whose boat.

My lower back stings from the enforcer's stunning spell. Someone left me on the floor even though there's a perfectly fine white leather couch. I get up and immediately topple over, banging into the floor and shouting. The door opens. There's time to morph, but there's no point. The owner of this boat knows who I am. I don't have much in the way of weapons, but I grab a marine biology textbook off the shelf because it's a lot heavier than my fist. My grip loosens immediately when the light catches the man's face.

The Senator. His suit is crisp, and his black hair is slicked back, and I never understood how someone who devotes so much energy to hating celestials can find the time for all this maintenance. But he always did say that appearances are everything.

"You're supposed to be dead," the Senator says, adjusting his glasses. He's not even looking me in the eye.

"You're supposed to be happy I'm alive."

The Senator reviews the remaining books on the shelf. "Yes, well, unfortunately your life puts me in a tricky situation this close to the election."

"Are you serious?"

"Quite. I've put years into this campaign."

"More years spent on politics than parenting, that's for sure."

"Only one of those paths was truly intentional, Eduardo."

I cannot believe I come from this monster. "Why haven't you killed me?"

"Believe me, the thought has crossed my mind." The Senator pulls bourbon out of the mini fridge and pours himself a drink. "Certainly wouldn't be the first time I tried."

It's as if he's thrown me overboard and is watching me drown. "That wasn't you. . . . Luna was responsible for the Blackout."

"We were united by a common enemy. The growing support for the Spell Walkers negated everything my campaign stood for. Not ideal when you're running against a celestial candidate. In exchange for my staying out of her affairs, Luna and I reached an agreement to eliminate the Spell Walkers."

There's no one in the world who truly knows the Senator or Luna. I was raised under his roof. I trusted Luna when she put shifter blood in me. Neither loved me.

"But why me?"

"Come on, Eduardo, you're smarter than this. I certainly paid for higher education, at least. The support I gained from your death was immeasurable. The grieving father who wanted justice for his son's death? Especially after losing his wife years before to more celestial violence? Hello, White House."

The Senator's smile fools the world, but I see him for who he really is.

I charge straight at him, and his fist catches me between the eyes. I'm seeing stars from the floor when his foot connects hard into my side, over and over. This is the person I feared so much that I risked death, hoping it would give me the power to hide from him. Someone who punches his son after telling him he coordinated his murder in the name of his own political agenda.

"You're a heartless monster."

"Monster? You're the one with unnatural blood. Luna is

crafty. It wasn't in our agreement to let you live, but I sup-
pose she took her precautionary measures in case I stepped out
of line and interfered with her dealings. Exposing you to the
world would've been my downfall. You must've pissed her off
significantly for her to reach out to let me know that you were
alive, knowing that I would send my guys to go collect you."

That chaos was because of me.

Did Emil get out alive?

"What do you want from me?"

"Your power could be very valuable to me. Impersonate
Congresswoman Sunstar and her committee and help me tank
her support. Then, after I've secured the presidency, we can
bring you back to life, but keep your powers discreet. There
will be plenty of opportunities to use them during my terms."

"I'll never help you," I say.

"Maybe some time in the Bounds will change your mind."

That's where we're headed. We're crossing the river to get
to the New York Bounds, where some of the toughest of celestials are locked up. Where they kill each other for survival and
sport.

"I'll expose you! Word will get out that your entire campaign is a lie!"

"You'll tell your fellow prisoners that you're the son of the
man whose policies are the reasons they're behind bars? Best
of luck surviving that. Eduardo, your time to reveal your truth

has long passed. But I'm being fair and giving you the option to either help me win this election or fight for your life in the Bounds." The Senator has no false smiles for me. "I need an answer fast. Who are you going to be?"

FORTY-THREE

SHINING BRIGHT

BRIGHTON

I turn away from my laptop and stare at the Crowned Dreamer from outside my window.

So much has changed since the constellation first returned to the sky. I was getting ready to leave for college. Emil and I were powerless together. But now the stars are shining their brightest before vanishing by morning, and Maribelle Lucero is sitting on my bed after the most game-changing month of my life. I'm famous; I have purpose. I've proven time and time again that Emil might be the one with powers, but I'm still powerful.

Maribelle is honoring Atlas with Instagram posts—my idea. She had the password to his account and decided she wanted to post three photos: Atlas's first day in New York, in front of a map that inspired his name; a selfie of Atlas and Maribelle during some rooftop date that was too hard for her to talk about; and the last of Atlas sleeping with a smile on his face. She doesn't speak to me when writing out her last caption, or any before, but after this, we're hitting the streets to find any leads on Luna's whereabouts. Wherever Luna is, June won't be far.

"Done," Maribelle says, pocketing her phone.

She's paying no mind to all the geeky Spell Walker stuff I have around the room, including the art print I have of her. Her eyes glow like sailing comets, but one is brighter than the other, as dark yellow flames burst between her palms. Maribelle's fire sounds different from Emil's—less of a screech and more of a roar. She has a greater handle on hers too. Let's see how Emil likes that.

"Let's go kill June," she says.

"You got it, Infinity Daughter."

She's not amused.

I still can't believe everything about Maribelle's true lineage. I thought we covered this ground already with Emil, but of course his own story is so huge that it involves a Spell Walker I've admired for years.

I'm about to close my laptop when a news notification pops up.

"Nova was attacked," I say. The school was infiltrated by

enforcers, and celestials were taken into custody. There's a warning for everyone to stay inside and wait out the constellation, as authorities believe the night will bring more chaos as celestials ride the high of the Crowned Dreamer. "Eight deaths have been confirmed. Give me your phone."

I lost mine in the cemetery. I don't know anyone's number but Emil's and Ma's—they were drilled into me when Dad was sick—and both their lines go straight to voicemail. But I can't assume the worst. There's a million reasons why they wouldn't have their phones—they left them behind, they didn't keep up with charging them since everyone they needed was under the same roof.

"This has to be Luna," Maribelle says. "She didn't make her move until we had something of hers that she couldn't get without help."

"What's our move?"

"We head for the church. Let's count on Luna having the phoenix. She'll have her entire gang backing her up too. We go hit them with everything we've got before they become unhittable."

"Emil is still alive," I say. The blood-and-bones feeling won't let me believe anything else. "He'll be there too."

"If anyone gets in our way, we strike them down. Got it?"

I nod. "I want to be a better soldier for you," I say.

"I'm listening."

Everything is a long shot—stopping Luna, killing June, getting out of the church alive, my big plan to put an end to all the insanity we've faced—but we leave the apartment with a dangerous amount of hope anyway, because the odds being unlikely don't make them impossible.

FORTY-FOUR
THE CROWNED DREAMER

EMIL

When will this end?

Phoenixes endure endless cycles of life and death, but I'm done being the Infinity Son.

I come home to an empty apartment that's straight wrecked. Brighton isn't here, and I'm out of ideas. If he decided to take off to Los Angeles and focus on school and start over and never talk to me again, I could make peace with that—as long as he's alive. I go in our bedroom, which smells like someone lit a match, and I collapse onto his bed and cry into his pillow because he might be dead, and there's no way Ma is going to survive her eldest dying, especially so soon after Dad.

Why did I have to be reborn into this?

When the pain becomes too much, I get out of bed. I go into Brighton's drawer and grab one of his favorite shirts that he must've missed when packing. Brighton was always going to stick his nose where it doesn't belong, but I didn't have to engage with this war. I drag myself to the bathroom to touch up my blazing wounds. I remove the baggy shirt in front of the mirror, and, to honor Ness, I keep my eyes on the body he claims is beautiful.

I shouldn't have involved him either.

Everyone I touch burns.

I press down hard with gauze, cleaning up the blood, and fix new bandages across my cuts. I pull on Brighton's white shirt with the minimalistic camera design over the pocket. The shirt is fitted, way snugger than anything I've allowed myself to wear in years. I'm going to rock it like armor.

The lock on the front door twists, but there are no keys jingling from outside.

I fight past the pain to conjure a fire-orb, but it's Prudencia entering with Iris and Wesley. I slam into her with a hug. Prudencia takes me to the couch and tells me everything. Ma and Eva are on their way to the shelter in Philadelphia where Ruth will watch over them. Other celestials have been spread out everywhere with short trips to New Jersey and longer journeys to Ohio. There's no sign of Brighton or Maribelle, but I have hope that maybe they're together when they tell me Maribelle recently uploaded some tributes to Atlas on his Instagram; that sounds like Brighton's doing. I tell them about Ness being exposed and taken captive.

Wesley stares at the constellation through the window. "We need to stop Luna. She's the heart of all this pain."

"We don't stand a chance," I say. "Four against however many acolytes and Blood Casters will be there. And Pru and I didn't grow up using our powers."

"Everyone gets a boost, but the Crowned Dreamer is on the side of celestials above all," Iris says. "Wesley will be faster, and I will be stronger, and Prudencia will be more powerful. We're not as outmatched as you think."

"Maybe it's time we turn it over to the authorities," I say. "Get the enforcers to take out Luna."

"They haven't cared before, and I don't see them starting now," Iris says. "We don't need to beat everyone. If we can get close enough to kill Luna or the phoenix, we can end this."

I shake my head. "No. Gravesend is a newborn. She needs to live long enough to grow that muscle. If anyone kills her now, she won't ever resurrect."

"Luna won't either," Iris says. "If we can save the phoenix, we will, but if we can't, we must do what has to be done. You're not calling the shots here, Emil. Especially not after you were ready to walk. But we do need you to fight alongside us."

It would be easier if I walked away from this battle. To spend tonight tracking my brother. "No lie, there have been times the past few days where I was hoping for a quick death. But what I want is a long life, and I know I can't have that if Luna lives forever."

Wesley nods. "It's what we all want, but I hear you. We got to grow into our roles, and you were pulled out of home suddenly. Honestly, I'm surprised you've stayed in for this long."

"This is the fight of our lives," Iris says. "If we don't move now, the sacrifices of everyone we've lost will have been for absolutely nothing."

If we lose, Luna can rise to power, and alchemists everywhere will stop at nothing to figure out her formula. And if they succeed, we'll have a world that's overrun with immortals fighting beyond the end of time.

We leave home.

During the ride over, we gear up in power-proof vests Iris had packed away. I wonder how much stronger I could be if I hadn't been cut up by the infinity-ender, but I'll take what I can get. During stoplights, Prudencia tests the elevated strength of her telekinesis out the window—lifting a parked motorcycle, knocking over a trash can. She's proud and hopeful, and I wish I felt the same.

We reach the Alpha Church of New Life. It isn't massive, but it's impressive. The bricks are dark gray with steeples as blue as Gravesend's feathers. We're spotted immediately when we get out of the car, and a sniper in the building next door fires a rapid bolt at me, which Prudencia sweeps away. Wesley takes the lead, faster than ever, and lays out acolytes left and right like a game of pinball, and he bursts through the front door. We run inside and there are murals of various creatures. It's refreshing to see them illustrated so peacefully and living their lives out in nature instead of the usual, like three-headed hydras viciously attacking cities or basilisks swallowing children whole or shifters deceiving loved ones or phoenixes being drowned.

I blast open a large door that leads us into the garden, and there they all are. Luna is in a ceremonial cape that drapes down to the floor, standing beside Anklin Prince. Stanton, June, and Dione are all dressed in gray jumpsuits with half a dozen acolytes surrounding them. Thankfully, there's no shield like the one in the cemetery.

Luna turns her back on us, muttering a prayer as she swings a massive scythe over the hydra's neck. The hydra roars in pain, and Stanton holds it down as Luna hacks away, yellow blood spraying and pooling into a metallic cauldron. Gravesend is screeching in her cage. We all break. June appears behind me and wraps her arms around my chest, kneeing me in the back repeatedly. I cast my fiery wings and take flight, shaking June off, and she crashes to the floor. I fly straight to Anklin as he twists open the urn, but a bolt from an acolyte's wand blasts me in the center of my vest. My world spins as I'm flipping toward the bronze spikes of the gate—suddenly I'm jerked in midair and fall into a cluster of bushes.

"That was close," Prudencia says as she helps me up. Before I can thank her, we see Iris being cornered by Dione and Stanton. "I'll do what I can."

"Be careful!" I shout as she runs off.

I knock out an acolyte with a fire-dart and fight past others trying to reach Luna. The ghosts have been released from the urn, and even though their mouths are moving, no words are coming out. It's the same howl as the night from the cemetery, except even more haunting and bone-chillingly empty. Everyone feels it too, but the battle keeps going. Luna isn't looking to capture this time. She's going to kill them with a dagger fully made of bone. I'm hurling a fire-orb when an acolyte tackles me, screwing up my aim.

Luna is swift as she runs the oblivion dagger across the necks of her mother and father, their gray blood spilling into the cauldron before their ghostly bodies fall face-first into the grass and fade away. She mixes the bloods with powders and liquids I don't know, and she turns to Gravesend's cage.

I finally wrestle the acolyte off me, and as Stanton charges me, a red bolt catches him in his side and he drops, his skin flaring as if being burned from the inside. I turn.

Brighton is standing at the entrance of the garden with a wand in each hand, and Maribelle has orbs of dark yellow fire rolling around her palms. The fire-orbs fly like arrows, and Dione drops to the ground.

I'm in shock, but I have to protect Gravesend. Anklin blocks my path, and I fight him like I've been doing this my entire life—punch to the gut, elbow to the chin, kick to the knee. I'm about to wind up a final blow when he quickly withdraws a dagger and slices my arm. Anklin holds the dagger above his head, and as he's driving it down, he's set ablaze.

Roaring streams of dark yellow fire flow from Maribelle's fists, and she doesn't let up until Anklin Prince's screams go quiet.

There is no remorse on her face as she helps me up.

"Why are you looking at me like that?"

"You killed him," I say.

"She's next," Maribelle says as she spots June across the garden and pursues her.

Luna opens Gravesend's cage, but I cast a fire-arrow into her shoulder, and she falls. I grab Gravesend out of her cage, holding her to my chest. Even with Brighton and Maribelle joining the battle, the tides are turning against us. Stanton and Dione have recovered and appear more vicious than ever. The potion is nearly done, and all it needs is Gravesend's pure blood.

I pick up the infinity-ender. "I'm sorry," I say to Gravesend as she looks up at me with adoring eyes. I was the first person she saw when she was born, and I have to sacrifice her for a world she never got to see.

This is wrong, I can't—

The blade is snatched out of my hand, and Luna drives it

straight into Gravesend's heart while she's still in my arms. Gravesend's brief cry sounds like all the pain in the world. I'm staring into her eyes as the fire goes out, and I'm completely frozen when Luna rips the blade out of Gravesend and stabs me in the stomach. The pain blazes as she twists the blade. She wrenches Gravesend out of my arms, and I slam on my back, staring up at the Crowned Dreamer, whose brilliant light fades from me as my eyes close.

I hear screams all around me, and I'm hoping my people are all good. I want them to run and hide—this is all a done deal. I pull the infinity-ender out of my stomach and press down on my wound while trying to breathe. I look up to find Luna draining Gravesend's dark blue blood over the cauldron. I'm too weak to call for help—every breath needs to be used to stay alive. Luna takes a step back from the cauldron and throws in a pouch of stardust, and it all erupts in see-through flames that smell of rainy evenings in the park and houses on fire. Luna is shaking as she scoops up enough potion to fill a round bottle that looks like an empty snow globe. The elixir looks like dirty seawater.

Red bolts strike through the air, blowing apart the cauldron and flying through Luna's stomach. Her eyes widen, and she falls to the floor, choking. Elixir splashes out of her bottle, but she's protected most of it. I try crawling to her. I'll spill it out myself and turn my back on Luna as she dies.

Brighton and Maribelle run up to me.

"You're going to be okay," Brighton says, kneeling beside me.

"Stop her," I say as Luna tries bringing the potion to her lips.

Maribelle steps on Luna's wrist and snatches the bottle. "So close," she taunts.

Brighton moves over to Luna, hovering over her face. "You thought I was nothing more than a pawn, and look who stopped you." He holds out his hand and Maribelle passes him the potion. "Who's the king now?"

"Pour it out," I say. But he doesn't, and it feels like someone is squeezing my heart. There's someone who wants power even more than Luna. "Brighton, don't do this, that potion is untested. You could die like Dad did."

Brighton stares at the elixir. "Better than living powerless."

My brother looks up at the Crowned Dreamer as he drinks every last drop of Reaper's Blood.

ACKNOWLEDGMENTS

Infinity Son destroyed me time and time again, but so many of my heroes pieced me back together.

Andrew Eliopulos is a brilliant and magnificent editor, who lived in this world with me so completely that he easily pictured celestials flying outside his window. I wouldn't have a book that I'm proud of without all his guidance, which helped me unlock this story that's been with me for well over a decade. And his patience after I missed my deadline so I could rewrite the book. And that other deadline. And yup, that one too.

Brooks Sherman got to geek out extra hard with me with this transition into the fantasy genre. We've talked about comics and superheroes for YEARS, and I'm so happy we're adding the Spell Walkers and co. to the canon.

My HarperCollins family: Rosemary Brosnan, Sari Murray, the epic Michael D'Angelo, Audrey Diestelkamp, Jane Lee, Tyler Breitfeller, Suzanne Murphy, indie queen Kathy Faber, Liz Byer, Caitlin Garing, and Bria Ragin. And so much love to my cover designer, Erin Fitzsimmons, who worked with artist Kevin Tong to give me a glorious and iconic cover that brought legit tears to my eyes. Thank you everyone for all you've done and all you do.

Thanks to my international publishers for making my stories more accessible to readers across the world and to my agencies for being that bridge.

Jodi Reamer was instantly charmed by my magical crew and flew right into this world with me as if she'd been here all along.

Julianne Daly very generously managed my website and so many requests so I could focus on writing.

My mom, Persida Rosa, never judged me as I cast spells with fake wands, drew demons in my Book of Shadows, and mixed potions with whatever we had in the fridge. And she always, always, always made sure I had notebooks and a computer to write my fan fiction so I wouldn't burst into flames.

Even though this is a work of fantasy, my contemporary crew helped me out so much along the way. Becky Albertalli's insta-love for Emil and Brighton made sure I never lost their humanity within all the magic happenings. David

Arnold continues to out-David himself, and I love him more than he loves using GIFs. Jasmine Warga is a blast of sunshine who reminds me to love my art and live my life. Nicola and David Yoon are the greatest neighbors ever, and they're mine, all mine! Angie Thomas pushed me to write the book that Little Adam never had and would've loved, and I believe I did that. Corey Whaley believed in this story back when it was going to be a dark fairy tale for kids. And Court Stevens pushed me to "Go for it!" with my ending, and I'm so happy I listened.

I would've never gotten through this draft without my New York crew. Arvin Ahmadi is the ultimate hype man. Dhonielle Clayton has always supported my Infinity dreams. Zoraida Córdova always checked in with my mental well-being. Patrice Caldwell made sure I didn't hold back on anything, especially the glory of being queer and powerful. Mark Oshiro hit me with expert notes. Laura Sebastian's high word counts during sprints motivated me to up my game. Emily X. R. Pan inspired me time and time again as we wrote (and rewrote) our heart-books.

So grateful for the friends who came outside their own fantastical worlds to check in on me as I created my own. Sabaa "Slytherin Hermione" Tahir always kept it super real with me because we didn't have time to pretend my story was great when it wasn't. Marie Lu's early passion for this story in 2015 was a powerful stamp of approval. Amie Kaufman

Skyped me in a Hogwarts T-shirt to help detangle this story's many threads. Alex London is my literary wingman with his own remarkable sibling story with fierce birds. Kiersten White generously—and hilariously—helped me brainstorm titles years before "Infinity Son" struck me like lightning one day. Victoria Aveyard inspired me and entertained me and ate tacos with me. Tahereh Mafi and Ransom Riggs have been so lovely and supportive since my bookselling days. Brendan Reichs grounded me when I was losing sight of the real work. Victoria Schwab's tweets and DMs kept the fire alive. Jay Kristoff kept asking me where the phoenix book was. Daniel José Older offered to guide me through the fantasy trenches like some foul-mouthed Yoda. Sasha Alsberg: YouTube icon who is way chiller than Brighton. Susan Dennard's summer sprints and writing tips were invaluable. Alexandra Bracken gave me a much-needed pep talk about the market—which I still think about. Roshani Chokshi quelled my fears about my writing my truth in this series. And huge thanks to Leigh Bardugo who kindly gave me her blessing to open this book with the perfect quote from *Crooked Kingdom*.

Thank you to Cassandra Clare for being the first author to show me that queer boys could save the day.

Amanda Diaz, Michael Diaz, Cecilia Renn, Luis Rivera, Sandra Gonzalez, Lestor Andrade, and Keegan Strouse have all championed me and this book for as long as we've known each other. And Elliot Knight came late to the game, but he's proven to be an invaluable player who kept me sane and happy and fed and loved, and helped me act out my favorite Emil/Ness scene so I could write it right. (Maybe we'll get more right in another lifetime, El.)

Infinite thanks to the booksellers, librarians, reviewers, and readers who've given me this life. Extra hugs to all the indie booksellers who united to help me reveal this gorgeous cover.

Lastly, I'm forever grateful to Harry Potter and the Charmed Ones and the Winchesters and the X-Men for helping this Bronx boy find magic.

INFINITY SON
BONUS MATERIALS

Turn the page for a glossary of terms,
a dramatis personae,
and a sneak peek at *Infinity Reaper*,
the gripping sequel to *Infinity Son*.

GLOSSARY OF TERMS

GLEAMCRAFTERS

Celestials—their true origins unknown, these people carry powers that have a connection to the stars and sky. Some powers are presented at birth, others surface later in life. The range of their abilities is wide. Celestials can be distinguished by the way their eyes glow like different corners of the universe as they use their gleam. Notable group: the Spell Walkers.

Gleam—extraordinary powers that have always existed and been known to the public.

Gleamcrafters—practitioners with powers. Applicable to both celestials and specters.

Specters—sixty years ago, alchemy was developed as a way to use the blood of creatures to give people powers. Gleamcrafters who receive their powers this way are specters, and the range of their abilities is limited to the blood of that creature's breed. Specters can be distinguished by the way their eyes burn like eclipses as they use their gleam. Notable Group: the Blood Casters.

CREATURES

Basilisks—large serpents whose fangs produce poisonous substances and who have heightened hunting senses.

Hydras—beasts who grow more heads when decapitated.

Phoenixes—birds of fire who resurrect. Notable breeds: gray-sun phoenixes, who come back stronger with each new life, and century phoenixes, who are reborn only every hundred years.

Shifters—animalistic beings who can morph into whatever form serves them best.

THE WORLD

The Blackout—another term for the massacre at the Nightlocke Conservatory. The day remembered as when the world felt dark, when the last remaining founding Spell Walkers were no longer recognized as heroes, but instead as terrorists, owing to their involvement in the massacre.

The Crowned Dreamer—a prime constellation that surfaces every sixty-six years and elevates powers to great heights for one month, reaching its zenith on its final night.

Gem-grenades—gemstones imbued with different elemental explosives.

Gleam Care—facilities designed for treating gleamcrafters.

Infinity-ender blade—a dagger that can permanently kill a phoenix.

Oblivion dagger—a dagger that can permanently kill a ghost.

Power-proof vests—designed to repel gleam attacks.

Prime constellations—special constellations that have influences over all gleamcrafters' powers, but especially celestials'. These constellations are beneficial for alchemists when transforming someone into a specter.

Spells—bullet-like attacks alchemically forged from the blood of celestials.

Wands—firearms charged with spells. Most notably used by enforcers and police, but can be used by anyone.

DRAMATIS PERSONAE

SPELL WALKERS AND ALLIES

Emil Rey—a reincarnated specter with phoenix blood who can cast gray and gold fire, self-heal his mortal wounds, sense feelings from other phoenixes, fly, and resurrect. Known as Fire-Wing and Infinity Son.

Brighton Rey—the creator of the online series Celestials of New York. No powers of his own.

Maribelle Lucero—a celestial who can levitate and glide.

Iris Simone-Chambers—a celestial with powerhouse strength and skin impervious to most gleam attacks. New leader of the Spell Walkers.

Atlas Haas—a celestial who can conjure winds.

Wesley Young—a celestial who runs at swift-speed.

Eva Nafisi—a celestial who can heal others but gets harmed in the process.

Prudencia Mendez—Emil and Brighton's best friend who has run away from her gleamphobic aunt to help them. No powers of her own.

Carolina Rey—Emil and Brighton's mother. No powers of her own.

Bautista de León (Deceased)—a reincarnated specter with phoenix blood who could cast gold fire, self-heal his mortal wounds, resurrect, and remember details from his past life. Founder of the Spell Walkers.

Sera Córdova (Deceased)—an alchemist and celestial who had psychic visions. Founding member.

Aurora Lucero (Deceased)—a celestial who could fly. Founding member.

Lestor Lucero (Deceased)—a celestial who could fly. Founding member.

Finola Simone-Chambers (Deceased)—a celestial with powerhouse strength. Founding member.

Konrad Chambers (Deceased)—a celestial with skin impervious to most gleam attacks. Founding member.

BLOOD CASTERS AND ALLIES

Ness Arroyo—a specter with shifter blood who can change his appearance at will.

Luna Marnette—a supreme alchemist who created the Blood Casters. No powers of her own.

Dione Henri—a specter with hydra blood who can grow extra/regrow missing body parts and run in bursts of swift-speed.

Stanton—a specter with basilisk blood who has serpentine senses and venomous, acidic, petrifying, and paralytic abilities.

June—a mysterious Blood Caster who can phase through solid objects.

Anklin Prince—an alchemist who specializes in necromancy.

Orton—a drug dealing specter with inexplicable powers.

Acolytes—followers who serve Luna in the hopes they will one day be turned into specters and join the Blood Casters.

POLITICIANS

Senator Edward Iron—a presidential candidate who opposes gleamcraft. No powers of his own.

Congresswoman Nicolette Sunstar—a celestial presidential candidate who can create burning hot dazzling lights.

OTHER NOTABLE CHARACTERS

Keon Máximo (Deceased)—an alchemist and specter with phoenix blood who could cast gray fire, self-heal his mortal wounds, and resurrect. He developed the alchemy to give normal people powers and became the first specter.

Leonardo Rey (Deceased)—Emil and Brighton's father. No powers of his own.

Kirk Bennett—the curator for the phoenix exhibit at the Museum of Natural Creatures.

Halo Knights—humans who have devoted their lives to protecting phoenixkind.

Enforcers—the government's special forces program trained to apprehend all gleamcrafters abusing their powers.

Turn the page for a sneak peek at *Infinity Reaper*,
the gripping sequel to *Infinity Son*.

The battle between the Spell Walkers and the Blood Casters has
reached its climax, but elsewhere, Senator Iron has abducted Ness,
intent on using his shifter powers for political gain.

PRISONER

NESS

Who am I going to be? The Senator's prisoner out in the world or one who's locked up in the Bounds?

We're below deck when the Senator invites me to get some air at the front of the ship to think over the big decision ahead of me. Between him punching me in the nose, getting shot with a stunning spell by enforcers hours ago, and the boat speeding towards the island, my balance is especially off as I go up the narrow stairway and step out onto the stern.

There are two men fully dressed in black outfits guarding the stairway, and neither pay me any attention, even though we know each other good and well. The Senator's head of security, Jax Jann, has always reminded me of an Olympian swimmer with his stretched torso and long arms and legs. He has thick eyebrows and red hair that's pulled into a ponytail. He's the most impressive telekinetic I've ever seen; there's no way any assassin will ever land a shot on the Senator as long as he's around. The other, Zenon Ramsey, has dark blond hair that completely covers his eyes, which lulls people into thinking he's not paying attention when in reality he's watching more than most. He has the rare ability to see things through other people's perspectives—literally. I've heard it only works on people in a short distance, but that's all he needs to be a security guard for a two-mile radius.

The Senator has always employed celestials to protect our family, and having celestial bodyguards when he's actively campaigning against the community always felt like a special sort of magic trick until I learned how well they were being paid to keep him alive. That's more than I can say for being a Blood Caster who was working to make Luna immortal. What is shocking to me is how Jax and Zenon regarded me like I wasn't supposed to have been blown to smithereens at the Nightlocke Conservatory.

How many others know that the Senator tried to have his own son killed so he could paint the Spell Walkers as dangers to society?

Even if there was some way I could take down Jax and Zenon and get away on a life raft, a piercing screech high above in the sky tells me that I wouldn't get very far. A phoenix that is four times the size of an eagle swoops down toward the river, its crystal blue belly skimming the surface as it searches for any intruders or escapees. This phoenix with drenched indigo feathers is a sky swimmer, which I can identify because the Senator once returned home from a hunting trip with the head of one; it might still be mounted in his office at the manor.

"Quite a sight," the Senator says as he follows me to the bow of the ship.

At first I think he's talking about the sky swimmer, but he's staring straight ahead at our destination. The New York Bounds is a collection of small stone castles, huddled together like someone pushed all the rooks of a chess board together. The towers are windowless, designed that way so inmates will be disconnected from the stars, dampening their abilities. Solitary confinement is the cruelest punishment, burying celestials so deep underground that it's as if all the stars have vanished from the universe.

I've seen this upfront.

The Senator brought me here after my mother was killed.

We toured the Bounds so I could understand the creative measures that the prison's correctional architects had to put in place to seal away their powerful inmates. On one level, there were two men floating inside tanks of water, with only their heads above the surface so they could breathe and eat; their waste was their own problem. The fire caster couldn't summon his gleam at all, and if the lightning striker wanted to make a move, well, that was his life to take. On another level, electric traps were installed around the edges of a cell to prevent a woman who could melt herself into a puddle from escaping. Her neighbor was a man who could camouflage himself against any surface, so the engineers installed sprinklers that sprayed paint of different colors to always keep track of him.

The last person we visited that day was a convict in solitary confinement. He'd been imprisoned for using his heating powers to boil the blood of his family. The screams echoing through the corridors had me so nervous that I had stayed hidden behind my then-bodyguard, Logan Hesse. But when the security guard opened the cell, I realized I had no reason to be scared. The inmate's hands and ankles and waist were bound by iron chains. He had no fight in him as we observed him like some animal in a zoo. The next day, the celestial was found dead in his cell, with red handprints burned onto his pale face. When the Senator told me the news, he mocked the dead man with an impression of his suicide. I laughed so hard before returning to my schoolwork.

I hate who I was.

The boat docks at the pier.

The island is known for having its traps, like sand basilisks waiting to swallow people whole, but when the Senator steps onto the beach before me, I trust that he knows more than I do right now. I'm weighing in my head if I'm ready for this steep climb with jagged rocks up to the prison when an older man walks out from a cluster of trees. The flashlight guiding his path illuminates his features and I recognize him instantly.

He runs this island.

Barrett Bishop is very pale, as if he only ever comes out at night. I haven't seen him personally since he first gave us that tour through the Bounds years ago, and there are now more wrinkles around his eyes, and graying hair that stops at his shoulders. He's dragging the maroon jacket for his three-piece suit because he doesn't care about appearances as much as the Senator. The contrast has worked for them this election cycle. The Senator is the put-together candidate who is best qualified to serve as president, but Bishop's everyman vibes paired with his experience as the Chief Architect of the Bounds have made him a dream choice for vice president. Their supporters cheer him on at every rally, even when he says the most dangerous things.

"Edward," Bishop says in a hoarse voice, regarding the Senator. Then his icy blue eyes turn to me. "You brought your ghost."

"I did indeed," the Senator says.

Bishop directs the flashlight towards my eyes, toying around with me like I'm some bored cat, before turning it off. "What are we doing with the ghost? Burying him deep in the Bounds?"

"It's his choice," the Senator says.

The little light spots fade, and Bishop's grin suggests he wants to make me his personal prisoner. If I were locked up, leaving me in a cell to regret all my wrongs would be punishment enough. But the correctional architects who hate gleamcraft have to show their dominance. They have to prove to all of us, everywhere, that our powers can be beaten by ordinary means. They have dark imaginations and enough hate to go home at night without feeling absolutely inhuman.

I once had that hate too.

Following our visit to the Bounds, the Senator asked me how I would've punished the man who killed my mother if we'd ever tracked him down. The celestial had cast an illusion and tricked Mom into believing he was her friend before gutting her. I spent all day thinking over the question and over dinner I told the Senator that I would chain the celestial to a chair, bring in his family, and kill them all in front of him. No illusions. Only reality.

"We can't murder people," the Senator had said.

But that's clearly a lie. He organized my death and pinned it on innocent celestials. The truth is that he can't be caught with blood on his hands.

So what's my move?

I hated being used by the Senator to spread messages to other young people that all celestials are dangers, but what he's got planned for me now is even more extreme. Back on the boat he said he wants me to use my shifting abilities to impersonate Congresswoman Sunstar and her team to counter the support she's being shown in the presidential race. I don't know the exact details of the plan, but if there's any chance of me posing as her somewhere public, then I might be able to flee.

Right now I stand no chance of escaping this labyrinth—four towers with multiple levels, armed enforcers, and traps galore.

I turn to the Senator to give him his answer, and the fading Crowned Dreamer is reflecting off his glasses. I have no idea what went down tonight with the immortality ritual. I hope Emil was able to find his brother and get away with the phoenix; I hope he didn't die for that bird. If I'm ever going to have a chance to see him again, I have to be as calculating and patient as Luna has been her entire life.

I have to become a pawn who takes down the king. To outsmart the man who fools the world without a single shifter's muscle.

"I'll work for you," I say.

"Smart choice, Eduardo," the Senator says with a quick that-settles-it clap.

"I was really looking forward to making a game out of your imprisonment," Bishop says. "But we'll make do."

"Let's go home then," the Senator says.

Home. That cold manor stopped being my home before the Blackout. It's a cage of a different kind. But if I can bide my time and wait for the Senator to leave a crack in the door, I can slip out and never look back.

Hopefully I can escape before helping the Senator become the president.